VOYEUR

ALSO BY DANIEL JUDSON

·

The Violet Hour

The Water's Edge

The Darkest Place

The Bone Orchard

The Poisoned Rose

DANIEL JUDSON

MINOTAUR BOOKS

NEW YORK

This is a work of fiction. All of the characters, organizations, and events portrayed in this novel are either products of the author's imagination or are used fictitiously.

VOYEUR. Copyright © 2010 by Daniel Judson. All rights reserved. Printed in the United States of America. For information, address St. Martin's Press, 175 Fifth Avenue, New York, N.Y. 10010.

www.minotaurbooks.com

Design by Kathryn Parise

LIBRARY OF CONGRESS CATALOGING-IN-PUBLICATION DATA

Judson, D. Daniel, 1962–
   Voyeur / Daniel Judson.—1st ed.
    p. cm.
   ISBN 978-0-312-38361-9
   1. Private investigators—Fiction.   2. Missing persons—
Investigation—Fiction.   3. Manhattan (New York, N.Y.)—
Fiction. I.   Title.
  PS3610.U532V69 2010
  813'.6—dc22

                           2010027428

First Edition: October 2010

10 9 8 7 6 5 4 3 2 1

for Kate Siner Francis

SAINT VALENTINE'S DAY

2003

1

He knew the equipment well, all the tools of his trade, and had already laid out the items he would need tonight on the empty seat beside him.

Hidden behind the heavily tinted windows of his panel van, he was free to watch without being seen, a simple necessity that, in theory at least, might someday prove to be nothing less than a matter of life and death.

His life and death.

Of course, Remer didn't care to dwell on that—or any of the potential dangers that came with observing people at their worst; to do so would be inviting fear in, and there was, he knew, no point in doing that.

He had parked on Gansevoort Street, in the heart of Manhattan's meatpacking district. An old-fashioned street, not paved but cobbled, it ran for several blocks through a neighborhood that was, despite the presence of the processing factories, nonetheless high-rent.

Shabby-chic, the Realtors called it.

Among the factories, dark now, were loft apartments, boutiques, several art galleries, bars, and cafés, one of which was Florent, a French bistro located, somewhat deceptively, in what had been decades ago, and still appeared to be, an old diner.

Small tables crowded close together on one side of the long room, a Formica lunch counter running along the other, lots of chrome fixtures and brightly lit, Florent was a place Remer had gone to only once—on a first date, years ago, with a dark and beautiful woman he had since worked hard to forget—but he remembered the layout well enough, both inside and out.

It was his job to possess a working knowledge of Manhattan—every street, every place of business and residence, all the ways in and all the ways out of every neighborhood, as well as the lines of sight from every corner. More often than not, success depended on this intimacy he maintained with the city—an intimacy that was a never-ending project and had long ago become a big part of who he was and, he believed, always would be.

So when he was told that tonight's tail would begin at Florent, Remer was instantly able to determine not only the advantages that would work in his favor but the disadvantages he would need to overcome.

At this time of night Gansevoort, despite its bars and cafés, was a desolate enough place, which meant he wouldn't have to deal with a lot of hectic street traffic. And yet it was busy enough—hipsters and A-listers roaming about, not to mention transsexual prostitutes lingering at the far corners and the trade they attracted—that his van, just a little beat-up, the logo of a nonexistent plumbing company marking its driver and passenger doors, wouldn't stand out completely as it waited at the curb.

These were the advantages. The chief disadvantage was that the meatpacking district was located on the northern edge of the West Village, which itself was a maze of narrow one-way streets.

Should the tail lead him south and into the Village, he would have his work cut out for him; following someone closely in that cramped place meant to risk being seen. Even with all the modern technology at his disposal, and the tools laid out beside him, success would come down to a mixture of instinct, experience, and, most important, luck.

Still, there were, he knew, worse places a mark could lead him.

▪

There was always the chance that the couple Remer had come to follow could remain inside Florent all night—it was a twenty-four-hour place—but a little over an hour after he had arrived he saw them exiting together.

They were an illicit couple—each married to another, and, according to the man's distraught wife, who had hired Remer, experienced at deception—so Remer didn't expect to bear witness to any flagrant displays of affection.

Still, both wore the kind of smile that could never be confused with innocent.

Knowing, familiar, provocative—difficult to misunderstand.

Mounted on the dashboard of the van was a digital camcorder, which Remer had already aimed at the ten-foot area spanning from Florent's front door to the curb. Having pressed the RECORD button the moment the couple emerged, Remer sat back and watched their faces and body language on the camera's color display screen.

The woman—tall, wearing a full-length fur coat—strode to the curb and, looking over her shoulder at the man, still smiling an indiscreet smile, raised her hand to flag down an approaching cab.

Starting the van's engine, Remer pulled the column shifter down and waited, both hands on the wheel and his left foot holding down the brake pedal.

On the passenger seat were two pairs of binoculars, standard and night-vision; a carrying case of impact-resistant plastic containing a state-of-the-art GPS tracking system; and a custom-made leather case containing a directional listening device equipped with its own digital recorder capable of storing over thirty hours of conversation.

There wasn't much more that he'd need tonight—he prided himself on knowing beforehand exactly what each job would require—but should some unseen situation suddenly arise, the appropriate tool was more than likely in one of the half-dozen metal lockboxes bolted to the floor in the back of the van.

Remer watched as the male followed the female into the cab.

A tall man, handsome, well groomed, and impeccably dressed.

A dangerous man, the wife had warned with both pride and contempt.

But who wasn't, Remer thought.

The cab turned left on Washington Street, heading south.

Remer kept the video recorder running so he could provide a real-time account of the couple's journey from Florent to their destination. The dashboard camera was connected to a small control panel mounted on the steering wheel that allowed him to easily direct the aim and increase or decrease the zoom.

While the van was in motion, the video was displayed on a screen built into the aftermarket rearview mirror. Remer quickly zoomed in on the license plate, should he need for some reason to track down its driver later, and then quickly zoomed back out again.

After that, he focused on maintaining the proper distance from the mark—too close and he could be detected, too far back and this cab could be easily lost.

A left onto Horatio, a right onto Hudson. *So, into the Village, then.* Hudson became Bleecker, after which the cab made a right onto Broadway and then a left onto Houston.

A little less than a mile, and then a series of quick turns onto Allen, Broome, and Orchard.

Finally, the cab came to a stop in front the Blue Moon Hotel.

Mindful of the distance he needed to maintain, Remer paused at the corner, midturn. Using the controls on his steering wheel, he panned the camera and followed the couple as they crossed the sidewalk and entered the brightly lit hotel lobby.

There were large windows on either side of the door, which itself was almost all window, so once he coasted forward and came to a stop, Remer was able to document the couple's behavior as they stood at the front desk.

The more he caught, the better.

It was here, his experience told him, that affection might be displayed. And soon enough it was.

The female was standing beside the male, not shoulder to shoulder with him but facing him. She had already taken hold of his left arm, was almost hanging on it as if it were a rope she eagerly wanted to climb.

As before, they were smiling. Remer thought of his client, how she would feel when he played the video for her.

So happy, these two—deliriously so.

Leave him, make a clean break and move on, Remer would advise his client. Of course, she wouldn't listen; no one ever did.

Once hurt, few had the sense just to walk away.

When the check-in was complete, the couple headed for the elevator just beyond the front desk. Pausing there, standing more or less in that same manner, their faces close now, they talked quietly. Still no kiss, though. The elevator arrived and they entered it, disappearing from Remer's line of sight.

Orchard, a quiet side street running north to south between Delancey and Broome, was like a long canyon of brick facades and wrought-iron fire escapes. The buildings here were slightly taller than in the West Village, many of them former tenements. Across from the Blue Moon was, in fact, the Tenement Museum, and surrounding it were several shops and offices, all closed now.

Pulling ahead, Remer parked the van at the eastern curb and killed the motor.

He had been lucky so far—first Gansevoort, now here. Both streets were relatively discreet, and he had found on each a place to park. Most of the time, to achieve a line of sight, he had to double-park with the flashers blinking and hope that he appeared to anyone who might take notice to be a plumber on some emergency job.

A good enough cover, but still, standing out was standing out.

Grabbing both pairs of binoculars and the directional microphone, he moved to the back of the van, sat on one of the bolted-down metal containers, and looked out the rear door window at the Blue Moon.

He took a quick count of the rooms with lighted windows and waited, watching for one of the darkened ones to illuminate.

If his luck held, the couple would have been given a room facing Orchard. Had they been given a rear-facing room, he would then need to abandon the comfort and protection of the van and seek out access to the building's rear windows.

Failing to find that would require him to return to the van and wait till the lovers exited the hotel, make a record of that, and, should they remain together, follow them again.

Should they part outside the hotel, which was the likely scenario, he would follow the woman to her residence, establish her address, and use it later to identify her. If *this* information wasn't sufficient and his client wanted more, then another tail would be planned.

Rarely did he get all that he needed on the first night out. Rarely were the logistics of working in this city anything less than a series of obstacles that he needed—was paid—to overcome.

Maybe, if his luck held, he'd have what he needed in a matter of hours, then actually find himself back in his apartment and asleep by midnight.

As he thought this, he removed the laser-sighted directional microphone from its leather case. Once he determined what room the couple was in, all he would need to do was aim the invisible laser at the window and listen to—and record—what was being said.

Or whatever noise they made.

It was as he pulled this piece of equipment from its case that Remer saw the two vehicles turn onto Orchard Street from Broome.

Moving quickly, a black sedan leading a black SUV, the windows of both vehicles as heavily tinted as the windows of his own.

His gut clenched instantly, seemed to know well before his mind what the presence of these shimmering, rushing vehicles meant.

But as the sedan skidded to a stop beside his van, positioning itself at a slight angle so its nose was just inches from the van's driver door, Remer's mind quickly caught up.

The SUV took position directly behind the van, its nose at the rear bumper.

There was no doubt now.

Cornered.

Remer kept a licensed handgun locked in the glove compartment. Dropping the directional microphone, he rushed toward the front of the van, but before he could even reach the passenger seat, its window shattered and a gloved hand reached in, unlocking and opening the door.

A *well-practiced move.*

He counted four men. Despite the confusion, he saw that two of them had handguns drawn and were holding them expertly.

Not one of these men, though, said a thing.

A third man leaned in through the open passenger door, reached back, and grabbed the handle of the cargo door, releasing it. That door instantly slid open, and before Remer could do anything, the fourth man lunged inside, his arm fully extended.

Something struck Remer in the chest.

He recognized it just before the 25,000 volts bit into his chest.

A *stun gun.*

It was this fourth man who dragged Remer from the van.

Though he was semiconscious, Remer saw the third man scrambling to get across the passenger seat and behind the wheel of the van. He saw, too, one of the two armed men holster his weapon and join the fourth.

There wasn't anything Remer could do as these two men lifted him and carried him back to the SUV.

He felt as though he were being rushed along by a swift current.

Once inside the SUV, seated between two men, Remer was hooded and his wrists were bound together with sharp wire.

The vehicle raced north for a few blocks, then turned right onto Delancey, heading east.

It was then that Remer felt a needle pierce his skin and enter his radial vein.

The last thing he knew was trying to breathe the already stale air trapped within the darkness of the canvas hood.

The last thing he heard was the sound of the SUV's thick tires thumping on the uneven surface of the Williamsburg Bridge.

▪

He opened his eyes to darkness.

It took him a moment to realize that he was no longer hooded but in an unlit room. When his eyes adjusted he could make out the shapes of high windows—whitewashed and honeycombed with security wire. *Opaque.* These windows were visible on all four walls, but some were nearby while others were a distance from where he sat. So this room took up an entire floor, and he was tucked away in one of its corners.

A factory? Maybe. Unused? Probably. The air was cold and smelled of damp and mildew. He could almost sense the dormancy.

He heard nothing for a long time—nothing from inside the building and nothing from outside it, not even the sound of distant street traffic. It was night still—but was it the same night or another? He could be anywhere—a few blocks into Brooklyn, or in any of the other boroughs.

For that matter, was he even in New York?

He was parched, he knew that much. A side effect of whatever they had injected into him? Or an indication that he'd been unconscious for a long time?

There was no way of telling. The only certain things were the cold and the smells and the pounding of his heart.

▪

Maybe an hour later—a long time, however long it actually was, to be bound to a chair in an empty room—Remer finally heard something: the sound of tires on the debris-covered asphalt below one of the windows.

A vehicle rolling to a stop, then its doors opening and closing.

This was followed by voices, first outside and then inside, far below him. Finally, Remer heard footsteps on stairs. One flight, then another, then another still.

Getting louder.

Then the footsteps were in the large room, moving toward him. He was able to determine that there were three sets. Hard-soled boots worn by big men.

Finally, these men were close enough for Remer to see them.

Two of them were dressed in army field jackets and jeans; the third, standing between them, was wearing a leather peacoat, dark knit sweater, and black slacks and shoes.

Hanging from his left shoulder was a leather bag.

By the way the others flanked this man, and remained always a step behind him, Remer knew he was the one in charge.

They stopped a few feet away. The man in the leather peacoat watched Remer for a moment, then said to the man to his right, "Get the light." His accent was French.

The man to his right disappeared back into the surrounding darkness. The echoes of his receding footsteps were the only sounds to be heard. The man in the peacoat continued to watch Remer in silence. Then the receding footsteps stopped, only to begin again a few seconds later.

The man reemerged from the darkness, holding now a six-foot standing lamp and an orange extension cord.

He placed the lamp beside Remer, then headed toward the nearest wall, uncoiling the cord as he went. Inserting the plug into an outlet, he returned to the lamp and switched it on.

The bright light cut into Remer's eyes. He blinked against it.

"I would imagine that you are at this moment very scared," the man in the peacoat said. His accent was heavy, muddy. He handed the leather bag to the man to his left.

This man knelt, placing the case on the floor and zipping it open. Remer said nothing.

"It is wise to be scared," the man continued. "You should be. We want you to be. It is natural. Fear is hardwired into all of us, put there by nature to protect and save us. Things can become very focused when we are scared. Only what truly matters gets our attention."

The kneeling man removed something from the bag.

Remer didn't recognize it at first. It was less than a foot long and had an electrical cord attached. The cord was rolled up.

Unrolling it, this man tossed the plug end to the man standing by the lamp, who connected it to the orange extension cord.

"Look at me," the man in the peacoat said.

Remer did, though the exact nature of the piece of equipment that had been removed from the bag was still very much on his mind.

"We all have jobs we must do," the man said. "Mine is to break people of bad habits. Do you know what your bad habit is?"

Remer said nothing.

"You pry into the business of others. That is your bad habit. No one makes you do this, you have chosen to do it—to make it your profession. Private matters, intimate matters—it does not matter to you. You follow, peek through windows like a voyeur, hide in shadows. This is the habit I have been asked to break you of."

The man holding the item stood.

Remer's eyes strayed toward his hand.

The handle of the item he held was clear plastic, and within it glowed a red light.

The other end of the item was a six-inch-long metal rod from the tip of which rose a thin, curling line of dark smoke.

Remer quickly looked back at the man in the peacoat.

"For all any of us know, I might just be doing you a favor," he said to Remer. "If you were to continue your habit of peeking, you might one day see something you will wish you hadn't. Of course, once a thing is seen, it cannot be unseen, can it?"

The man in the peacoat held out his hand.

The grip of the soldering iron was placed into it.

The man by the lamp stepped to Remer and tore open his shirt, exposing Remer's broad chest.

"I find it is best to leave a little reminder," the Frenchman said. "This way you will be unlikely to forget the lesson you are about to learn. Think of it as a note from your teacher."

Remer struggled to get free of his restraints, couldn't help himself; it was reflex, a result of the adrenaline streaming into his blood.

He felt the bare wire cutting into his wrists but didn't care; all that mattered was getting free, somehow, and escaping the agony that awaited him.

The two men moved to either side of Remer and placed their hands on his shoulders, holding him steady.

The man in the peacoat took a step toward him.

Again, Remer flailed, fighting against the wires.

He felt them cutting into his wrists, zipping open his skin. He knew he was bleeding, but he also knew that this was the very least of his problems.

The man in the peacoat took another step, then leaned down. "Lucky for you, my pride is my penmanship."

Remer said the only thing he could.

"Jesus."

The Frenchman pressed the red-hot metal tip into Remer's flesh and began to carve.

All Remer could hear then was his own screams.

DECEMBER 20

2008

2

Sitting in his dark apartment, Remer listens carefully for the sound of sirens.

His business—a liquor store on Job's Lane, less than a mile away—is equipped with a state-of-the-art security system, so there is no need for him to keep this closing-time vigil of his; he would be notified instantly by a text to his cell phone should one of his employees trip the silent alarm.

But a month ago a man walked into a Westhampton liquor store minutes before closing and gunned down the owner and his wife, making off, it was later learned, with only a few hundred dollars.

And a week after that, in Hampton Bays, the same thing occurred in a family-owned drugstore, except it was the pharmacist who was killed and a large supply of painkillers, not cash, that was taken.

There was a time when such acts of violence against merchants were unheard-of this far out on the island, which is one of the reasons why Remer chose to come here and begin his second life.

Times, though, have changed, there is no escaping this fact, and knowing that a murdered employee cannot trigger an alarm, Remer finds himself these days, as he waits for nine o'clock to come and go, listening more and more intently for any and all indications that trouble—the worst kind of trouble—has crept its way east into Southampton.

Of course, he has his herbal "blend" to help ease the tension and pass the time.

So far tonight he has taken only a half dose—enough to relax but not disable him, in case the worst happens and he is required to leave.

Also, it is Saturday, and his upstairs neighbor, Angela, will, as she does every Saturday, come by after her shift at Red Bar. Remer will take more then—a full dose, as will she—after which they will wait till the effects begin to manifest and then fall into bed.

Made of herbs—skullcap, lavender, passionflower vine, larch, and wormwood, the hallucinatory ingredient in absinthe, all of which are available in tincture form in the health food store on Main Street— Remer's blend dulls emotions and slows thoughts to a crawl but leaves an almost heightened awareness of his body.

A painkiller for the mind, a sleeping pill for the soul—so nothing left to sense but the body.

A harmless vice, as far as he is concerned, it was introduced to him in a slightly different form by the first woman he met when he came out here nearly six years before. A waif of a thing named Patti who taught yoga and fancied herself a healer.

Remer knows he was lucky to have met her when he did; the word burned into his chest only just beginning to heal, and hooked on pain pills, he was a walking time bomb, all rage and grief and fear, unable to care for anyone but himself.

Though their affair didn't last long—Remer's affairs simply don't— he has over the years perfected her original design by adding ingredients and tinkering with percentages, refining it till its effect on his mind is both powerful and consistent.

He could probably sell the thing if he chose to, bottle it and make a small fortune, but he is doing well enough providing the public with the standard range of intoxicants.

And anyway, it isn't in his nature to give up his secrets.

■

By nine fifteen Remer has neither heard sirens nor received an automated text, so he rises from his chair and, crossing the dark room to his desk, checks his notebook computer.

By the log he sees that the security system was armed at a few minutes past nine. Accessing the live feed to the surveillance cameras mounted throughout his shop, he pulls up the four-way split screen that shows real-time images of the front and back doors, the register area, and the safe in his office upstairs.

Everything appears to be in order.

Back in the living room he stands at his window, looking down at the courtyard below. His apartment is on the third floor of a four-story building set behind a private home on Hampton Road, as it passes the eastern edge of Southampton Village. An old barn once, converted into a rental property—a four-bay garage on the first floor, divided into storage units, and six apartments above, two on each floor—it is the only apartment building, as such, in all of Southampton.

For Remer there is security in being one among many, which is why he lives here even when he could afford something better.

There is security, too, in being close to the village but not within it.

To the right of the courtyard, through a line of bare border trees, stands Red Bar, its parking lot full. Bars and restaurants are still doing decent business on weekends, but most have reported a significant weekday drop-off. Several shops on Main Street are already closed for the season, while others have closed their doors for good. The only businesses able to claim actual increases are the thrift shop on Main, the cobbler on Newtown Road, and the three liquor stores within the village proper.

A Christmas out of Dickens, the mayor was quoted saying in a recent article in the *Southampton Press* about the debate whether or not the town could afford to install its seasonal decorations this year.

An accurate assessment, perhaps, but hardly good for morale.

It doesn't help matters that so far this is a colder-than-usual winter. Since Thanksgiving there have been already two snowstorms, both arriving on Fridays and keeping the out-of-towners away. The town's annual decorations—lighted six-foot pine trees set every fifty feet along both sides of Main Street and Job's Lane, and an elaborate wreath strung across Main from the Hildreth's hardware store to the Masonic Building—inevitably did go up, but they only seem this year to call attention to the mix of shops advertising slashed prices and the shops for rent. And the First Presbyterian Church on the corner of Meeting House Lane and South Main reprogrammed its electronic bells to play "Deck the Halls" every hour from 8:00 A.M. to 10:00 P.M., another village tradition.

But the tune merely echoes a bit mockingly along empty sidewalks.

A Christmas out of Dickens, indeed.

At half past nine Remer gets a text from Cynthia, one of his two employees working the late shift. Sent nightly by whoever closes, this text is to communicate two things, both equally important to Remer: the day's take, and that his closing employee has made it home safely.

Tonight's text reads: *$11,756.93.*

Not bad, he thinks.

Of course, he pays a high rent for the Job's Lane address, and he has the salary of six employees, including benefits, to cover, not to mention his own.

It wouldn't take much of a drop-off in business to push him into the red.

For now, though, a good day's haul, and his employee home safe.

What more does he need?

Pocketing his cell phone, he remains by the window, feeling against his unshaven face the cold coming off the glass like a breeze.

▪

A little after midnight, and no sign yet of Angela.

He is back in his chair in that dark corner of his room, clean-shaven now and eager for both his full dose and her company. Usually her shift is over by eleven thirty, sometimes even earlier than that, and he hopes this delay means a better-than-usual night for her.

There is precious little he knows about Angela. She spends her weekdays in the city, staying with a girlfriend as she works to complete her nursing degree. On Friday nights she waits tables in a well-established restaurant on the Upper West Side, and Saturday mornings she catches the early train to Southampton, walks the three blocks from the station to her apartment above Remer's, then works three shifts—lunch and dinner on Saturday, brunch on Sunday—before taking the evening train back to the city.

Those few hours she has between closing Saturday and opening Sunday she spends with Remer.

By quarter past twelve there is still no sign of her, nor at twenty past, nor at twenty-five past. Finally, though, at twelve thirty, Remer hears the main door downstairs open, followed by the familiar sound of Angela, in her work shoes, making her way up to her apartment.

He listens as she moves through it—first in her shoes, then in bare feet. Minutes later—just long enough for her to shed her work clothes—he hears her leave her apartment and start down the stairs.

Seconds after that, she knocks gently on his door, and he tells her to come in.

Still in his chair, Remer watches as she approaches. In the summertime she comes down barefooted, often dressed in nothing but a simple white slip. Tonight she is also wearing a cotton bathrobe and thick socks.

Reaching Remer, she places her hands on the arms of his easy chair and bends down, kissing him. They have not seen each other since Sunday afternoon, and the length of their kiss reflects that.

Leaning back and standing straight, she looks down at him and smiles.

"Hey, stranger," she whispers.

"Hey, you," he says. "How was your night?"

"Busy."

"It looked that way."

"Sorry it's so late. I had a table that didn't want to leave."

"Don't worry about it."

"How was your week?"

"Quiet. How'd your finals go?"

"I did better than I thought I would."

"That's always good."

She is his age, forty-two, recently divorced after twenty years of marriage. *Starting her life over, making smart choices this time around— only smart choices.*

She and Remer have this in common.

Her ultimate goal, once she completes her studies, is to land a job at Southampton Hospital, which is just a few blocks south. Working there would provide her with the option of walking to work, like Remer does.

If these tough times last, every corner that can be cut should be cut.

A few inches shorter than he, she has thick shoulder-length hair, light brown with highlights the color of hay. A sturdy woman, athletic, quick to smile, with a glimmer in her green eyes and a laugh that at times is like the blast of a tenor saxophone.

"I'm beat," she says. "I'll make you a deal, lover man. I put the kettle on and you start the tub."

"I think I can live with that."

She leans down and kisses him once more. They don't generally communicate during the week; her life is nonstop, and when she is in the city there is only time for work, classes, studying, and sleep.

It is an arrangement that suits Remer.

Certain intimacies he is good at, while others are simply beyond his reach.

One more kiss, and then Angela stands and heads into the kitchenette. Remer's apartment is somewhere between a loft and a studio, so she doesn't have far to walk.

As she grabs the teakettle from the two-burner stove and begins filling it from the tap, Remer rises from his chair and heads for the bathroom, also not that far away.

Long and narrow, the room approaches half the size of the rest of his apartment. Sitting on the edge of the tub—claw-footed and rust-stained, but with a high rim and deep to the point of cavernous—he inserts the plug into the drain and opens the spigots. The crash of the falling water echoes to the dark end of the room.

Above the tub is a window. It, and the one in the living room, are the only windows in Remer's place. Through it he sees fragments of white swirling frantically against blackness.

"Jesus, it's snowing again," he says.

Angela calls from the other side of the apartment. "Did you say something?"

He raises his voice. "I said it's snowing again."

"I know. It's not supposed to amount to anything, though. It's supposed to be just flurries."

Remer watches the snow for a moment. Some flakes fall fast while others rise, twisting upward on a sudden gust of wind. Others still are swept past the glass, some coming from the left, some from the right, but never colliding.

The chaos is entrancing, but he grows tired of it and dips his hand into the water collecting in the bottom of the tub, testing its temperature. He adjusts the flow from the dual spigots, and once he has the proper ratio of hot to cold, he steps to the old wooden trunk he uses as a hamper and pushes it across the tile floor, setting it beside the tub.

Steam is already collecting in the air when he exits the bathroom.

Angela is standing by the stove, waiting for the kettle water to heat up. She has set out a small tray and placed two coffee cups on it.

Thrift shop purchases, both, one plain china, the other elaborately decorated with etchings of roses and vines.

Remer keeps his blend, once mixed, in a vial made of blue-tinted glass. Retrieving it from the bedside table, he begins rolling it between his palms, to mix and warm the fluid inside.

Back in the bathroom, he rechecks the water, then lights the two nearly melted votive candles on the back rim of the sink. The lack of wax causes both flames to sputter and spit. Still rolling the vial between his hands, Remer returns to the tub and sits on its edge, monitoring the rising water.

A few moments later Angela enters and places the tray on the wooden chest. Removing her robe, she steps to the door, closes it partially, and hangs the robe on its knob.

Naked, she steps to Remer's side and places her hand on the back of his head, running her fingers through his thatch of dark hair.

He looks up at her and whispers again, "Hey, you."

"Hey," she whispers back. "I'm glad I'm finally here."

"Me, too."

When the tub is full, Remer spins the spigots shut and pours in the rosewater he keeps in a plastic bottle by the soap tray. Still seated on the tub's edge, he holds out his hand for Angela. She takes it and carefully straddles the high rim, then lowers herself till she is seated in the hot and silky water.

"Good?" Remer asks.

"Yes. Perfect."

He gives the vial a few more quick rolls, then removes its cap. Attached to it is a glass eyedropper. He places twenty drops into one of the cups, fills the dropper again, then drips another twenty into the other.

As Remer undresses, Angela pours the heated water from the kettle into both cups, filling each only halfway.

He waits to remove his T-shirt last. As he lowers himself into the water, Angela glances at the square patch of scarred skin at the center of his chest.

Of course, she says nothing. When she first saw the scar, during their first encounter a year ago, she assumed it was the mark of a tattoo that had been removed. She teasingly asked Remer what the tattoo was, but he didn't answer. The manner in which he avoided the subject told her never to ask again.

Settling into the water, Remer wraps his legs around Angela's hips and crosses his ankles behind her. They are sitting face-to-face. Angela takes both cups from the tray and hands Remer the more elaborately decorated one, keeping the plain one for herself. He knows that it amuses her to see a man like him holding such a dainty cup.

She offers the same toast she always offers at the start of their Saturday nights together.

"Here's to swimmin' with bowlegged women."

Her green eyes shine in the candlelight, and she laughs once, a coarse, deep, joyful laugh. Her last name is Syc, pronounced *sigh*, as in, she likes to say, "to breathe out softly." It is a name that strikes Remer as ironic—or at least does every time she laughs.

Tapping the cups together, they down their contents. Remer returns both to the tray as Angela leans back, resting her neck on the tub's rim.

She rolls her head till she is comfortable, then closes her eyes and says, "God, I needed this."

Remer watches her face, sees the relaxation coming over her. A total surrender, a complete *letting go*. It pleases him greatly to be able to share this with her.

He, too, closes his eyes, and it isn't long at all before he feels the effects of the full dose begin. Starting as a warmth in his stomach, it quickly rises through his chest and into his face, where it spreads like a blush.

A tincture is created by soaking herbs or flowers in alcohol, which stabilizes the chemicals extracted. The resulting liquid can contain up to 65 percent alcohol, which no doubt contributes to the initial effects.

Once the blush arrives, Remer knows it won't be long before what comes next.

Tonight he feels it almost suddenly: a steady surging in all his limbs, from his shoulders out to his hands, and from the lowest part of his gut down through his thighs and calves to his feet and, finally, his toes.

The closest thing to laudanum you'll ever find, he was told when he was given his first taste.

Maybe, maybe, but he knew that night there would be no living without this.

Soon the surging becomes a deep and pleasant throbbing, and it is at this point that his mind is at last cast adrift, and his body is carried, as if by powerful currents, toward a place where very little at all can find him.

▪

She finds him, though.

Her voice is a whisper reaching him across a great distance.

"The water is starting to get cold," she says.

Remer opens his eyes, sees that Angela is sitting up now, leaning forward and looking at him with eyes that are glassy and half closed.

"Let's go to bed, okay?" she says.

Remer nods. Standing, water running down his skin, he feels cold air attack him from all directions. At this instant his heightened sense of touch is a downside, but there is nothing he can do about that. He pulls a towel from the nearby wall rack and holds it open as Angela rises from the water.

Wrapping it around her shoulders, he begins patting her skin, as much to warm her as to dry her off. Then, leading her from the tub and standing her on the mat, he kneels, begins to dry her from her toes up.

As he does, she watches him. Once she is dry, he quickly dries himself, then takes her by the hand and leads her across his dark apartment to his bed.

They hurry to get under the covers, where Remer smells the familiar mix of rosewater, damp hair, and clean skin. His arousal is instant. Lying on their sides, facing each other, she reaches for him and, using his body as an anchor, pulls herself closer to him with strong arms.

■

Afterward, Angela falls fast asleep, but Remer, his heart pounding beneath his scar, lingers in consciousness.

Eventually, though, he feels himself starting to calm and employs the old trick of imagining his long day as a shore and his body as a boat sailing away from it. This gets him to the very edge of nothingness.

He is there, and about to drop off, when from the other side of the room his cell phone suddenly rings.

It is not, however, the ring of an incoming call.

It is the tone—one long ring followed by three quick rings— assigned to a specific incoming text message.

Hurrying from his bed, he crosses to his desk, pulls the phone from its charger, and sees on the display screen the exact thing he expects to see.

Notification of Silent Alarm.

Below it, the time and date. And below that, the number 4, indicating that it is the back door alarm that has been triggered.

He closes the phone, turns to head into the bathroom to get his clothes, but before he can take more than a few steps, his phone rings again.

This time it is the ring assigned to an incoming call.

On the display, though, is a number he doesn't recognize. Nonetheless, he answers it quickly, for the sake of the woman sleeping nearby.

"Yeah," he says softly. He looks back toward his bed as he continues toward the bathroom. All he hears through the darkness is the long and steady breathing of sleep.

From the phone's earpiece comes a male voice.

"Mr. Remer, this is Sergeant Spadaro, Southampton police. I'm calling to inform you that someone has attempted to break into your business."

Remer, being a business owner, knows most of the cops in town, is even on a first-name basis with many of them, including Spadaro.

It is odd, then, for Spadaro to address him so formally.

But that isn't what really confuses Remer. What confuses him is the fact that the call came so quickly.

He makes a point of keeping from his voice any hint of surprise or suspicion.

Closing the bathroom door behind him, he says, "Yeah, I just got the alert on my cell."

"We'd like you to come down and secure the premises as soon as possible."

"Yeah. Of course. I'm on my way."

There is a silence that causes Remer to believe there is still more information to come. After lingering for a moment, this silence ends finally not with words but with the line going dead.

Remer stops in his tracks and looks at his phone.

There is something not right about this, and despite tonight's full dose, he feels a sense of alarm spreading through him.

▪

Dressed, he hurries from the bathroom to his desk.

Lifting the lid of his notebook computer, he reopens the program displaying live feed to his shop's surveillance cameras and studies the four panels on the screen.

He sees nothing unusual in any of them.

Front and back doors are both closed, the register is still in its place, and the safe upstairs is shut.

Pulling on his boots, he wonders if he should wake Angela but decides not to. If the ringing of his cell and his subsequent movement through his apartment didn't stir her, there's little chance that she'll awaken anytime soon.

Grabbing his coat—a long wool greatcoat from the Second World War that he found at the thrift shop during his first week in town—he leaves quietly, making his way down the stairs and out into the snowy night.

It isn't that cold, easily well above freezing, but he is a man who has just been pulled from the warmth of his bed, so it's cold enough.

In his midsized pickup, Remer steers out of the courtyard and down the narrow driveway. Turning left onto Hampton Road, he heads toward the heart of the village.

3

■

The Christmas trees lining Main are unlit, the brick sidewalks and wide street empty.

As Remer rolls slowly through town, the only motion his eyes can detect is the snow crisscrossing in front of his windshield.

At the end of Main Street he turns right onto Job's Lane; his store is a little more than halfway down the block. A narrow alleyway runs between his building and the one next to it, allowing access to the large, well-lit municipal parking lot. Turning into this alleyway, Remer sees right away two vehicles parked not far from his back door.

An unmarked sedan and a patrol unit, headlights and roof lights dark.

He pulls into his designated parking spot, kills the motor and lights, and gets out. The patrol unit is nearest to him, sitting in the shadow of the small cluster of trees that separates his small back lot from the larger, well-lit town lot. Despite this shadow, Remer is able to see through the windshield of the patrol car and identify the officer seated behind the wheel.

Billie Clarke—young, in her late twenties at the most. Though she is looking directly at Remer, she makes no move to get out and meet him.

So, the unmarked sedan, then.

Just as Remer looks at the vehicle, its driver door opens and Spadaro emerges. He hurries around to its passenger door.

In his early forties, he has a stocky build, dark, curly hair, and a square face. Though Remer can't remember ever seeing the man out of uniform, Spadaro is dressed tonight in street clothes—jeans, sneakers, and a red-and-black-checkered hunter's coat.

Before Remer can say anything, the sergeant opens the passenger door and helps a woman out.

The very sight of her tells Remer that something is, in fact, up.

At first Remer can't understand why Kay Barton would need help getting out of a vehicle. He walks around the patrol unit to meet her, and the instant he is standing face-to-face with her, he sees why.

She is also dressed in street clothes—jeans, work boots, and a familiar green parka that has seen better days. Even though the garment is zipped closed, and is just a bit too big for her, it cannot hide the fact that she is pregnant.

Smiling warmly, Barton says, "Long time no see, boss."

Remer's eyes linger on her protruding stomach, and then he looks at her face. Even in this darkness he can see that very little else about her has changed.

Still pretty, in her plain way, still wearing her brown hair straight and long, still gifted with steady and confident eyes.

"What's going on, Detective?" Remer says.

Barton nods in the direction of his shop's back door. "Sorry about the drama. Obviously, no one tried to break in. I needed you to meet with me right away, so I tripped the alarm myself."

"It might have been easier just to call me."

"No, it wouldn't have been, actually."

Remer says nothing, is reluctant, considering how this conversation is starting, to see it go any further.

Barton knows him well enough to understand this.

"It'll only take a few minutes," she says. "And it is important, otherwise I wouldn't bother you, you know that."

Remer glances at Spadaro, who is surveying the small back lot. It is obvious that the man is concerned someone might see them all gathered together here.

Before looking back at Barton, Remer checks out the cop behind the wheel of the patrol car one more time.

No longer staring at him, she is busy writing something on a clipboard she has balanced on the steering wheel.

"Do you think we can talk?" Barton asks.

Remer looks at her and nods. "Yeah, sure. Let me take care of the alarm first."

∎

Minutes later, Remer is seated in the back of the unmarked sedan, Barton beside him.

Spadaro is up front, watching them in the rearview mirror.

Every now and then a gust of wind whistles past the vehicle, buffeting it and sending the softly falling snow into tiny, furious tornados.

"Sorry to drag you out in this," Barton says.

Remer wonders if she can smell the rosewater—or the scent of Angela—on him.

"Don't worry about it," he says. He looks down at her rounded stomach again. "How far along are you?"

"Seven months."

"Congratulations."

"Thanks."

Last Remer knew Barton was living with her boyfriend, a guy ten years younger than she, in an apartment across from the train station, on the corner of Elm Street and Powell Avenue. He asks her if she's still there; it is the only way he can think of—only delicate way—to ask if she and her boyfriend are still together.

It has been, after all, almost two years since he and Barton have last spoken. More than enough time, as far as Remer is concerned, for things to have fallen apart and for Barton to have moved on.

"Still there," she answers.

"Good for you," Remer says. He waits a moment, then decides to cut to the chase. As warm as the inside of this unmarked sedan may be, it is not his bed.

"So, c'mon, Kay," Remer says, "what's with the runaround tonight?"

"It's important that we cover our tracks like this, at least for now."

"Why?"

"I'm assuming you know about the new chief of police."

"Yeah, I heard about that."

"Have you met him yet?"

Remer shakes his head. "No."

"He used to be a precinct captain in the city. He's very hard-nosed, expects everything to be done by the book and proper. He made it perfectly clear his first day in that he wouldn't tolerate anything less."

"So I gather a call to my phone would be considered improper."

"More or less, yeah."

"You could have used a pay phone."

"I didn't want to risk it. Pay phones are out in the open. And in case we were seen together, I needed a reason for us to have met. This way was the best, trust me."

This is a side of Barton Remer has never seen before.

And her concerns are ones he hoped never to have to deal with again.

"Actually, I'm surprised you haven't met Manfredi yet," Barton says. "He had this big meet-and-greet when he first came in last year, invited all the local business owners. You didn't go?"

When he heard there was a new chief, Remer learned what he

could about the man. The fact that Manfredi had been a New York City cop for twenty years was all Remer needed to know.

What needed to be done to avoid the man, Remer would do.

Better safe than sorry.

"Couldn't make it," Remer says.

"Right now Officer Clarke is filling out a statement. You know Billie, right?"

"I've seen her around."

"It'll say that someone triggered your back door alarm and that you were called to secure the premises. Would you have a problem signing that?"

"No." Remer waits a moment, says finally, "Kay, what's going on?"

Barton sighs, glances at Spadaro, then looks back at Remer. "There's someone I'd like you to meet with."

"Who?"

"You remember Tommy?"

Tommy Miller is her boyfriend. Remer knew very little about the man except that he, too, had been a private investigator for a number of years before retiring suddenly at the ripe old age of thirty.

A property owner and landlord now, Miller keeps an even lower profile than Remer does.

He couldn't help but wonder what Miller is hiding from.

"I've actually never met the guy," Remer says. "But yeah, I remember him."

"Tommy was approached by a woman who wanted to hire him to find someone who has gone missing. He had to turn her down, obviously, but I'd like to help her out. I thought maybe you could do that."

"Back up a minute. Why did he 'have to' turn her down?"

"Because he gave up his license and has no intention of doing that kind of work anymore. But also because if he helped her, it would put me at risk with Manfredi. How could the guy I live with take on a missing persons case without me knowing about it? Manfredi won't even tolerate the appearance of impropriety, and I worked too hard to get where I am now to risk losing it."

"But yet you have Billie filling out a false statement for me to sign."

"Like I said, I want to help this woman if I can."

Remer thinks about that, then says, "What exactly made you think to come to me?"

"Aside from the obvious reason?"

There are some things—some things—that Barton knows about his past life.

"Yeah," Remer says.

"Because the person who has gone missing is someone we both know."

There is no need for Remer to ask Barton to elaborate.

"Mia," he says.

Barton nods. "Yeah."

Remer looks out at the snow and does his best to keep what's suddenly inside him from showing.

Finally, though, he looks back at Barton and says, "Let me guess, the woman who tried to hire Tommy is her mother."

"She seems genuinely concerned. She's afraid something has happened to Mia, says she's been running with a bad crowd."

"From where I'm sitting, Kay, I can see three cops."

"There isn't much we can do, officially. You know that. Mia's an adult. And her mother was hoping to hire someone who can make it his only priority."

"I've got a business to run, Kay."

"I know that. But, like I said, she believes Mia's in trouble."

"There's a surprise."

"Listen, I know she's the last person in the world you'd want to help out. But all things considered, I figured you might want to track her down and maybe get back what she took from you."

"That money is long gone by now, Kay. We both know that." Remer glances at the rearview mirror. Spadaro's eyes are fixed on him. Remer quickly looks away.

Barton says, "If she is in trouble—serious trouble, like her mother thinks—then I'd like to try to help her. I need to."

"Why?"

"Because I worked side by side with her for two years. Because I know things about her you don't. And because I don't believe people are born rotten. Someone made her the way she is. I'm not saying what she did wasn't wrong, because it was, but I think I understand why she did it, why she couldn't stop herself."

Nearly six years ago, when it became obvious that she would not advance under then chief of police Roffman, Barton quit the department. Needing work, she walked into Remer's store one morning. He hired her on the spot.

A woman as attractive as she, and a former cop—how could he not?

Barton had been at the shop for three years when Mia Ferrara came in looking for work. It was Barton who suggested that Remer hire Mia despite her lack of experience.

A thirty-year-old woman who had never held a job in her life.

A troubled daughter of privilege wanting to make it on her own.

It was over a year before Remer and Mia actually got together.

And it was less than a year after that that Mia disappeared with the eighty grand Remer kept in his office safe.

Barton waits for Remer's response, and when none comes, she says, "Mrs. Ferrara offered Tommy some serious money. I know the shop is doing okay, that you haven't been hit yet like everyone else, but that can change. Everyone is folding. You're right, the money is probably long gone by now, but here's a chance for you to maybe get back what was taken from you. Maybe just a part of it, maybe all of it. Mrs. Ferrara kept throwing numbers at Tommy. You should have heard her. She's desperate, and you know she has the money to spare."

The Ferrara family—Mia and her mother being all that is left of it—owns, among other properties throughout the world, an estate in the south end of Southampton and a triplex on Fifth Avenue.

It has been a while since Remer thought of Mia, but there was a time when her departure—so sudden, so *rude*—disturbed him deeply, when all he could do was wonder where she had gone and what man she was with now, if they were happy in any of the many ways she and Remer couldn't be.

"If not for yourself or for her mother," Barton says, "then maybe you could find Mia for me, before she turns up dead and I spend the rest of my life wondering if I should have done something more."

Though this is a concern Remer can relate to, he finds himself unwilling to say anything.

"I know this is a lot to ask," Barton says, "but she was a friend to me during a bad time in my life. Believe me, she has her flaws, but like I said, I know some things about her that you don't. It would mean a lot to me if you found her. If you do and she meets with me and refuses my help, then so be it, she's on her own. I've done everything I could, and you've gotten at least some, if not all, of your money back. Last I knew you were looking to buy your own building in the village. Why pay a lease when you can be paying a mortgage, right? The way the bottom has dropped out of the market, now might be the time for you to do that."

"What things?" Remer asks.

"What do you mean?"

"What things do you know about her that I don't?"

"I promised I would never tell anyone. Everyone has secrets, right?"

It takes a moment, but finally Remer says, "So how would we do this? If I agreed, I mean."

"I'll arrange a meeting and call you later with the details."

"What about covering our tracks?"

Barton says to Spadaro, "Hand me the phone, please, Ricky."

Spadaro passes a cell phone over the top of the seat to Barton. She offers it to Remer.

"It's prepaid, so any calls made to it will be untraceable. And just to be safe, we'll be calling it from another prepaid cell."

It takes Remer another moment, but finally he takes the phone.

"This isn't exactly police procedure, is it?"

"No, it isn't," Barton says. "So what do you say?"

"Yeah, alright. I'll at least meet with the woman, see what she has to say."

"I appreciate this, boss. I really do."

"How long do you think before I'll hear from you?"

"A few hours."

"I might not be able to answer when you call. Will you leave a message?"

"If you make certain to delete it after you've listened to it."

"Of course."

Barton smiles. "Do you have company tonight?"

There is no reason Remer can think of to deny that. "Yeah."

"I'm glad."

"Me, too," Remer says.

He opens the door and steps out into the cold night.

Barton leans across the seat and says, "You'll sign Billie's statement before you leave?"

"Yeah," he says. "No problem. I'll see you, Kay."

He swings the door closed.

4

■

The unmarked sedan leaves, and Remer steps to the patrol car, quickly reads and signs the statement Officer Clarke has written, then watches as she, too, drives off.

Alone in his back parking lot, he waits till all he can hear is the wind, then enters his shop through the back door and heads up the steep and narrow stairs to his small office.

Sitting at his desk, he turns on the monitor that shows the same four-way split screen image he can view from the computer in his apartment.

After a moment, he rises and crosses the small room to his safe. Entering the combination into the keypad, he pulls the heavy door open.

Inside are several bottles of absinthe, collectibles he picked up at auctions over the years. Each is from the mid-1800s—Czech, French, and a very rare Transylvanian. *In case he ever becomes immune to his blend.* He no longer keeps large amounts of cash here, only the day's tally and enough money for the register.

Each night the closing employee puts the day's haul inside an envelope and drops it through a slot that feeds into the safe. The next afternoon Remer transfers that cash into a deposit bag and walks it to his bank on Main Street.

He sees now, below the slot, the envelope containing the cash and the register receipts, but this isn't what he is looking for.

On a shelf at the back of the safe sits a small fireproof box. He takes it out, opens it, and removes a single DVD disc.

He inserts the disc into the computer tower below his desk and opens up the media player from an icon on the desktop and waits for the only video file stored on that disc to play.

It begins, showing the view of his safe from the surveillance camera. There is nothing to see for a moment, and then a figure enters the frame.

It is Mia.

He is caught off guard by how sharply his gut tightens at the sight of her. He watches as she enters the code into the keypad and opens the safe door.

He presses the PAUSE button, freezing the frame. She is standing profile to the camera, and he can see the side of her face clearly now.

Exquisite features—nose, jaw, cheeks—framed by long, dark hair. Pale skin—he can almost smell it now, recalls instantly the pull her scent had on him, that heady mix of testosterone, dopamine, and adrenaline it would trigger.

Attraction is an addiction, there is no getting around that.

Even seeing her in this poorly lit black-and-white surveillance footage causes a little of that mix to enter his blood and rush to his brain.

He lets the video continue, watching as Mia reaches inside the safe and removes from the small fireproof box the manila envelope containing Remer's eighty grand.

Knowing this footage well—how many times has he viewed it?—he freezes the playback again at the right moment, then, clicking the mouse, moves Mia forward frame by frame till he has the clearest image of her this recording allows.

She is wearing black jeans, a wool sweater, and, as always, her leather harness boots. *Her beloved boots.* He remembers clearly the sound their hard soles would make as she walked across the wood floor of his shop. And then, later, his apartment. A tall woman—Remer's height—Mia had what Barton called a cowgirl's walk, which was both a compliment and completely accurate. Whether she was walking down the street or from one side of his shop to the other, Mia would take long, determined strides, and do so without moving her hips, as though some gun belt were hanging low on them. The fact that she was just slightly bowlegged only added to the illusion.

It was Mia's walk that first got to Remer. Strange, maybe, to be caught by such a thing, but then again, maybe not; the manner in which a person moves says so much.

Remer lets the video continue, watching as Mia, leaving the safe door open, swiftly exits the frame.

The playback stops seconds later, and the screen goes blank.

Many memories—too many—rush to fill his mind right now: the winter morning Mia came into his shop looking for work; their first night together a year later; the nights that followed; the day she moved into his place.

The only woman, of those he has known, to actually live with him.

The start of something, or so he thought.

He remembers, too, her smile—strangely knowing, at times even wicked—and how, he later learned, it was only a mask that she wore to hide a deep, almost paralyzing insecurity.

A nest of contradictions, Mia Ferrara: well educated but naive, beautiful but self-conscious, bright but troubled.

It eventually became obvious to Remer that there was between Mia and her mother some kind of battle going on, one that had begun, as far as he could tell, when Mia was just a child.

It was a battle that escalated into something more—something terrible, something darker—on the day Mia learned that her father had been killed in a late-night car crash.

In the weeks that followed Mia changed, her various contradictions giving way to one simple and consistent state of mind: paranoia.

It was as if she had been replaced, overnight, by a stranger.

Their already strained relationship was pushed to the breaking point. Remer did what he could for her, was determined to hang in there and bring her back to her old self, but her hurt was beyond his abilities to heal.

The more he tried to help, the angrier she grew.

Their last week together was a blur of late-night arguments. Mia would disappear in the evenings, be gone for hours at a time, and, when she finally returned, refuse to tell Remer where she had been.

On what would turn out to be their last night together, during a standoff neither was about to win, Mia blurted out what became her last words to Remer.

"I think my mother is going to have me killed."

It was an anguished outburst, childlike. Panicked and angry and frightened, Mia stormed out of his apartment. Tired, knowing their end was near, Remer let her go.

After a sleepless night spent waiting for her to return, Remer was sitting on the edge of his bed and considering driving around to look for her when the call from his opening-shift employee came, informing him that the safe was open.

He knew even before he checked the surveillance footage what that meant.

In the days that followed, Remer left dozens of messages on Mia's cell phone, and sent dozens of texts. He got nothing but silence back.

Nearly a week later a letter addressed to him arrived at the store. It had been slipped through the mail slot in the front door during the night.

All it said was *Please leave me alone.*

Why wasn't he surprised?

And with his past being what it was, how could he go to the police?

▪

Removing the disc from the DVD tray, Remer returns it to the fire-proof box, then closes and locks the safe.

He is lost to these memories for a long moment, then finally finds himself thinking of something Barton said to him.

I know things about her that you don't.

Maybe that is true, but if she was aware of Mia's fears about her mother—fears real enough to Mia to send her running—would she really be helping the woman find her daughter?

Switching off the computer monitor, Remer makes his way through his dark office and down the steep stairs.

He is back out in the snowy night, crossing his small back lot, when the call from Barton comes.

Answering it after the second ring, he says, "That was fast."

Barton explains that they were able to get hold of Mrs. Ferrara right away, then asks if tomorrow evening at seven works for him.

Remer would have assumed that a meeting as urgent as this one—a mother desperate to find her only daughter—couldn't wait, but before he can express his surprise, Barton says, "She's in the city and has a meeting in the morning she can't reschedule. Tomorrow at seven is the soonest she can get out here."

"Where am I meeting her?"

"She has certain security concerns we had to work around, but we came up with the Southampton train station."

Remer pauses. The apartment in which Barton and Miller live has a clear view of that station.

He considers that for a moment, then says, "Yeah, okay."

"You're going to have to take some precautions, and they may seem a little . . . elaborate, but it's the way she says she needs things to go."

Remer reaches his pickup, gets in, and pulls the door closed.

His windshield is covered with a fine layer of wet snow. Turing the ignition, he activates the wipers. One fast sweep and the glass is clear.

"Just tell me what I have to do," he says.

■

Angela is still asleep, so Remer undresses in the bathroom.

Taking off his shirt, he pauses to look at the scar on his chest in the mirror above the sink.

To remind you to mind your own business, the Frenchman had said.

The word that had been branded is gone, removed by a plastic surgeon a few months after Remer arrived in Southampton.

Erased from his flesh but not his mind.

Leaving the bathroom as quietly as he can, Remer opens a bureau drawer and finds a T-shirt, pulls it on. Despite his efforts to be silent, Angela awakens.

"Where are you?" she asks.

"Right here."

"Can't sleep?"

"The alarm went off in the shop. I had to run into town. You were out, so I didn't wake you."

"Everything okay?"

"Yeah. False alarm."

"Oh."

He slips in next to her, as close as he can get, and lies on his back.

"You're cold," she whispers.

"Sorry."

"No, it feels kind of good." She drapes her right arm across his chest, hooks her leg around his, then, resting the side of her face on his shoulder, brushes his neck with her nose.

It isn't long before she is asleep again. And it isn't long after that that all traces of the cold Remer has brought to their bed are gone.

Even though he is smelling Angela's hair and skin and feeling the steady rhythm of her breath, Remer's thoughts are of another.

▪

In the morning they linger in bed for a while.

Eventually, though, it comes time for Angela to get ready for her brunch shift, after which she'll catch the train back to the city.

Rising from his bed, she crosses to his bathroom and reaches around the door, grabbing her bathrobe off the knob. As she puts it on, she turns to Remer and says, "You know, I don't have classes this week. Christmas break. I was thinking maybe you could come in with me and hang out."

This is something Angela has never suggested before.

Remer, seated on the edge of his mattress, says, "I have a meeting tonight." His answer, he knows, is just a bit too quick.

"My roommate is going skiing with her parents for the week, so I'll have the whole place to myself. You could come in Monday. Or Wednesday. That's Christmas Eve, right? There's a working fireplace, and the market on the corner sells these little bundles of firewood."

He hesitates, doesn't want to respond as quickly this time, says finally, "I don't really like the city that much."

"Oh. Okay."

"Also, it's a busy week at the shop. The holiday rush."

"It was just a thought." She waits a moment, then says, "This thing of ours doesn't have to be anything other than what it is. I'm busy, you're busy, and when you get to be our age, there's a lot to be said for convenience. But I can't be afraid to ask for a little more if I want it. I'm not a big fan of being afraid. Twenty years of that was plenty."

"That's fair."

"If you end up changing your mind, you know how to reach me. The apartment is in the West Village, so all you'd need to do is walk out of Penn Station and catch a cab down Seventh."

"I'll think about it."

She pauses. "I didn't make things weird just now, did I?"

"No. No."

"You sure?"

"Yeah." He shrugs. "I used to live in the city, that's all."

"I didn't know that."

"It was a long time ago."

"Bad memories?"

"Something like that."

"Hey, trust me, I understand bad memories. Sometimes the thing to do is face them, you know?"

"That's what I hear."

"And then there's that other approach—replace them with good memories."

"It's tempting, Ange. It really is. We'll see."

She smiles. "I had a mother; I know what 'we'll see' means."

Remer wants to say something, offer her something, anything, but he comes up blank.

Certain intimacies he is good at, while others are simply beyond his reach.

Angela walks to him, then leans down and kisses him.

"Have yourself a merry little Christmas," she says.

"You, too."

Standing up straight, she looks down at him for a moment, then turns and heads toward the door.

Opening it, she says, "I'll see you next Saturday, lover man."

"I'll be here."

The door closes, and all that is left of Angela is her scent on Remer and the sound of her footsteps in the hall.

5

Remer's store closes at six on Sundays.

Once that hour comes and goes with no automated text to his cell or sound of sirens in the distance—and once he receives the text from his closing employee with the day's tally twenty minutes later—there is nothing left for Remer to do but sit in his chair and wait till it is time to leave for his meeting with Mrs. Ferrara.

The train station is a ten-minute walk away, so he has a half hour.

A long time to be alone and lucid.

His blend is on the windowsill in front of him, within easy reach. Usually by now he has taken a full dose, is already adrift, and though he comes close to reaching for the blue vial a dozen times, he never actually does.

There are things he wants to know, questions of his own he would like answered.

He will need, for now, to remain clearheaded.

▪

At six forty-five he puts on his boots and greatcoat, then grabs a small duffel bag, per Barton's instructions, and tosses a few random things into it to give it weight.

Leaving his place, he heads across the courtyard toward the narrow driveway leading to the street, glancing through the row of bare trees at Red Bar as he goes.

Angela should have left for the city by now. Still, Remer moves quickly and quietly while in view of the restaurant, just in case.

He crosses Hampton Road, walks west for a half block, then turns right onto Elm and follows that to its end. The train station is straight ahead, across a wide street called Railroad Plaza. Crossing it and stepping onto the long platform, Remer places the duffel at his feet and begins waiting.

Nothing more than a man come to catch the 7:30 eastbound.

A few moments pass before he finally looks over his right shoulder at the two-story building standing on the corner of Elm Street and Powell Avenue.

A French-Moroccan restaurant called L'Orange Bleu occupies the ground floor, and above it is the apartment in which Barton and Miller live.

The restaurant is closed, its windows dark, the tables beyond empty. The windows above, three in a row, are dark and empty, too.

Well, not completely.

In one Remer can see a small red light glowing steady.

Stand within twenty feet of the pay phone, Barton had told him. He estimates that he is farther away than that, so he picks up his duffel and moves till he is no more than six feet from the phone, then drops the duffel again and continues his act.

Mrs. Ferrara was supposed to meet him at seven, which would give them plenty of time to talk before the 7:30 arrived. But there is no sign of her—or anyone, for that matter—anywhere. When Remer first checks his watch, it is 7:04. When he checks it again, it is 7:09. Glancing again back at the row of dark windows, he thinks of calling Barton on the prepaid cell phone but decides not to—yet.

Finally, though, at 7:14, a car appears, turning onto Railroad Plaza from North Main.

He watches it approach. It is a Mercedes sedan, a brown four-door, not new but not vintage, either. The vehicle pulls in close to the platform steps and parks. A moment passes, and Remer begins to doubt that this is Mrs. Ferrara. But then the driver door opens and a woman exits.

He looks forward then, glancing westward down the tracks. He hears her climb the stairs and cross the platform. Reaching its edge, she aligns herself with Remer but keeps a distance of about six feet between them.

She, too, looks westward down the tracks.

Two strangers waiting for a train.

Remer is startled by the resemblance between mother and daughter.

The same height, the same length of limb, the same long, dark hair. Had he watched her approach, would he have seen the same lanky walk?

And though Mrs. Ferrara is, of course, older—even under the dim lights of the station Remer can see lines around her eyes and the edges of her mouth—her facial features are nearly identical to Mia's.

The only real difference Remer can observe is that this woman is well tended in that way wealthy women of a certain age often are— groomed to the point of being polished—while Mia, on the other hand, seldom wore makeup and often got out of bed and started her day with little more than the quick running of a brush through her hair.

Remer glances at his watch. 7:15.

Before he can say anything, Mrs. Ferrara—*how could this not be her?*—says, "It took longer than I thought to get here from the Hampton Bays station."

While Remer is to appear to anyone who may be watching as

a man waiting to catch the train east, Mrs. Ferrara is to appear as a woman waiting to meet someone arriving from the west.

She no doubt dropped off the person she is here to meet at the Hampton Bays station—the next station west—then drove here.

"We still have fifteen minutes," Remer says. He pauses, then introduces himself. *It is the polite thing to do.*

Smiling, quickly looking Remer up and down, Mrs. Ferrara says, "I'm Evelyn. Thank you for meeting with me like this."

"No problem."

He wants to ask why it is she needed to meet in this manner but doesn't. Precautions as such—granted, ones less elaborate than this— were common enough back in his PI days.

"Since we're short on time, I'll get right to it. I understand you were involved with my daughter at one point."

"I was."

"May I ask for how long?"

"Close to a year."

"And when was the last time you saw her?"

"A year ago last October."

"About a month after her father died."

"That's correct."

"That's when I lost touch with her as well." Evelyn Ferrara pauses a moment, then looks westward down the tracks and continues. "Mia and her father were close, in a way she and I weren't able to be. He indulged her and, for the most part, left all the parenting to me. I was, therefore, by comparison, the bad guy." She looks at him and smiles again. "I'm certain you've heard a horror story or two about me."

Remer shrugs once but says nothing.

"It's okay," she says. "I've long since stopped caring what my daughter tells people about me. What she doesn't tell anyone, and probably never will, is that she and I are probably too much alike. Too strong-willed, too stubborn. Maybe you saw a little bit of that in her when you were together."

Again, Remer says nothing.

Evelyn Ferrara waits a moment, then says, "My daughter worked in your liquor store here in town for two years, correct?"

"Yeah."

"I'm curious, was she a good worker?"

"Why do you ask?"

"After college she went through a particularly difficult period, one that lasted many years. She saw a number of doctors but didn't stay with any one of them for very long. Certainly not long enough for them to be of help. Finally, though, we found someone she liked, and after a few months he diagnosed her with narcissistic personality disorder. Do you know what that is?"

"Not exactly."

"It's more than a case of one being in love with his or her own reflection. The most common symptoms are a need for admiration and a complete lack of empathy. But there are others—a sense of entitlement, wildly inaccurate interpretations of what others say and do, and a belief that one's conduct is always correct, no matter how painful to others it may be. Mia, we are told, has moderate to severe impairment, as indicated by her inability to hold a job, her tendency to take advantage of others, and her willingness to alienate friends and family at the drop of a hat. Does any of this ring a bell?"

Remer nods once.

Evelyn Ferrara studies his face, then continues.

"Narcissists tend to be aloof and avoid intimacy, though they *can* attach themselves to someone they deem worthy, or necessary, but only for as long as that person remains worthy or necessary. Because of her sense of entitlement, my daughter has always considered most things to be beneath her. Other people, organizations, work. So I find it interesting that she was able to work as a simple store clerk for so long. Perhaps your relationship with her allowed her to . . . get away with things. Take days off, avoid certain tasks, that kind of thing."

"She did what everyone else did," Remer says.

"Perhaps you're the kind of boss who lavishes praise."

I'm the kind of boss who is hardly there, Remer thinks.

Then, another thought: *Perhaps it was Barton's friendship that allowed Mia to change—for a while, at least.*

"I'm sorry to say this, but my daughter has a long history of getting involved with men who can help her, only to abruptly disappear on them once she has taken all she can get. Or once she has found someone else, someone she believes to be more . . . deserving. Looking the way she does, and being from a well-to-do family, meant there was never a shortage of men willing to go along for the ride."

When Remer hired Barton, there was an increase in business during her shifts. It was the same when he hired Mia.

And when the two of them worked the same shift together . . .

"She's not an evil person," Evelyn Ferrara says. "You were with her for almost a year, so there had to be some reason why you stuck around so long. And, of course, there had to be a reason why you got involved with her in the first place. From what I understand there is some debate among doctors whether this disorder is an irredeemable one or not. Is it an abnormality of the brain or learned behavior? I think the fact that she held a job for two years and stayed with you for so long means she was capable of change—was, in fact, trying to change. Obviously, the death of her father—the one man who loved her unconditionally—triggered something within her and sent her running back to her old ways."

Remer thinks about that, then says, "I'm told you want to find her. Why now, so long after she took off?"

"About a week after she disappeared, I got a letter from her. A long letter recounting all the terrible things I had ever done to her. You could hear the mania as you read her words. She ended the letter by saying that she never wanted to see me again. Its postmark indicated it was mailed from Southampton. Naturally I was concerned, so I hired a PI firm in the city to send someone to find her. It took a year for them to track her down, at which point they kept her under constant surveillance."

Remer wonders which PI firm Evelyn Ferrara had hired; he knew them all, or did once.

He wonders, too, how much their work had cost her.

He says nothing, though, letting her continue.

"She was living in Bridgehampton with a bartender who was, frankly, much too young for her. The firm did a background check on this man, and it turns out there are some things in his past that are, well, alarming."

"Like what?"

"He has several aliases, for starters. And there is no indication that he ever held a job, under any of his names, for very long. There had to be a reason, knowing my daughter's condition, for her to be with a man like that. When the investigators dug a bit deeper into this man's past, they discovered that he was once a suspect in a murder-for-hire scheme up in Canada, where he is from. Just days after my investigators learned this, as her doctor was going over all their reports, Mia and the bartender disappeared again."

"Did your men see any indications of violence between Mia and her boyfriend?"

"No."

"I don't understand. I was told you were concerned about her safety."

"It's not hers I'm worried about. It's mine."

"I'm sorry, I'm not following—"

"I'm afraid my daughter is planning to have me killed. And I think her disappearing is the first step in executing that plan."

6

It takes a moment before Remer is able to speak again.

"Why would she want that? Why would she have you killed?"

"If hating me for all the wrong I supposedly inflicted upon her isn't reason enough, there is always the money. She is my only child, and per her father's will, she stands to inherit everything when I die. There is nothing I can do to change that."

"But what good would finding her do?"

"I have her doctor ready to tell a judge that she's a danger to herself and others, which is required for involuntary commitment in New York state. She needs care. She needs to be locked away before she does something that can't be undone."

"The firm you hired found her once already. Why don't you have them do it again?"

"They recently went out of business. The man I worked with directly, and his several partners, are all a bit difficult to get hold of right now. Apparently they're dodging several lawsuits. I paid them a hefty retainer, only a little over half of which was used. My lawyer looked around for someone else, and he was referred to a man named Miller. Unfortunately, he is retired, but he suggested that I talk to you. He says you used to do this kind of thing for a living."

"That was a long time ago."

"I'm certain you've retained the necessary skills."

Remer says nothing.

Evelyn Ferrara seems to be deciding something. Finally, she says, "I understand that Mia took a large sum of money from you when she left. Eighty thousand dollars, to be exact."

Remer never filed a police report, so this information—the fact that Mia had stolen from him, and the exact amount she had taken— could have come only from Barton.

Not a betrayal, exactly, but he would have preferred that this matter remain private.

Again, Remer says nothing.

"That must have been . . . emasculating."

What could Remer say to that?

"Find her and I'll pay you what she took. Frankly, her having stolen from you will only help matters when we get in front of a judge."

To this, Remer knows exactly how to respond.

"I'm sorry," he says. "I mind my own business these days."

"But you'd be helping yourself as much as you'd be helping me. So that makes this your business. Doesn't it?"

Remer shakes his head.

She takes a step toward him, closing the distance from six feet down to three.

The same long stride as her daughter.

It is doubtful that their conversation would appear now, to anyone watching, as a casual one.

In a low but determined voice, Evelyn Ferrara says, "Do you know what it's like to live in fear? In fear for your life? Knowing that there is someone out there waiting for the chance to kill you—planning for it—is just paralyzing. The fact that that someone is your own child, well, I don't expect you to understand that. But I can assure you that it is unbearable."

"Hire a bodyguard," Remer says flatly.

"I have. And if he weren't on the train right now, on his way here, he'd be standing right behind me, trust me. Fearing for your life is not living. You must be able to understand that."

It has been a long time since Remer has had to wonder what is known about him by someone. As is always the case at times likes these, his mind goes to his last days in New York.

No matter how well one covers his tracks, the risk of a trail being found is always there.

Glancing past her, Remer sees in the distance the lights of the train. A half mile away and approaching fast.

"I can give you five grand right now," Evelyn Ferrara says. "If that'll help you make up your mind."

It seems to Remer that no matter what he says or does here, regret will be the result. Long seconds pass, and then he says, "I can look, but I can't guarantee anything."

"I understand that."

"And all I need to do is find her?"

"That's all I'm asking. Just find out where she is living. My lawyer will contact the proper authorities."

"And you'll pay me eighty grand."

"Plus five for your troubles."

"You can keep that."

"Does this mean you'll help me?"

He already feels regret.

"What was the bartender's name?" he asks.

"David Brazier. For some reason, he is using his real name."

It doesn't ring any bells. "Where was he working?"

"A place called Pintauro's."

That, on the other hand, Remer has heard of.

It is a restaurant and nightclub on Montauk Highway, in that stretch between the villages of Water Mill and Bridgehampton.

Was that where Mia had gone all those nights she disappeared for hours on end?

Was that the place she ran to the night she left him?

Evelyn Ferrara has to raise her voice to be heard over the train, which is only a few hundred feet away.

"According to my investigator, Brazier quit Pintauro's at the same time he and Mia disappeared. My investigator went there to get information, but Brazier didn't leave a forwarding address—or so the manager claimed. Maybe you'll have better luck."

The train pulls in. To be heard over the noise, Remer shouts.

"I'll be in touch," he says.

Evelyn Ferrara smiles, seems genuinely grateful.

She either says or mouths the words "Thank you."

■

Only one passenger disembarks from the eastbound train.

A man in his late twenties, maybe early thirties, tops. He is dressed in a suit and a dark overcoat. Remer's height, but with a significantly more powerful build, thick like a tree trunk from shoulder to thighs.

Evelyn Ferrara's bodyguard.

He has an intense look on his face—stoic but alert, focused to the point of sternness. It is a look Remer knows well. Following his discharge from the Marine Corps, where he'd seen that same face on every other kid in his unit, Remer himself had worked as a bodyguard. He did this for several years before working his way up to investigator and eventually being hired on by a Manhattan law firm.

After five years of corporate life, he finally branched out on his own, had by then allowed all those sharp edges the Corps had carved in him to round off and fall away.

So he knows a fellow former marine when he sees one.

He knows, too, a marine who is, more or less, fresh out of uniform—at least not out of uniform so long that his edges have begun to round.

Evelyn Ferrara introduces the two men. *Mr. Remer, Mr. Smith.* This is per the instructions Barton passed on. If Remer decides to turn Mrs. Ferrara down, he is to simply get on the train. If he agrees to help her, he is to remain a moment and shake hands with this man, at which point the man will pass to Remer a small flash drive containing all the information that has been gathered so far on Mia and her boyfriend.

Smith's grip is, of course, fast and firm. He has blue eyes that seek out Remer's with a directness bordering on assertion.

Remer wants to smile, remembers clearly those days when seeing the world through a marine's eyes was all he knew how to do.

He doesn't smile, however, nor does he revert to old habits by offering this kid a dose of what he's giving Remer.

Too old for that nonsense.

As they end their handshake, there is a slight turning of the wrists so that when they break their grips and withdraw, Remer's hand will be facing palm up.

He feels the postage-stamp-sized flash drive pressed against his skin. Keeping it there by wedging it securely between two creases, he picks up his small duffel packed with random things and boards the train.

Taking a seat, he watches from his green-tinted window as Evelyn Ferrara and her roughneck bodyguard move down the platform steps and head toward her Mercedes-Benz.

As they reach the vehicle and the bodyguard opens the passenger door for her, he touches her elbow in a way that catches Remer's attention.

He was once paid good money to recognize gestures of intimacy between a man and a woman.

His professional eye—or what remains of it—tells him that what he is seeing could very well be an indicator of a relationship beyond that of bodyguard-client.

But it could also be a gesture of simple courtesy.

Not his call to make anymore.

When the train pulls away from the platform and they are gone from his sight, there is nothing else for Remer to do but look at the stark shadows racing by in a blur outside his window and occasionally focus on the faint reflection of his own face on the cold glass.

▪

He is one of three passengers to disembark at the Bridgehampton station.

The cab that Barton arranged is waiting for him, standing not at the platform but toward the back of the parking lot, to avoid being approached by someone other than Remer.

As he walks to it, he sees on its drivers door lettering that reads EDDIE'S CAB COMPANY. Below it is a phone number, simple enough for even the worst drunk to remember.

Seven sevens.

Nothing short of genius, Remer thinks.

He knows of Eddie, pretty much everyone in town does, but it is not Eddie, an elderly Jamaican man, seated behind the wheel. It is, instead, a young woman.

She looks over her shoulder at Remer as he slides into the backseat. She is in her midtwenties, is wearing a wool hat that covers shoulder-length hair, and has a face that is round and broad. Her jawline and cheeks, however, are sharp and angular.

"You're Remer?" she says. Her voice is deep for a young woman. The eyes looking back at him in the rearview mirror are dark brown.

Remer nods.

As she steers the cab toward the lot's exit, Remer glances at the license mounted on the backseat, finds her name. Brianna Ruocco.

The photo shows her with no hat on. Her hair is a fountain of dark twists and twirls.

Leaving Bridgehampton Village, they head west toward Southampton. Remer looks out the window to his right; he knows it will come up soon enough, and it isn't long before it emerges out of the darkness.

Pintauro's.

Like a number of the restaurants and nightclubs on the East End, it was first a private residence, then later adapted for commercial use. California Spanish: two stories, a red tile roof, stucco walls painted yellow—but not recently, that much is certain.

Its parking lot is a narrow, tree-lined lot of worn grass, its driveway a mix of sand and dirt, woefully uneven. Remer sees, during the few seconds that the building is visible, only a handful of cars parked in that lot, but then again it is early, and it is a Sunday night in December.

Ten minutes later, the Southampton train station is outside Remer's window. He thinks of suggesting she take him home, but if this is what Barton instructed the driver to do, it was for a reason.

Glancing forward at the rearview mirror, Remer meets the young woman's stare.

"What do I owe you?" he asks.

"It's taken care of."

Remer nods and says, "Thanks for the ride."

"No problem."

Climbing out, he is hit by a cold he almost forgot about. Pulling up the collar of his greatcoat and slipping his hands into its deep pockets, he looks up at the apartment above L'Orange Bleu.

Its windows are still dark, but the small red light he saw earlier is now gone.

No sign of a soul anywhere.

The cab drives off, and Remer begins retracing his steps along Elm.

Returning to his apartment and inserting the flash drive into his laptop, Remer sits down and one by one opens and scans the dozen of documents.

The reports from the PI firm remind him of the reports he used to write. The name of the firm, listed on the letterhead, is one he has never heard of, but he has been out of the business for almost six years now.

The first report he reads recounts how Mia was located, and the next one tracks, day by day, at times hour by hour, her subsequent activity.

Another report chronicles the background of David Brazier, and confirms, as Evelyn Ferrara stated, that this name is not one of his many aliases but in fact his actual name.

Odd, Remer thinks, but he has known people—career criminals like Brazier—who have done things more reckless than that.

By skimming this report, Remer gathers enough information to know that Evelyn Ferrara does indeed have reason to be concerned. There are a number of arrests in his jacket, his first being for auto theft and his last for stealing drugs from a hospital in which he worked as an orderly.

It is from this report that Remer learns Brazier's age.

Twenty-five. Nineteen years younger than Remer. And seven years younger than Mia.

A glimpse—albeit a painful one—into something that has always been a mystery to Remer: *Who did Mia run to when she ran from him?*

Finally, Remer turns his attention to a folder on the flash drive marked PHOTOS.

Opening it, he watches as the tiny thumbnail previews blink into view. Even without opening these photos he can tell that they are the exact kind that he used to take. Surveillance photos, many taken from a distance, some even through windows. Still, despite their small size, he can see Mia clearly enough in most of them.

He spots, halfway down the folder, a thumbnail with two people in it.

He opens it, and a photo instantly fills the screen of his computer.

It is a shot of Mia and Brazier walking to a car. Mia is laughing, has her arm hooked around Brazier's.

A happy couple—at least at this particular moment.

Opening up a few more photos, he sees more of the same. His first instinct is to find his vial and down a dose of his blend. His mind is crowded with too many chemical reactions. But instead he remains at his desk, opening a few more photos till he has had enough.

He moves to a final folder. Inside it are reports from not one but three psychiatrists. He barely skims those, feels that to do more would be an invasion of Mia's privacy.

And anyway, what could they tell him that he doesn't already know, and from firsthand experience.

He should not have said yes to this, that much is clear. But it is too late for that; the part of him that needs to know—has always wanted to know, must know—has taken over.

He drags and drops each folder to his hard drive, storing them in an encrypted folder to keep them secure. From there copies will be automatically uploaded to an online backup facility.

He selects two photographs—two that look the least like surveillance photos, one a shot of just Mia, the other a shot of just Brazier—and queues them up to be printed out.

As the printer goes to work, he removes the flash drive and places it in the top drawer of his desk. Checking the time, he sees that it is almost nine.

When the photos are done, he removes them from the printer tray and, without looking at either, folds and pockets them as he heads out the door.

As he approaches his pickup, he sees that a slip of paper has been placed under the driver's-side windshield wiper.

He looks around, then takes it.

It is a note from Barton reminding him, should he need to reach her, to use the prepaid cell phone she provided. He pockets this note as well and is getting into his truck when he realizes there is something on the passenger seat.

A carrying case made of impact-resistant plastic.

He opens it, and inside, held securely within compartments of molded foam, are several pieces of equipment.

Each item is something he may require during the course of tonight's job.

The tools of his trade.

He knows them well.

Closing the case, he turns the ignition and switches the heater to its highest setting, then steers toward the end of his driveway.

He pauses there, then makes a right onto Hampton Road, heading eastward toward Bridgehampton and the place he believes Mia may have gone the night she walked out his door.

7

By the time he reaches Pintauro's, the number of vehicles in its grassy lot has at least doubled.

Still, the lot is nowhere near full.

Parking his pickup in a dark corner, he kills the motor and lights and gets out. Though this lot is little more than a perimeter of darkness, Pintauro's itself is aglow, illuminated by a number of floodlights mounted along its foundation and aimed upward at steep angles.

Inside, the only light sources are dimly lit track lights mounted on the low ceiling and the illuminated shelves behind the long antique bar.

The sound system is playing soft jazz loudly. Though there are dozens of people seated in the dining room—in booths and at tables for two—Remer can hear only the music and, beneath it, the faint and steady murmur of hushed voices.

A lovers' destination, Pintauro's, designed with intimacy—and discretion—in mind.

The long bar is to the left of the room. At it three people—a couple and, one stool away, an older man—are seated. Right away Remer can tell by the couple's body language that the solitary man is intruding upon their privacy.

Wanting privacy of his own, Remer chooses to sit at the far end of the bar, nearest to the door and a good dozen stools away from the unhappy threesome.

The bartender, a woman in her early thirties, is dressed in black leather pants and a tight, sleeveless T-shirt. Complex sleeves of tattoos—swirling blacks, greens, and reds—cover her forearms. On her wrists are a variety of bangles and bracelets and strips of raw cowhide, and on her feet are high-top sneakers, their black canvas faded and worn. Her hair, as dark as a Bible, shimmers, her bangs, long and jaggedly cut, all but hiding her eyes.

A rock 'n' roll chick, if ever Remer saw one.

She approaches the moment he sits down, is probably herself eager to get away from that lonely old man. She offers Remer a fast and warm smile, showing teeth that are perfect, and says, "What can I get you?"

He orders tequila, neat.

"I like the sound of that." She places a bar napkin in front of him. "Patrón? Sauza?"

"Cuervo Gold is fine."

"Water back?"

"Please."

She nods, puts a second napkin next to the first one, and steps away.

Remer removes the photos from his back pocket and places them, still folded, beside the napkins.

The bartender returns with a tumbler of Cuervo and a highball glass of water, setting them on the napkins. "Lime?"

"No, this is fine."

"Just so you know, in case you're hungry, the kitchen closes in about a half hour."

"I'm good, thanks." He unfolds the photos. "Actually, I was wondering if you might be able to help me."

"With what?"

He slides the photos toward her. "I'm looking for some friends. I was wondering if you might know them."

Smiling, she says, "You a cop?"

"No."

She picks up the photos, looks at the one, then the other. Her smile doesn't diminish, but in the way it lingers, Remer can tell that it is forced.

"Who are they?" she says. "I mean, what are their names?"

"The woman is Mia. The guy is her boyfriend. He used to work here."

"What's his name?"

"Dave Brazier."

"He must have left before I started. Sorry, I've never seen either of them before." She hands the photos back to him. "Why are you looking for them?"

"She used to work for me. I need to know where to send her W-2 next month."

It is the best lie he can come up with.

"You certainly came prepared." She nods toward the photos.

"I used to be a Boy Scout."

She doesn't laugh.

"Actually," Remer says, "I'm leaving town for a few months, and I need to get this taken care of before I go."

"Wish I could help you."

"Maybe someone who was around when Dave used to work here knows where he went. Someone in the kitchen, maybe. Or the manager."

"If I spoke better Spanish I'd ask the kitchen guys. And the manager ran out to get some smokes. He shouldn't be long. I can ask him when he gets back."

"I'd appreciate it."

"No problem. Do you want to start a tab?"

"No, I'll pay up now."

"That's nine fifty."

He hands her a twenty, tells her to keep the change.

"I like the sound of that, too."

▪

Remer sips his drink and waits.

The couple at the end of the bar finally have enough, pay their tab, and leave, after which the rock 'n' roll chick bartender is all that is left to entertain the lonely man. He compliments her far too often, tells her about his sailboat, that he'll be heading south soon and that she should come with him. She tells him she can't, that she boxes out of a gym in Riverhead and has a fight coming up soon. His smile is condescending, his doubt obvious, so she demonstrates by shadowboxing— a combination of jabs and hooks capped off with a cross and uppercut. Her body mechanics are perfect, her form flawless. It took, Remer knows, years of training to achieve this level of proficiency.

Shortly after this the bartender ducks into the kitchen, is gone for several minutes. Remer passes the time by observing the man. Eventually he wonders what it was that made this man so lonely that he insists on going out and finding—stealing, if he must—the attention of others.

Even at Remer's worst, in the very bad months following Mia's rude departure, he never got so miserable that he felt compelled to venture out into public and take his grief out on others.

Sorrow—real sorrow—is best kept hidden.

After the bartender returns from the kitchen, Remer senses that something has changed.

She doesn't look at him—doesn't even once look his way—and is suddenly more than happy to give the lonely man her undivided attention.

The change in her demeanor doesn't in itself concern Remer, it is what the change could mean.

When in doubt, get out.

He downs the rest of his drink, folds up and pockets the photos, which he kept out in case the manager did return, then stands and readies to leave.

It is only then that the bartender acknowledges him.

The suddenness of her attention is, for Remer, telling.

"Where you going?" she says.

"It's getting late."

"I should have told you, the manager called while I was in the kitchen just now. He's on his way back. I told him someone was waiting for him."

Maybe the truth, maybe not—Remer heard no ringing phone, though the call could have come to a cell phone in her pocket and set on vibrate.

"Maybe I could give him a call tomorrow," he says.

"Seriously, he'll be here in, like, five minutes. You should wait, have another drink. On me."

Remer knows a stall when he hears one.

"Can't, but thanks."

The bartender's smile gives her away—she is uncertain what exactly to say or do next.

Remer doesn't give her the chance to figure her problem out, has already stepped away from the bar and is heading toward the exit.

Outside, he makes his way across the dirt driveway and enters the dark edge of the grassy lot. He reaches his pickup and is about to get in when he hears from behind him the sound of a door opening, followed immediately by the sound of someone calling after him.

The door Remer heard is the back door to the restaurant, and the someone calling after him is male.

"Hang on, hang on."

Remer stops and turns to face the man as he approaches.

"You looking for Dave?"

"It's no big deal," Remer says.

"I'm Rene. I'm the manager." The man's accent is French, and Remer is briefly but instantly back in that empty warehouse in Brooklyn.

He shakes the memory off—the memory of that man's voice and what he said—and says, "I thought you were out."

"I must have come in the back door just as you were going out the front."

The man stops just a few feet from Remer. He is tall, imposing, and with the only source of light coming from behind him, his face is entirely featureless.

"I'm running late," Remer says.

"Casey tells me that Dave's girl used to work for you and that you're trying to get her W-2 to her."

Remer nods. "That's right. Any idea where she is?"

"A guy came here about two months ago looking for them. In a suit."

"I don't know anything about that."

The more Remer hears this man's accent, the more he can detect differences between the way he speaks and the way his tormentor spoke.

His tormentor had a muddier accent, while the man standing a few feet from him in the dark now has a cleaner one and is clearly better educated.

Of course it isn't Remer's tormentor, can't be.

Still . . .

Rene says, "I told the man in the suit that I didn't know where they went. I'm afraid that hasn't changed."

"It was worth a shot."

"You said Dave's girl used to work for you, right?"

"Yeah."

"Would you mind telling me where?"

"Why?"

"If you are really who you say you are—Mia's former employer—then maybe we can help each other out."

Remer isn't keen on the idea of giving up the location of his business because to do so would be tantamount to surrendering his identity.

So far, to this man, and the bartender inside, he is nobody.

He'd like to keep it that way, but if revealing himself in this way will get him the information he needs . . .

"I own a liquor store in Southampton," Remer says.

"Where in Southampton?"

"Job's Lane."

Satisfied, Rene nods, then says, "Dave gave me an address when I hired him. I went by it a couple of times myself after he quit, but it looked pretty empty."

"What does 'pretty empty' mean, exactly?"

"There was a mattress on the bedroom floor, some other things here and there, but other than that, the place was bare. Maybe they were squatting. A lot of rental units are sitting empty these days. Or maybe he was using the address as a mail drop. Who knows?"

"I'm curious," Remer says. "Why were you looking for him?"

"The little scam-artist bastard cleaned out my register the night he quit. It was just a couple of grand, but I'd still like to have a word with him, if you know what I mean."

Remer does, though he is careful not to indicate this.

"The problem with hiring the wrong people," Rene says, "is that you don't know they're the wrong people till it's too late. I'm sure as a fellow employer you must have experienced that."

Does this man know?

Did Brazier—or Mia, for that matter—boast about what had been done to him?

Remer ignores the comment.

"I'll tell you what," Rene says. "I will give you that address on one condition."

"What?"

"If you find him, you let me know where the bastard is."

"Can't do that. Sorry."

"Why not?"

"For all I know, you'll kill the guy."

"Not over a couple of grand."

"Things might get out of hand. Things like that usually do."

Rene shrugs. "Fair enough."

Though he still can't see the man's face, Remer senses that he is smiling.

"I'd be happy to share his whereabouts with the police, if that helps."

"I suppose it'll have to. I don't remember the exact number of the house, but the street is called Magee Drive. It's over in Southampton. Not Magee Street—I made that mistake myself already. This one is across from the college. Do you know it?"

"I'll find it."

"The street itself is only a block long, and the house is the only yellow one on it, so it should be easy."

"Thanks. I appreciate this."

Remer turns away and heads toward his pickup.

"Good hunting," Rene says.

Remer ignores this, too. Reaching his pickup, he gets in.

As he drives out of the lot, he sees the man walk past the restaurant's back door, which he has left slightly ajar, and head toward a Range Rover parked in a far corner.

Remer sees the man pull something from his pocket—it is difficult to tell what, though—and look down at it as he walks.

Maybe a cell phone, or a set of keys.

Or maybe just a pack of smokes.

8

A half hour later Remer is parked a few doors down from a small cottage on a dark Southampton side street.

From the outside the place looks unlived in, but so do most of the other dozen or so single-story homes on this street, three of which have FOR SALE signs posted in their front yards.

Two of those signs indicate that the homes are bank owned.

These places are most likely rental properties, and even in a good year many of them sit unused from October to April.

After several minutes pass and Remer has gotten a sense of the quiet neighborhood—not a hint of motion at all, from anywhere, and every house dark—he grabs his flashlight from under the passenger seat and exits his pickup.

Backtracking to the cottage and crossing onto its property, he follows its driveway around back.

The rear face of the single-story cottage is a series of three large windows, each one several feet from the other, and, between the first and second windows, a back door.

Remer shines his light into the first window and sees a living room empty save for a large Persian rug.

Looking through the back door, Remer sees a long mud porch, its floor cracked tile.

The next window shows a kitchen that is completely empty.

The final window is the largest of them all. Remer pauses, then shines his light through it and sees a bedroom with just two items in it: a single folding chair leaning up against a wall and, on the floor, in the center of the bare room, a mattress covered with a rumpled blanket.

Remer doubts now that this is a rental property since summer rentals are generally furnished, and a chair and a mattress could hardly be called furnished, even by the most unscrupulous of land-lords.

An abandoned house, then, one of the many in the limbo leading up to foreclosure—a long limbo these days, due to the record number of homes being lost.

None of this matters, though. What does matter is the presence of that mattress.

And, too, the folding chair.

Making his way around to the front of the house, Remer quickly scans the neighborhood, then approaches the mailbox and opens it, but finds nothing inside.

Back in his pickup, he tries to decide what to do next. It is difficult to imagine Mia living in such a manner. "Slumming it" with Remer in his modest apartment was one thing, but squatting in an unrented cottage across from the college is another.

And if they were living there, wouldn't Remer have seen some signs of use in the kitchen?

No, this doesn't add up.

There is only, as far as Remer can see, one other purpose that an empty house with only a mattress could serve.

A place for a couple to be alone.

Mia and Brazier had disappeared on the men sent by the investigator Evelyn Ferrara had hired.

They could be sleeping on someone's couch and have no privacy. An empty home Brazier used to get his mail—something a "scam-artist bastard," as Brazier's former boss had called him, would do—could suddenly, easily become a place for them to fuck.

The mattress and the chair—Mia, Remer recalls, had a real fondness for sex in a chair—makes this even more likely.

The only thing Remer can think to do now is wait and watch.

It has been six years since he has does this kind of thing—waited in a vehicle on a dark street in hopes of catching a couple in the act.

The last time, in fact, was that night on Orchard Street.

Of course, he doesn't care to dwell on that memory.

A number of times he feels a real compulsion to leave—to flee, return to a state of ignorance and remain there.

But the compulsion to stay is stronger.

A chance to get back what was taken from you, Barton had said.

He'll give it an hour, maybe two. If necessary, he'll come back again tomorrow night, and the night after that.

Opening the case on the passenger seat, Remer busies himself by prepping the various pieces of equipment Barton has provided.

A digital camcorder, mini notebook computer, tracking device, pad of paper and pen, and binoculars.

A small collection, but everything he would conceivably need, so carefully selected.

State-of-the-art gear, all of it.

▪

It is a little over an hour later that a vehicle turns onto the far end of the empty street.

As it approaches the house, Remer, several doors down, identifies it as an old Volkswagen Scirocco.

He writes this down on the pad.

The vehicle pulls into the driveway of the yellow cottage and parks.

Remer can see that there are two people inside, but they don't exit right away. Though he can't hear them, and can only make out their silhouettes, it becomes clear to him quickly enough that whoever they are, they are arguing.

Using the binoculars, Remer zooms in on the rear license plate. He copies down the number.

Eventually the driver of the Scirocco, a male, gets out and storms across the lawn, heading toward the front door of the cottage. Stopping midway, he abruptly turns and calls to the passenger.

Despite the distance and the closed windows around him, Remer can hear what this man says.

"*Mia, c'mon.*"

Remer's heart stops suddenly, then, just as suddenly, is pounding.

The Scirocco's passenger door opens, and Mia emerges.

He would have known it was her even if this man—Brazier, he assumes—hadn't said her name.

He would have known it just by watching her rise from the car and stand.

She is dressed tonight in a long overcoat, black turtleneck sweater, and black jeans. And, of course, her leather harness boots.

Just as she was dressed the night she left.

Though she has gotten out of the car, she is refusing to follow the male. They face each other over the roof of the Scirocco. There is no mistaking what this is: a lovers' standoff.

Remer aims the binoculars at the male and identifies him as the man in all the surveillance photographs Evelyn Ferrara provided. Just as the file on him stated, he is a kid of twenty-five.

Brazier's demeanor tells Remer that the guy is close to losing his temper, and, in turn, Remer's instincts and experience observing men and women at their worst alert him to the potential for sudden violence.

"Just *c'mon*, Mia," Brazier calls.

His voice carries across the quiet neighborhood like a dog's bark.

Brazier waits, and when Mia doesn't immediately obey or respond—she remains by the open passenger door, rigid—he takes several steps in her direction, enraged, then, as he had done before, stops himself short.

An overt threat from a man who has had about enough.

Remer's left hand reaches down for the door handle. It takes all he has not to grab it and pull it up.

What he would do after that isn't clear to him.

But he does, for an instant, imagine the look on Mia's face were she to see him approaching out of nowhere.

Reacting to Brazier's threat, Mia swings the door closed and hurries around the vehicle, meeting Brazier on the front lawn and standing face-to-face with him.

Though Remer and Mia had their fair share of arguments—stupid arguments—he cannot remember ever seeing her behave quite in this way before.

Then again, he never once made an angry charge toward her, as Brazier did.

Still, the Mia Remer knew, while often quick to start a fight, was always the first one to turn away, either offer her back and go silent or simply leave the room—or apartment.

A narcissistic trait? Remer wonders.

This Mia, then, is a Mia he has not seen before. More than that, though, her current behavior is, to his eye, a clear indication that her relationship with Brazier is currently as strained as his own relationship with her ever was, perhaps even more.

What Mia says to Brazier Remer cannot hear. She does not yell, instead speaks quietly. Brazier tries to take a step back, but Mia grabs both his hands, won't let him retreat from her.

Yet another thing that seems out of character.

Brazier is still angry—Remer can tell this by the fact that the kid is unable to look Mia in the eyes.

She says something else. Something *earnest*. And then, finally, Brazier looks at her.

Letting go of one of his hands, she reaches up and touches his face.

It is a loving gesture.

Remer closes his eyes, and when he reopens them, Mia and Brazier are kissing.

He watches this, has no other choice, his hand still hovering over the door handle, the binoculars on his lap. It is only after the kiss, as Mia and Brazier are walking around to the back of the cottage, that Remer takes his hand away.

He watches the cottage for several minutes, needs that time to center himself. With the threat of violence gone, there is nothing now to keep back the shock of seeing Mia again, seeing her with the man she left him for, seeing her keeping him from pulling away from her, seeing her kiss him.

All this hits Remer like the concussion wave from a nearby explosion.

Not enough to kill him, but enough to knock the wind out of him for a moment.

Mia and Brazier, he realizes when the shock passes, were both completely empty-handed. Mia wasn't even carrying a purse. If they were squatting, here to sleep through the night, wouldn't they have brought *something* in with them? Food, changes of clothes, an extra blanket?

After several minutes not a single light can be see in any of the windows visible to Remer.

There is little doubt now what this place is for them.

And there it is, just as Remer predicted.

Regret.

There are, though, things that need to be done, tasks that will, for a short period of time at least, distract Remer enough so he won't have to imagine what is going on inside that cottage right now.

Mia naked. Standing. On that mattress. In that chair.

Lovemaking that bordered on worship.

The smell of her hair and skin.

Removing the magnetic tracking beacon from the foam-lined case, Remer places it in the pocket of his greatcoat with his right hand as he reaches for the door handle with his left.

Activity is his only hope right now.

This time he pulls the handle up and nudges the door open with his shoulder. As before, he makes his way down the street and onto the property. Crossing the driveway and crouching on the far side of Brazier's vehicle, he attaches the beacon to the frame behind the right rear wheel. The strong magnet grabs the metal fast, holding the device firm.

Back in the pickup, Remer powers up the laptop. His mouth is dry, and there is a lump in his throat, as hard as a fist. His hands shake a bit from the adrenaline in his blood.

When the computer is up and running, he opens the tracking program and immediately locates the signal from the device.

The equipment is working fine.

With these activities done, there nothing left for Remer to do but resume his waiting.

And get control over his imagination.

He is surprised by the emotions he is feeling, though he knows he shouldn't be. It isn't, after all, just the sight of the lover who scorned him that is causing them.

Settling into his seat, Remer puts his hands deep in the pockets of his coat, wrapping the thing around himself like a blanket against the growing cold.

■

An hour passes, during which nothing disturbs the stillness of the block-long neighborhood.

Then, shortly after midnight, there is sudden movement.

Brazier appears in the driveway. He hurries to the Scirocco and gets in, starting the motor. Instead of backing onto the street, he pulls forward, turning into the backyard, disappearing behind the house.

Remer does not understand this. He waits for something more to happen. Nothing does for ten minutes, and then, suddenly, the Scirocco is backing out from behind the house and onto the driveway.

Reaching the street, it rolls to a stop, pauses as the driver shifts gears, and then takes off.

Quickly, though, jolting forward.

Before the vehicle makes it to the end of Magee, Remer sees one more thing that doesn't make sense.

Only the driver's silhouette—Brazier's silhouette—is visible through the rear window.

Remer quick-checks the computer. The signal from the beacon shows that the Scirocco is moving away steadily, has already reached Montauk Highway and is heading west.

He half expects it to turn around. *This is yet another spat, certainly. At any minute Brazier will calm down and come back for Mia. After all, men don't leave Mia, she leaves them.*

But the signal continues, moving through the Shinnecock Hills, approaching Hampton Bays.

It takes Remer a moment more to decide to check the cottage. Even if Brazier did turn around, it would take him at least another two minutes to make his way back to Magee Drive.

Now or never.

Grabbing the flashlight again, Remer exits his pickup and crosses onto the property for a third time. Reaching the first of the three back windows, he pauses to listen but hears nothing. Finally, peeking through, he detects no motion inside. Only then does he turn on the flashlight and shine it through the glass.

A quick look tells him that nothing is different.

It is the same with the door to the mud porch and the kitchen window.

He reaches the last window, the bedroom window, knows that if Mia is still in the cottage, she would have to be in this room.

Pausing beneath the window, he listens again, hears, again, nothing.

Then, rising up, he dares to sneak a look through the glass, feels his heart pounding as he does this.

He sees, though, nothing.

Shining the light inside, he notices right away that the rumbled blanket that had covered the mattress is now in a tousled heap on the floor beside it.

He sees this but no sign of Mia.

He sweeps the room with the light, looks for the folding chair he had seen leaning against the wall, but something else catches his eye, on the wall where the folded chair had been.

A collection of dark dots.

He moves the light to the floor directly below that part of the wall and sees something just as strange there.

A large dark stain.

As Remer moves the light over it, he knows that what he is seeing is blood.

For a second he freezes, but only a second. Reaching the door of the mud porch, he pulls the cloth liner from the pocket of his great-coat and, using it as a glove, tries the doorknob.

Locked.

Leaning back, he raises his right leg and stomps at the door, the sole of his boot landing just below the lock. It takes several thrusts, each one a solid blow with every ounce of strength Remer has behind it, to splinter the wood frame and send the door flying open.

Moving inside, Remer rushes into the bedroom, stopping at the door. He is surprised by warmish air. There must be some kind of heating device somewhere, or maybe even though the home was unrented, its owner kept it heated for the sake of the water pipes.

But Remer doesn't care about that.

Aiming the light at the wall, he recognizes that the collection of dark dots is, in fact, spattered blood.

Jesus.

If Brazier was alone in the Scirocco, then Mia has to be here somewhere.

Dying, or already dead.

Frantic, Remer begins to search. He opens the closet door—nothing—then rushes into the kitchen, shining the flashlight into every corner. He even calls Mia's name several times. All this, and yet no sign of her.

It is only when he is standing in the last room—the living room, the first room he looked into upon arriving hours ago—that he realizes what is going on.

The Persian rug that was there is now gone.

Brazier spent close to ten minutes out of Remer's line of sight before taking off.

Plenty of time to roll Mia's body up in the rug and place it into the back of his vehicle.

Feeling the impulse to bolt again, Remer this time gives in to it. Fleeing the cottage, he tears down the driveway, crossing the empty street at a diagonal and reaching his truck in seconds. Removing his greatcoat and tossing it onto the passenger seat, he gets in behind the wheel and starts the motor and shifts into gear.

He doesn't care about breaching the quiet of the neighborhood now.

He takes off after Brazier.

The computer screen shows that the Scirocco is a few miles ahead and still in motion.

Remer stomps on the accelerator, makes his way to Montauk Highway quickly, then races westward, locking himself willingly, and with no concern for the consequences, on a collision course.

9

There are no Christmas lights on display in the village of Hampton Bays, but Remer barely notices as he enters the business district.

The Scirocco has already cleared the town and made the turn onto Sunrise Highway.

Remer gets a break, catches a series of green lights before finally being stopped by a red one. He waits only a few seconds before jumping it.

Beyond this light is the entrance to Sunrise Highway. He turns onto it, checks the screen, and determines that the Scirocco is still westbound, and only a little over three miles ahead.

It makes sense to Remer that Brazier isn't speeding. If Mia is in fact wrapped up in that Persian rug in the back of that vehicle, then Brazier wouldn't dare risk getting pulled over by a cop.

Remer, on the other hand, doesn't care about cops.

Let one pursue me, call for backup when I don't pull over.

Let every damn cop on duty tonight be on my tail when I overtake Brazier.

Gunning the engine, he reaches ninety, at which speed the pickup begins to shudder. He pushes through that to one hundred.

He is in the long stretch of nothingness extending between Hampton Bays and Westhampton known as the Pine Barrens. The highway, more or less a straightaway here, skims along a series of shallow hills—long rises and drops, barely perceivable at the posted speed limit but decidedly so at almost twice that.

He is closing the distance fast, feels rage joining with the adrenaline in his blood. A dangerous mix, a demon's blend—he knows this but still doesn't resist it.

There is less than a mile between him and the Scirocco, and a steep rise ahead, when Remer sees the signal suddenly come to a stop.

He eases back on the accelerator, the pickup dropping down to eighty, and then seventy, as he approaches the crest of the hill.

He isn't certain whether he should stop before his pickup reaches the top and his presence is exposed. He realizes quickly, though, that this is an old instinct—he isn't tailing the Scirocco but attempting to overtake it.

With that in mind, he pushes down on the pedal again, watches as the speedometer flips almost instantly back up to ninety.

The pickup reaches the apex, is almost free of gravity for a second, then, caught by it again, drops down suddenly—nothing short of a carnival ride.

Remer sees the taillights ahead, at the bottom of the decline, realizes quickly that the vehicle is not on the road but rather alongside it.

Nose-first in a ditch.

Slowing to fifty, then to thirty, Remer pulls onto the shoulder and closes the remaining distance cautiously.

He stops a good fifty feet away and positions his pickup so the headlights fall squarely on the Scirocco. It is hard to tell if the vehicle lost control and careened into the ditch or was parked there on purpose.

The driver door is open, the interior light on. Remer sees, however, no activity in or around the vehicle. Grabbing his flashlight, he gets out, doesn't even feel the cold around him. Pausing at the nose of his truck, he studies his surroundings carefully.

Finally, he takes several steps toward the Scirocco. He shines the light down into the ditch; he searches the immediate area.

Nothing.

He continues forward, then climbs down into the ditch. Reaching the vehicle, he aims the light through the glass of the rear hatch door.

The Persian rug is there, but partially unrolled and empty.

Remer moves around the rear of the vehicle and checks the passenger side. As before, nothing. He aims the light toward the edge of the scrub pines on the rise at the other side of the ditch. Beyond them is a thick woods of dwarf trees.

He listens for the sound of someone moving through them but hears instead a vehicle pulling to a stop behind his pickup.

The headlights, set on high, stand a good foot above his vehicle's headlights. Another truck, then, but a full-sized one, or maybe an SUV or a Jeep rigged for beach-running with oversized tires.

Remer climbs out of the ditch, has to shield his eyes with his hand. He knows better than to look straight into a bright light at night, was taught that in basic training some twenty-odd years ago. To do so could cause night blindness, which may last for as long as a half hour.

As he reaches the top of the ditch, a floodlight mounted on the driver's side of the vehicle comes on suddenly. Significantly brighter than the headlights, it catches Remer at a moment when his guard is down, hitting him straight in his eyes.

The night blindness is instant and causes Remer to stagger a little on the uneven surface. He hears the sound of car doors opening and closing, then of footsteps walking toward him. Two doors, so two people, at least.

"Can you kill that light?" he says.

No one responds.

He makes his way onto the edge of the pavement. Despite the fact that the damage is already done, he is still holding his hand up to shield against the light.

"Kill that light already."

He again gets no response. A single set of footsteps approaches him. He senses that someone has stopped just a foot or two in front of him.

He smells perfume and hears what sounds to him like the jingle of bangles.

"What the fuck—" he says.

But his words are cut short by the sound of a sharp grunt.

A boxer's grunt.

But more than that, too.

A *woman's grunt.*

Suddenly something hard slams into his skull. Despite his blindness, he sees a flash of white-blue light. It fills his eyes and lasts for several seconds.

Once this light is gone, he is overtaken by darkness.

▪

He hears what sounds like a cacophony of ringing bells. Frantic and tuneless, sometimes near, other times distant.

He is confused, knows that he is down, and on cold pavement, but despite these vivid specifics, he has no idea how he got there.

Other sounds begin to penetrate the din of the bells—the winter wind, a car coming to a stop on the shoulder of the road, footsteps, then, from directly above him, a male voice saying, *Jesus, man, what happened to you?*

The next thing Remer knows there are flashing lights in the sky. He is on a stretcher, though he has no memory of being placed there. Then he is in the back of an ambulance, the interior of which is so bright his eyes ache.

A female EMT is tending to the wound on his head. She asks if he knows his name, what month it is, who the current president is. He has no idea if he answers her or not, but the fact that she keeps asking probably means he doesn't.

It goes like this for a while, Remer seeing and hearing and feeling only bits and pieces. The ambulance is in motion, and then isn't. Suddenly he is out in the cold night again, and then he is indoors again.

After that he is being stitched up by a doctor who can't be more than twenty-five years old, then wheeled down a hallway—again, the lights above him are just too bright. He hears two people talking, saying things like *concussion* and *X-rays*.

Passing out, Remer comes to in a dimly lit room. Eventually he realizes there is whispering nearby. Looking around, he finds an open door and sees two people standing in the lighted hallway just beyond it.

Barton is one, this he can tell right away. The other is an older man in a long parka. There are patches on his shoulders.

A cop.

The whispering between this cop and Barton is heated.

"I'm not too close to this."

"You are, Kay. You know the rules."

"Tommy will be here in a few minutes."

"I don't want your boyfriend interfering. Do you understand me?"

"When you see the videotape you'll understand."

"What's there to understand?"

"Just watch the tape, Chief. Please."

"You saw the blood. His goddamned boot prints are all over the place, inside and out. They're on the door he kicked in."

"Just wait till Tommy gets here with the tape."

Remer can no longer keep his eyes open. His lids fall, and he tries to at least listen, but the ringing has returned, drowning everything else out.

At one point he forces his eyes open by sheer will and sees that a third person has joined Barton and Chief of Police Manfredi outside the door of his hospital room.

Tall, big-shouldered, with dark hair and beard.

Because the light of the hallway is behind him, this man is to Remer little more than a hulking shadow.

This is the last thing he sees for a long time.

FEBRUARY 17

2003

10

■

At midnight, in his apartment in Gramercy, Remer waited for the phone call.

The burns on his chest were only three days old, and though covered with a thick layer of ointment and a fresh bandage, the sickening aroma of seared flesh still reached his nose. Whether the smell was real or simply memory, Remer didn't know, and anyway, did it matter either way?

He was in that span of time when the painkillers he took earlier were beginning to wear off but it was still too soon to take another dose.

The gauntlet, he had come to call it.

His apartment, though sparsely furnished simply because he worked too much and never had the time to tend to it, was always a comfortable and safe place for him, good for sleeping.

Now it felt like a trap, and he hadn't come close to sleeping in days.

He had been able to determine, with help, that the woman who had hired him, and the couple he had followed from Florent to the hotel on Orchard, were all part of the setup. He was not, however, interested in finding them.

The Frenchman was a different story.

Like Remer, he was a man for hire, which meant that he counted on being found by those looking to pay him to make his living. It took a handful of phone calls to select people, but Remer eventually learned the man's identity. He was waiting, had been for hours now, to be informed of the man's whereabouts.

If that call was the last one he would ever get, he didn't care.

By 1:00 A.M. the pain was too great. He downed a pill, broke a second in half and downed that as well, then continued to wait.

▪

The call came finally at two.

The ring of the prepaid cell phone he had bought specifically for this line of communication echoed through his near-empty apartment.

Answering, he simply said, "Yeah."

On the other end was a male voice, the very one he expected to hear. "The Rodeo Bar in Williamsburg. You know it, I'm sure."

"Yeah."

"Apparently our Frenchman likes rockabilly."

"His two friends?"

"No sign of them. He doesn't look like he's on the job. Maybe it's his night to go out and spend his hard-earned money."

Remer said nothing.

"You there?"

"Yeah."

"Want me to come with you? In your condition, it might be better if—"

"No."

"You sure?"

"Yeah. What about who hired him?"

"It was a man named Daley. Ring any bells?"

It did. An errant husband with a penchant for call girls that Remer had exposed about six months ago.

"We sure on this?" Remer says.

"Very. Listen, why don't I take care of it for you."

"No, it's my problem."

"I owe you that much, at least."

"You don't."

"You sure?"

"Yeah."

"I'll get a call if the Frenchman leaves in the next hour. If you don't hear from me, that means he's still there. Good?"

"Yeah. Thanks for this, man."

"Semper fi. You know that."

Remer nodded. "Semper fi."

He hung up.

On the chair by his door was a leather knapsack, in it the things that he would need tonight.

The tools of his trade.

Grabbing it, he left.

▪

The L train was delayed, as it often was late at night, so it was close to three when Remer emerged from the Bedford Avenue station and walked to the corner of North Seventh Street.

It was a bitterly cold February night, but the overcoat he had picked up yesterday specifically for this purpose, at a secondhand clothing shop across town, kept him warm enough.

Still, there was no avoiding the fact that he was shaking.

He wore a black knit military hat with a brim, to keep his head warm but also to help hide his identity from the surveillance cameras at the two subway stations. This being a weeknight, Williamsburg was quiet—almost no street traffic, and only one pedestrian visible during his first five minutes there.

The luck he would need—the luck he always needed—was holding so far.

The dead center of the block was the darkest part of the street, so Remer moved there. The Rodeo Bar was a small neighborhood place, the ground floor of a four-story building. The three floors above it were dark, as were the other buildings on that side of the street.

From where Remer was standing he had a clear view of the entrance. But he was far enough down the block that it wouldn't look like he was watching it.

He reached into the pocket of his jeans and removed the cell phone. He would have been unreachable while down in the subway, and any voice mail message would have certainly caught up to him by now.

But there was none.

So the Frenchman was still inside.

He returned the phone to his pocket, then reached into his overcoat. In his right pocket, wrapped in a large clear plastic bag, was the Glock, its serial numbers filed down. In all the time he had owned it, he had never once touched it with his bare hands. Still, earlier today he had disassembled it and wiped every piece down with a rag.

He did the same with each of the hollow-point bullets he thumbed into the clip. The plastic bag that contained the gun wasn't to protect his gloved hand and the cuff of his overcoat from powder burns, though it would do that, but rather to catch the bullet casing that would be ejected upon firing.

A redundancy, perhaps, considering the precautions he had taken while loading, and that he would dispose of the gun at his first opportunity.

But counting on luck was one thing, and pushing it was something else.

▪

The Rodeo Bar closed at four, and the Frenchman was, as far as Remer could tell, the last patron to leave.

Most importantly, he was alone. Remer saw right away that he was, too, drunk.

The man walked north to the end of the block, turned west onto Seventh and disappeared from sight.

Remer, still on the other side of the street, made his way to the northern corner and looked westward but saw no sign of the man. Quickly crossing Bedford and continuing on Seventh, Remer realized soon enough that there was an all-night store about halfway down the block.

The Frenchman had to have gone in there.

Remer stopped and waited for a moment, but that didn't look natural, so he pretended to pat his pockets as if he had maybe forgotten something, then continued on, walking past the store at a steady gait.

Just a man heading home in the cold.

As he passed the shop, he glanced inside, and sure enough there was the Frenchman, standing at the counter and paying the cashier.

Remer passed too quickly for either man to see him. Ahead was a row of residential buildings. No place there for Remer to stop and take cover, so he passed them, too, making it to the end of the block and stopping there.

Seconds later, the Frenchman emerged from the store and headed in Remer's direction. He was staggering, his head down, a bag under one arm. Chances were he would pass Remer without even looking at him.

Still, it was better not to push it, so Remer headed south, stopping halfway down that block where it was the darkest. From there he watched the Frenchman pass and continue west. The East River was two blocks away, and Remer guessed that was where the man was headed.

There wasn't much else down that part of Seventh.

Remer backtracked to the corner and followed the Frenchman, keeping the distance of about a half block between them. The closer to the river they got, the more desolate the neighborhood. *Luck was holding.* When he wasn't watching his target, Remer studied his surroundings, and he was growing more and more certain that they were the only beings present.

Picking up his pace a little, he began to overtake the staggering man.

There were twenty paces or so between them when the Frenchman reached the edge of the river.

Stopping there, he stared across the water at Manhattan for a moment, then reached into the paper bag and removed a bottle. Dropping the bag to the pavement, he twisted the cap from the bottle and took a long sip.

Remer was close enough to see that it was a pint of booze, but he couldn't tell which kind.

Though the Frenchman was standing still, it would have been obvious to anyone just now looking at him that he was drunk. He wavered as though he were being buffeted by high winds. Remer reached into the pocket of his overcoat, wrapped his gloved hand around the plastic-covered grip of the Glock, then began to close the remaining distance.

It was now or never.

He stopped just a few feet from the Frenchman. Still he kept the Glock in his pocket. He watched the man watch Manhattan, saw him take several more long sips. Remer could see the label now. Brandy, of all things. It was clear that the Frenchman was transfixed by the lights.

A pitiful man right now, there was no mistaking that. There were drinkers, and then there were men who were addicted to drink. The Frenchman was the latter. He must have lived somewhere near, was too drunk to be too far from home.

Too drunk and still drinking.

Still, pitiful or not, barely able to stand or not, he was the man who had three nights before mutilated Remer, branding into his chest a singe word.

VOYEUR.

There was simply no point in a man like that walking this planet.

The Frenchman took another long sip, then began to turn, almost losing his balance as he did. He had looked at the lights long enough and was ready to head home, or so it seemed to Remer.

The man completed his turn, took a single step, then stopped when he realized someone was standing in his way.

He looked at Remer—first at Remer's feet, up Remer's body, reaching, finally, Remer's face.

There was no hint of recognition in the man's eyes.

He mumbled something in French, then attempted to step around Remer, only to stumble and fall to the pavement.

"Merde!"

Remer stood there, looking down at the man. He attempted to stand, asked for Remer's help, but Remer, of course, offered none. Scanning his surroundings again, Remer saw nothing but empty streets and sidewalks in three directions.

He removed the Glock from his pocket and quickly adjusted the ziplock bag so it covered the entire length of the weapon. Even with the silencer affixed, the gun fit the bag with room to spare.

The Frenchman was still trying to stand. Remer stepped back. Finally up on his feet, or as close to it as he was going to get, the man looked at Remer again.

His eyes this time were on the plastic bag in Remer's hand.

Remer waited for the man to look him in the eye, which the man finally did.

Maybe there was recognition, maybe there wasn't, but Remer didn't care about that anymore.

He raised his arm and fired.

One shot in the heart, two more in the head.

Tap.

Tap tap.

The Frenchman was dead before he hit the pavement.

▪

Quickly Remer walked a block south.

He tossed the bag containing the Glock and the three ejected shell casings into the East River, then did the same with the prepaid cell phone.

Placing the leather knapsack on the ground, he took off his gloves and overcoat and knit hat, laid them beside it. He opened the knapsack, removed a North Face jacket, and put it on, pulling the hood up over his head.

All that remained in the knapsack was a two-pound dumbbell for weight.

Placing the overcoat and gloves and knit hat into the knapsack, he buckled it closed and, grabbing it by its strap, flung it as far as he could out over the water.

The effort caused the dressing covering the burns on his chest to pull free, but he ignored it.

He waited till the knapsack hit the water, watched as it sank immediately below the choppy surface.

Gone.

He continued south, didn't see a soul for the entire twenty minutes it took him to reach the Williamsburg Bridge. Crossing it on foot, he was passed in both directions by the occasional vehicle, but with his hood up, no one could possibly see his face.

The bridge fed into Delancey Street. Remer walked four blocks, passing Orchard Street, where the Blue Moon Hotel stood. He didn't even look in its direction. Turning right a block later onto Allen, he walked three blocks north, where, just above Houston, Allen became First Avenue.

It was a straight line from there, more or less, to his apartment twenty-six blocks away.

▪

He made it home by daybreak.

On the corner of Twenty-fourth Street he removed his North Face jacket and dropped it into a nearby garbage can, then crossed to Second Avenue.

Just two blocks to go.

He was exhausted, but once he was inside his apartment, he didn't know what to do with himself, and that included whether he should sleep or not.

He hadn't really thought this far ahead—what, really, did one do after such a thing?

The only thing he could think to do was go into the bathroom and wash his hands. As he dried them, he looked at his face.

He saw a man lost to pain and crazed by sleeplessness.

He saw, too, something in his eyes, an unmistakable look, one he was surprised to see staring back at him.

Fear.

Raw and rooted deep, the kind of fear that drives men to run.

DECEMBER 23

2008

11

■

Remer comes to in a dark room.

The first thing he realizes is that he is in a strange bed, lying between clean, stiff sheets.

The next is that he is dressed not in clothes but in a hospital gown.

It is then that he begins to remember.

And it isn't long after this that he becomes aware of the sharp ache deep behind his eyes.

He looks for a clock but can't find one, then starts to search the room for a window. Is it day or is it night? There is only one window, on the far side of the room, and he sees blackness beyond it.

Night, then.

But what time? Just after sunset, right before dawn, that long stretch in between?

He looks toward the door. It is closed, but there is a considerable gap between its bottom edge and the floor, one that allows light from the hallway to show through.

He asks if anyone is there. Considering the argument Barton and the chief were having, he half expects a cop to be standing watch outside his door. But he gets no response. Searching his bedside, he finds the call button and presses it.

A half minute passes, and then he hears coming from the hallway the rubbery squeak of sneakers on linoleum.

The door opens, the hallway light, harsh to his eyes, spilling in. He turns his head, and when he hears the door close, he looks back and sees a nurse standing beside his bed.

She is tall, his age, maybe older, wears her long brown hair pulled back in a sleek ponytail. The name tag pinned to her colorful scrubs reads GALE.

"You're awake," she says. "You had us wondering."

"What about?"

"You're okay now," she assures him. "But you had a concussion. You took a blow to the head. Do you remember that? Getting hit in the head."

Remer nods. "Yeah."

"That's good. That you remember, I mean. You never really know exactly what to expect with a concussion. Any nausea or lightheadedness?"

"No."

"Sensitivity to light."

"Yeah."

"Headache?"

He nods again.

She picks up a large plastic cup from the table by the bed. "Drink some water. You must be parched." She carefully places the straw in his mouth.

Remer draws a mouthful, swallows it. He is aware suddenly that he is very weak. Drawing another mouthful, he swallows that, too.

"What time is it?" he asks.

"It's almost seven."

"Night?"

"Yes."

"I've been out since last night?"

"The doctor will be by in a little bit. He'll talk to you."

Despite his condition, Remer can tell that she is skirting the question. And only now does he notice the IV in his forearm.

"How long have I been out?" he says.

Gale hesitates, then says, "Two days."

"Jesus."

"Listen, the good news is now that you're conscious, we can give you something for the pain, if you think you need it."

Remer's headache is only getting worse by the minute, but he isn't even remotely tempted; the last pain pill he took six years ago was, as far as he was concerned, the last pain pill he would ever take.

"No, thanks," he says.

"You sure?"

"Yeah."

"If you change your mind, just buzz me, okay?"

"Okay. Thanks. Listen, do you have any idea what's going on?"

"What do you mean?"

Remer wants to ask her if she overheard any conversations that might concern him—conversations between cops—but decides not to pursue the matter. He saw what he saw at the cottage on Magee, and right now that is both all that matters and all he can handle.

Sooner or later, he'll be made aware of the rest.

"Forget about it," Remer says.

"Would you like more water?"

He nods. She holds the cup for him, watches his face closely as he takes another sip. Something about the way she looks at him makes him wonder if during the course of the last two days and nights she caught a glimpse of the scar on his chest.

When those few who have seen it first saw it, they each had a similar expression on their faces. A desire to ask what that scar was, but uncertain if they should.

When Remer has had enough water, he nods. Gale returns the cup to his bedside table.

"The doctor will want to have a look at you and ask you a few questions," she says. "But you'll probably be able to go home tomorrow. Your friends dropped off some clothes for you." She nods toward a chair against the wall by the door.

Remer sees the vague shape of folded clothes upon it.

"What friends?" he asks.

"That detective. Barton. And her boyfriend."

Beneath the chair is a pair of hiking boots. Remer does not own such boots.

Someone else's clothes.

"Listen, is there any chance I can go home tonight?" he asks.

"No, sorry. But I'll try to get the doctor up here first thing."

"Please, if you can,"

She smiles. "Of course."

▪

The next morning at nine a doctor stops by, and by ten Remer, his belongings in a manila envelope, and dressed in the clothes left for him—clothes just a bit too big—is discharged.

Though his place is only a few blocks from the hospital, he is weak from days of nothing but inactivity and intravenous glucose, so he calls for a cab.

Even the simple act of standing and waiting for it to arrive takes considerable effort and concentration. And the gloomy winter light spilling in through the tall lobby windows is more than enough to cause the ache deep behind his eyes to sharpen.

Less than five minutes after he calls for the cab, it pulls up to the door. As he gets in he sees that the driver is the same one who picked him up at the Bridgehampton train station.

He can't, though, remember her name, has to look at the hack license mounted on the seat back in front of him.

Brianna Ruocco.

They say nothing during the short drive to his home. She watches him in the rearview mirror much of the way; he watches the familiar streets dusted by a snow he hadn't seen fall.

When the cab swings into his driveway and passes the main house, he sees that his pickup is sitting in his parking spot outside the back building.

"They had it towed here from the impound lot," Brianna says.

She must have seen the brief look of confusion on Remer's face.

"Let me guess," he says. "Barton and her boyfriend."

Brianna nods. Remer isn't sure what to think of this; there is, after all, a fine line between benefactor and manipulator.

But he decides to add it to the list of things he'll think about later.

The cab comes to a stop, but Remer doesn't at first make a move toward getting out.

He isn't all that sure he can stand, let alone walk.

"You okay?" Brianna says.

He nods. "Yeah. I'm fine."

He reads the meter mounted on the dashboard and pays the fare. Climbing out, he stands on legs that don't feel like his own. Before he has a chance to close the door, the cabbie wishes him a merry Christmas.

He wishes her one as well.

As the cab drives off he realizes that he has no keys. The last time he touched them, that he could remember, was when he was outside the cottage on Magee. *Turning the ignition so he could chase down Brazier.* They must still be there, then.

He steps to his truck. The driver door is unlocked. Opening it, he sees his greatcoat on the passenger seat. He sees, too, an empty ignition. He flips down the visor. Nothing. Finally, reaching under the driver's seat, he locates his keys. Grabbing them and his greatcoat, he heads inside.

Upstairs, he finds that his apartment is strangely silent. It is as if he—or anyone, for that matter—hasn't been here for years. Dormant, like a museum after hours. Around him, relics and remnants of a long-ago life.

He wants to stay on his feet and move around, shake the feeling of weakness and fatigue. He wants to get back to his shop and his routine as soon as possible. He is, though, suddenly uncertain what day it is, exactly. It takes checking his computer to find out.

Wednesday, the twenty-fourth.

The day before Christmas.

Days from his life are missing. The world had turned twice as he lay oblivious.

A long time to be out of commission, considering the events prior to his slipping into unconsciousness.

He checks his cell phone, sees that he has received a number of texts in the past two days, the most important of which are the ones after closing time on Monday and Tuesday, informing him of the day's take. Another tells him that the bank deposits—a task he usually performs when he comes by in the afternoons—have been made.

The rest, from each member of his staff, are get-well wishes and promises to keep the business running smoothly till he gets back.

So life goes on.

In an effort to reclaim his apartment, he draws a bath. Stripping out of the strange clothes, he slips into the hot water, mindful not to get his head—specifically, the six stitches keeping the gash on his forehead closed—wet.

His mind wanders, not away from thoughts now but toward them. He is aware of the mess he made back at the cottage in Southampton. Footprints beneath every back window, footprints in every room, the forced entrance, the fact that he happened to be there to catch his ex and her current lover.

How could no one think that he was involved in Mia's murder? How could the police not be waiting for him outside the hospital when he was discharged?

His recollection of the heated discussion between Barton and Chief Manfredi, which he overheard as he fought for consciousness, is sketchy at best.

But he does recall Barton saying to the man, *Just watch the tape, Chief. You'll understand then.*

What tape was she talking about?

The more Remer tries to think about this, the more holes he finds in his memory. It is like watching a movie with random chunks of footage missing from every scene. Even events prior to the blow to his head aren't fully accessible. His conversation with Evelyn Ferrara is only bits and pieces. It is the same for his visit to Pintauro's.

The only vivid memories, in fact, are of Mia walking from the Scirocco to the cottage, and the grunt—the woman's grunt—he heard just before being sent to the pavement.

How could that—meeting a bartender who boxes and, just hours later, getting his skull cracked by a woman—be a coincidence?

Still, what it means, he is nowhere near certain. The only explanation his currently less than reliable mind can find is that he was set up to witness Mia's murder.

But set up by whom? And why?

▪

When he realizes that the bathwater has turned cold, Remer steps out of the tub and dries off, then puts on a clean pair of sweatpants and a T-shirt.

He knows that at this moment overcoming his fatigue can be his only concern, and to do so will require yet more sleep.

Everything else will have to wait.

Passing his mirror, he catches sight of the bandage on his forehead. Stark white, it is, at first glance, simply by virtue of the contrast between it and his olive skin, shocking

There is, of course, another reason why the sight of it shocks him.

It has been nearly six years since his last encounter with violence.

The result of a different kind of setup, but a setup nonetheless.

The reemergence in his life of both things is, at best, disconcerting.

As he heads toward his bed he sees the blue vial on the windowsill. Grabbing it, he rolls it between his palms quickly, then removes the cap and downs a dose like a shot.

No need to bother with the ritual of heating up water, no desire to carefully measure out the proper dose.

Put me under, and keep me there for as long as I need.

Within sheets that smell faintly of Angela, Remer closes his eyes, eager to feel himself beginning to drift. His hope is to do so fast and to sink so deep that dreams cannot find him.

The very next thing he knows is that a cell phone is ringing and he is once again in a room that is utterly dark.

■

It takes him a moment to find his phone, and when he does he realizes the ringing isn't coming from it.

It is coming from the manila envelope on his desk.

The envelope given to him when he was discharged.

He hurries for his desk, reaches into the envelope, and grabs the phone, answering it just as the fourth ring ends.

The voice on the other end says, "It's Kay."

He is still groggy, and only just now aware of the fact that there is yet more darkness around him.

His first concern is that he has somehow missed another two days.

It is a concern bordering on panic, and he speaks without thinking.

"What day is it?" he says.

"You okay?"

"Yeah. I was asleep. What day is it?"

"It's Christmas Eve."

Once Remer is able to process this information—it takes several seconds—he is relieved. "Oh," he says. "What time is it?"

"Almost eight. I was going to ask you if you were up for a visit."

"What's up?"

"I was thinking of a swap of info. I can come over."

Remer rubs his eyes, and is reminded by this of the pain behind them.

Not as bad as before, but still there.

"I'll come to you," he says.

"You sure?"

"The fresh air will do me some good. I hope. I'll be there in a little bit."

"The downstairs door will be unlocked, so come right up."

He closes the cell phone. It takes a moment before he can stand. He feels a bit stronger but can't be certain how long that will last.

Turning on his bedside lamp—its dim light causes him to squint—he gets some clean clothes from his bureau drawer and dresses.

Gathering together the clothes Barton left for him, he folds them as best he can and gets a plastic bag from the cupboard under his kitchenette sink. He places the hiking boots into the bag and lays the folded clothes upon them. Then, putting on his own boots and coat, leaves.

The cold has the effect he hoped for. Awake now, his legs strong and getting stronger, he decides to walk to the building at the end of Elm.

12

■

The door is old and weatherworn, in need of a good scraping and a fresh coat of paint, but the brass lock is new and shiny.

Remer tries the knob, which turns freely. Climbing the creaking wooden steps to the apartment above, he knocks on a door only slightly better than the one below.

Barton leads him through a kitchen and into a large open room. It is the front room, at the far end of which is a row of three windows—the three windows that look out over the end of Elm and the train station across from it.

Looking around the large room, Remer realizes that he and Barton are alone.

"Tommy's running an errand," she offers. "He'll be back in a little while."

Remer nods. Their place is more or less a larger version of his own—an open loft to his somewhat cramped studio. Past the kitchen, though, are two doors. Bedroom and bathroom, he assumes.

He sees a minimum of furnishings—table and chairs in the kitchen, couch and coffee table in the living room—and finds no knickknacks displayed or photographs hung. Just bare plaster walls, bare wood floor made of wide pine planks.

The only indication of the season is a two-foot-tall Christmas tree standing on a corner table. It is strung with tinsel and lights that are unlit, and beneath it are several wrapped presents.

Remer suddenly thinks of Angela alone in her girlfriend's West Village apartment.

If only he could go there.

"How are you feeling?" Barton asks. She glances at the bandage on his forehead.

"Better, thanks."

"Can I get you anything? Coffee, tea? Something stronger?"

She is dressed in jeans and work boots and an oversized turtleneck sweater made of thick wool. Though loose on her, the sweater does not conceal her round belly, the top of which she touches often, and tenderly, with the palm of her right hand.

"No, I'm good." He holds up the plastic bag containing the clothes. "Thanks for these."

"No problem." She places it onto a nearby chair.

There is a brief moment of silence. Because they are old friends, it isn't at all uncomfortable. Still, there are things he wants to ask, and things he wants to say, so Remer dives in.

"You said something about a swap of information."

"I figured you'd want to know what's been going on."

"That would be helpful."

"And there are a few things I need to know."

"Okay." He wants to ask if Mia's body has been found yet but doesn't. He trusts Barton, probably more than anyone else he knows.

Still, his instincts tell him it would be better to let her lead things right now.

In his condition, his instincts are close to all he has.

"The reason Tommy and I were quick to suggest the train station as the location for your meeting with Mrs. Ferrara was so we could be there to make a record of it. It was a precaution Tommy used to take back when he was a PI."

Remer recalls the red light in the window.

He recalls, too, the heated discussion between Barton and Manfredi in the doorway of his hospital room.

"You made a videotape," he says.

Barton nods. "Tommy placed a microphone under the pay phone. That's why we had you stand within twenty feet of it. The microphone provided the audio, which Tommy synched up with the video."

"Which you gave to Manfredi."

"Yeah."

Remer thinks about that for a moment, about how differently things might have gone had they not done this.

"I appreciate that, Kay," he says finally.

"It wasn't looking good for a while there. You were found out in the middle of nowhere, not far from a vehicle with a rug in the back that contained blood and hair. That and all the boot prints you left back at the cottage had Manfredi thinking he had his man."

A thought crosses Remer's mind. "Wait a minute," he says. "How did Manfredi find the cottage so quickly? Or, for that matter, at all?"

"There were directions to it on the front seat of the Scirocco. When Manfredi found them, he sent a patrolman there. When the patrolman saw that the back door had been kicked in, he entered and found all the blood. The videotape gave a reason for you being at the cottage, but it still didn't clear you completely."

"What did?"

"The tracking program in the laptop we gave you records GPS

coordinates, miles traveled, and the time it took to travel those miles. It doesn't only record the location and movement of the tracking device, though. It also records the location and movement of the laptop monitoring the tracking device. The program shows that your pickup not only left a few minutes after the vehicle the device had been planted on left—the Scirocco—but that your pickup was obviously racing to catch up to it."

"Lucky for me I had that gear, huh?" Remer says.

Barton nods. "Manfredi hung on to a little hope for a while longer, but when the forensics came back on the Scirocco and your prints weren't anywhere on it, he finally gave up."

"So I'm in the clear?"

"Yeah."

A pause, then he says, "Thanks."

"Would you mind going over what happened?"

"Are you a cop right now?"

"Do you even need to ask?"

Remer shakes his head. "I guess not, no." Another pause, then, "It was Brazier."

"What did you see?"

"They arrived an hour after I got there and walked into the place together. An hour later, Brazier came out alone and pulled the car around back. Ten minutes after that he takes off. From what I can see, he's alone."

"What did you do?"

"On their way into the cottage they had an argument. I thought maybe by the way Brazier took off, they had another one inside. I went to see if Mia was still there. I looked through the window and saw the blood, so I kicked in the door. When I figured out what had happened, I went after Brazier."

"How did you figure out what happened?"

"When I first looked inside that place, before they arrived, I saw a Persian rug on the living room floor. It wasn't there anymore."

Barton nods, thinks for a moment, then says, "What happened when you caught up with the Scirocco?"

"The car was nose-first in a ditch. The only thing inside was the rug. I looked for Brazier, but I couldn't find him."

"So who hit you with the blackjack?" Barton asks.

"It was a blackjack?"

"That's what the doctor says."

Remer knows the weapon. A lead pellet the size of a thumb attached to a six-inch coil, the whole thing wrapped tight in black leather. Easily concealed and designed for nothing less than cracking skulls.

"I don't know for sure," he says.

"But you have an idea?"

Remer nods. "Yeah. Brazier's old boss, a guy named Rene, told me to check out the cottage. A bartender was working there, a woman named Casey. A boxer."

"And you think it was them."

"As I was leaving Pintauro's I saw Brazier walking to a Range Rover. The vehicle that pulled up behind my pickup when I was look-ing for Brazier was an SUV." Remer pauses, then shrugs. "And any-way, how many other female boxers are there out here?"

"So you saw her?"

"No. They shined a light in my eyes. I couldn't see a thing."

"Then how do you know it was her?"

"I don't know that it was her. Whoever hit me, though, was a woman, that much I do know."

"How do you know that?"

"Mainly because I heard her grunt. In that way boxers grunt when they throw a punch."

"Any idea why they were there? And why they would attack you?"

"According to his old boss, Brazier helped himself to the register the night he quit. Maybe this Rene guy used me to flush Brazier out."

"You don't sound so convinced of that."

"I'm not. I mean, why bother involving me? If that was Mia and

Brazier's regular place, and if he really wanted to find the guy, he could have gone there himself. Or paid someone to watch it."

"Maybe he saw the fact that you were looking for Brazier as his chance to get revenge and have someone else take the blame."

"Maybe. But Mia and Brazier showed up an hour after I got there."

"Tommy has always insisted that all investigations are about eighty to ninety percent luck."

Remer, from his own experience, knows this to be very true.

Still, there is being at the right place at the right time, and being exactly where someone wants you to be, when they want you to be there.

"I was set up, Kay. There's no way around that. I was there to witness Mia's murder."

"Set up by whom, though? Brazier's boss? Brazier? That doesn't make any sense."

"Tell me about it," Remer says. A thought comes to him. "Who's running the investigation?"

"Manfredi put Spadaro on it."

"That's a bit unusual, isn't it? Spadaro's not a detective."

"I think Manfredi did that so he could run the thing himself."

"What have they found?"

"The blood and the hair on the rug in the back of the Scirocco, and the blood and hair in the cottage, are all Mia's."

"Where'd they get a sample of Mia's blood and hair to match it to?"

"Manfredi contacted her mother. At one point Mia was on a whole bunch of meds and had to have regular blood tests. One of her many doctors has his own lab, and he still had a sample of her blood."

"And the hair?"

"Mrs. Ferrara was able to find a few strands in a brush Mia left behind."

Remer thinks about that. He sees no point in avoiding the question that keeps coming to mind.

"Have they found her body yet?"

"No," Barton says.

A pause, then Remer asks what else she can tell him.

"The Scirocco was stolen three months ago from Queens. The license plates were taken from a vehicle registered to an address in Brooklyn. It was parked on the street, and the owner came out one morning to find his plates gone."

"And the cottage?"

"The owner says it has been empty since September."

"Any connection between the owner and Mia?"

"None yet."

"What about the previous tenants?"

"No."

"What about the inside of the cottage?"

"According to forensics, height and spray of the blood spatter on the wall is consistent with a victim being struck in the head while on his hands and knees. There was a smudge mark of blood on the base-board nearby. In it were a few strands of what turned out to be Mia's hair, as well as the imprint of wood. The grain is consistent with the grain of a wooden baseball bat."

"All the qualities of a rage killing."

"That's what it looks like."

"Yeah, but there's a problem with that," Remer says.

"What?"

"The bat would've had to have been inside already. Mia and Brazier were both empty-handed when they entered the cottage. You're telling me that place is empty except for a mattress and a Persian rug—and a baseball bat?"

And a folding chair, Remer thinks, though he leaves that item out.

"You said Brazier came out an hour after they went in and pulled the car around back. He was out of your sight for, what, ten minutes, you said? He could have gotten the baseball bat out of the car then."

"Maybe."

"And they had an argument on the lawn, right?"

Remer nods.

"I don't know, it sounds like a rage killing to me," Barton says.

It is an unpleasant thing for Remer to imagine—Mia on her hands and knees in that all but empty bedroom, Brazier striking her in the head with a baseball bat with enough force to cause such a large spatter.

Was it postcoital? Was she naked, in the dark, afraid?

At this moment Remer longs for the confusion that marked his first few hours home.

The black holes in his memory, the lingering weakness sapping his ability to think.

A state not unlike the effects of his precious blend.

Clearing his head of any and all imagery, he is left, once again, with that one thought.

"All the makings of a rage killing," he says, "and yet I just happened to be there."

Barton says nothing. Remer can tell by the look on her face that she wants to say something but simply hasn't a clue what she could say.

"When I came in you told me Tommy was running an errand," Remer says.

"Yeah."

"What kind?"

"He wasn't specific."

"But it has to do with this, right?"

"Yeah."

"Won't that piss Manfredi off?"

"Probably. Tommy doesn't let things go very easily. I learned a long time ago not to try to stop him." She pauses, then says, "And anyway, Tommy knows what's at stake. Manfredi won't find out."

"He's that good, huh?"

"Tommy's father was the chief of police here for a long time. Over twenty years. This was before you moved out here. I think Tommy actually learned to read from police reports his father would bring home. This is in his blood. It's who he is."

"But he doesn't do this anymore. For a living, I mean."

"No."

"Why?"

She shrugs, seems at first reluctant to answer, then finally says, bluntly, "It almost got him killed once."

Remer nods but says nothing.

"And, to be honest," Barton says, "he really only got into the business because of his father."

"Tradition?"

"Just the opposite, actually. His father was as corrupt as they come, and then some. Tommy needed to prove that he wasn't his father. At least he needed to prove it to certain people."

Again, Remer says nothing.

For a moment Barton is silent, then says, "This must not have been easy for you. Seeing Mia with Brazier, realizing what he'd done to her while you sat outside. Maybe it's a good thing you didn't find him after all."

"Maybe."

"Manfredi's going to want you to swear out a statement. It's just a formality. The doctor told him to give you a few days. Just tell him everything you told me."

"I will. Thanks, Kay. For everything."

"At least we tried to help her, right?"

"She made her choice. She didn't just disappear on me, she disappeared on you, too."

He shrugs. What else could he do?

Barton watches Remer closely, studying his face, then says, "What are your Christmas plans?"

"I think I'm just going to rest up."

"Will you have company?"

"No."

"You're welcome to stop by tomorrow. We'll be here all day."

"Thanks."

"It was good to see you again, boss."

"It was good to see you, too, Kay."

"Let's not be such strangers. Okay?"

Remer nods. They shake hands, and he turns to leave.

As he exits the living room he passes the small Christmas tree with the wrapped presents beneath it.

Barton walks him to the doorway, then stands in it as Remer makes his way down the stairs. The strength he felt earlier is starting to leave him. Negotiating these steps requires a bit of concentration and care.

More, in fact, than it should.

"Maybe I should call you a cab," Barton says. She must have seen Remer's effort.

"No, I'll be okay," he says. "I just need some air."

"Get home safe."

"I will. Have a good night, Kay."

"Merry Christmas, boss."

13

■

Cold night air greets Remer as he steps onto the sidewalk.

Pausing, he looks toward the train station parking lot across the street, sees in it only three vehicles. He determines with quick glances that there is no one seated inside any of them, then takes note of the make and model of each.

An old habit, revisited.

Necessary for now, all things considered.

Though he sees nothing unusual, he knows that this, of course, doesn't mean anything.

None of the people he watched back when he watched people for a living ever saw him.

He begins the walk back to his place. The homes that line Elm Street—middle-class, for the most part—are all decorated for the season, and the already well-lit stretch of three long blocks is as bright as a New York City street.

Remer walks with his hands in the pockets of his greatcoat, hears only the sounds of his own footsteps till, after maybe a hundred feet, he hears from behind him the sound of a car engine starting.

Looking back, he sees nothing at first. Then, abruptly, headlights swing in an arc along the front of Miller's building, indicating that a vehicle in the parking lot across the street is in motion, making its way toward the lot's exit.

Standing this far down Elm means Remer cannot see the vehicle, nor the exit. All he can do as listen as that unknown vehicle—one of the three he took note of—moves west on Railroad Plaza, passing the long platform as it heads toward North Main Street with its engine gunning.

Quickly enough the sound dissipates—the vehicle has made the turn onto North Main—then disappears completely.

After that all Remer can hear is the winter wind moving through the bare trees that line Elm.

▪

Sitting on the edge of his bed, he takes the two cell phones from his pocket—his own, and the prepaid Barton had provided—and, setting the prepaid phone aside, opens his and pulls up Angela's number.

It is listed under her last name, Syc. *To breathe out softly.* Smiling at that, Remer looks at her number but does not press TALK.

He would like to call her to tell her that he is on his way into the city, that he wants to spend Christmas with her, *needs to.* But he knows he can't do that—can't make the call, and can't go back there.

Six years ago he left his apartment, walked to the corner, and hailed a cab, offering the driver two hundred dollars on top of the fare if he would take Remer to Southampton.

It was a town Remer had visited once just a year before, with a certain dark-haired woman.

They had spent a long November weekend together there, and it seemed, on that long-ago February morning, a good enough place for Remer to go and wait to be caught.

It was after a few weeks there—living in a motel on the edge of the village, perpetually stoned on pain pills, wandering around like a ghost—that he decided it was here that he might start over again.

He remembers now sitting in the backseat of that city cab, downing two pain pills just to get him through the ride.

By the time the cab had emerged from the Midtown Tunnel, Remer, his brain tingling, didn't care about anything, not even the word burned into his chest.

■

The sound of bells coming from the village pulls him from these memories.

"Deck the Halls," muffled by distance and the wind and his two windows shut tight against the winter cold.

He knows he needs more rest, but something keeps him from lying down. He stares at his window for a long time, and then his eyes move to his easy chair a few feet away.

The chair in which he sits every night, waiting for closing time and any and all indications of trouble.

The same chair in which Mia first revealed to him her fondness for the particular pleasures she got by straddling a seated man.

Remer at her mercy, hers to control.

Mia, his to watch.

It takes a moment for the significance of what he is seeing to make its way through the dark maze that is his tired mind.

Once it does, though—once it reaches *him*—he drops his own cell and grabs and opens the prepaid one.

There is only a single number in its CALL HISTORY file.

Remer pulls it up and presses TALK.

On the third ring, Barton answers.

"It's me," Remer says.

"You okay?"

"Yeah. Listen, I was wondering if you could do something for me."

"What?"

"Your buddy Spadaro, he has access to all the reports, right?"

"Yeah."

"There should be a list, an inventory, of everything the cops found inside the cottage, right?"

"Yeah."

"Would you call him and find out what's on it and call me back?"

"What's going on?"

"Please just do this, Kay And find out what was in the Scirocco, too."

"Okay. I'll try to reach him and get right back to you."

Remer closes the phone but keeps it in his hand.

As he waits, he stares at his window. It isn't long before his eyes go to the vial sitting upon its sill.

Three minutes later, Barton calls back.

"Got it," she says. "It's a short list, actually, for both the cottage and the car. Inside the cottage was a mattress, two blankets, and a small kerosene heater. The only thing in the Scirocco was the rug."

"No mention of a chair."

"No. Why?"

"Because I swear there was one. A folding chair, leaning against the wall where all the blood ended up. I saw it when I first looked inside the place, but I don't remember seeing it when I went inside after Brazier left. I kind of forgot all about it when I saw the blood. If it's not listed in the cottage's inventory, then Brazier must have taken it with him. And if it's not listed in the car's inventory, he must have removed it when he removed Mia's body."

"Why would he do any of that?"

"I don't know."

"And why would a chair be there to begin with? I mean, the bed, yeah, and the rug, but why a chair?"

Remer hesitates, then says, "Our mutual friend had a thing for chairs." Another hesitation, then, "Sex in a chair."

"Oh, yeah."

"You knew?"

"She talked about it a few times. Listen, I was debating just now whether or not to call you. Tommy found some things I think you should know about. Why don't you come back over and we can talk?"

Remer tells her about the vehicle leaving the station parking lot shortly after he left her.

"It was probably nothing," he concludes, "but no point in pushing our luck, right?"

"The shop?" Barton suggests.

"That's what I was thinking."

"When?"

"As soon as you can get there."

"We're leaving now."

"The back door will be unlocked. I'll be up in my office."

The connection ends, and Remer closes the phone.

14

He doesn't put on his greatcoat.

He has been seen in it, tonight and all month long, so he pulls from his closet a heavy hooded sweatshirt and a black North Face Windstopper jacket, putting them on as he heads into the bathroom, where he removes the large white bandage covering his stitches and replaces it with two flesh-colored Band-Aids.

They only barely cover his wound, but the less about him that stands out now, the better.

Taking a zigzagging route into the village—Hampton Road to Little Plains Road to Meeting House Lane, at the end of which he crosses Main and heads down Job's Lane—he reaches his store but continues past it, turning right at the end of the block, then right again, doubling back through the large municipal parking lot around which the village's business district is laid out.

The entire journey has taken him fifteen minutes, and he probably glanced behind himself two dozen times.

Not once, though, did he see any indications that someone was tailing him.

It would be difficult, now that he is paying attention, for anyone to tail him through these quiet streets without giving himself away.

Remer passes through the cluster of pine trees that separates his back lot from the municipal lot, then, removing the keys from his pocket as he approaches the well-lit rear entrance, quickly unlocks the door, and slips inside.

Deactivating the security system and leaving the door unlocked, he climbs the narrow back stairs to his office.

Sitting at his desk, he leaves the light off but switches on the monitor that displays in a four-way split screen the view from each of his four security cameras.

Its pale glow is more than enough.

He waits in this weak light, then at last hears the sound of the rear door below opening.

In one corner of the screen, Barton and a large man Remer assumes is Miller can be seen entering and starting up the stairs.

The steps creak and groan under the man's feet.

■

There is barely enough room in his office for three adults to gather comfortably.

They manage, though—Remer standing by his desk, Barton by the small two-person couch a few feet away, and Miller just inside the door.

A hulk of a man, he all but fills the doorway.

His hair and beard, both a little on the scraggly side, are dark. *A man without a boss.* Remer knows that Miller is only in his early thirties, but facing the guy now for the first time, he sees that there is something about Miller that makes him somehow appear older than that.

Something in the way he looks, and in the way he carries himself— a conscious effort, it seems to Remer, to keep all movements to a bare minimum and the expression on his face as neutral as possible.

As if to do otherwise might give something away.

A man, like Remer, tainted by regret?

Dressed in a black army field jacket, jeans, and work boots, and wearing leather gloves covering hands that promise real power, Miller studies Remer closely.

Remer can't help but wonder at this moment what Miller knows about his past. What Miller may have been told, or maybe found out on his own, as a precaution.

It is, of course, likely, Remer thinks, that Miller is wondering the same.

Barton introduces them. Since the office is small, Remer need only take a step from his desk to accept Miller's extended hand.

A firm but quick handshake followed by a mutual release, then Remer returns to his desk, leaning against it with his arms folded across his chest.

Miller wastes no time. "Kay says you saw something when you left our place tonight."

"Not exactly. When I was about a hundred feet down Elm, a car in the train station parking lot started its engine and drove off."

"So you didn't get a look at it."

"No. But there were only three in the lot. A silver Lexus, a black Chevy Avalanche, and a purple PT Cruiser."

"The Lexus and PT Cruiser were the only vehicles there when we left just now."

"So the black Chevy, then," Remer concludes. "Like I said to Kay, it's probably nothing. But considering the past few days, any coincidence is worth pausing at."

"I'll have Spadaro run a DMV check," Barton says. "It's a popular truck, but maybe we'll get lucky, maybe there aren't too many out here."

There is a pause, and then Remer says to Miller, "So what have you found out?"

"Kay filled me in on what you told her. There are, for both of us, things that don't add up."

"Like what?"

"According to Spadaro," Barton answers, "the owner of the cottage stopped making his mortgage payments back in September. But the bank has yet to get around to foreclosing on it. Apparently, they're all a little overwhelmed right now, and a number of places are sitting in limbo—abandoned by their owners, and not yet seized by the mortgage holder. When his summer tenants moved out, and he couldn't find someone to rent it for the winter, the owner knew he wasn't going to be able to hang on to it, so he emptied the place out, drained all the pipes, said he left not one thing behind. Which means someone else brought in the mattress and rug and heater after that."

Miller jumps in. "If we assume it was Mia and her boyfriend, that means they were there at least once before the night you saw them there. And according to Brazier's old boss, that was the address Brazier gave him when he was hired. Assuming that's true, then why would Brazier need directions? And why would he be so stupid and leave them behind?"

"Criminals do stupid things all the time," Remer says.

Barton continues, "You're right, they do. But why leave the rug behind, too? A rug with blood and hair on it. The directions led Manfredi right to the cottage, where fibers found on the living room floor were a perfect match with the fibers of the rug in the Scirocco. Add to that the fact that the blood on the rug and the blood in the bedroom were both Mia's, and there is little doubt that she was murdered there."

"Maybe Brazier panicked," Remer says. "Or maybe he was going to take everything with him but his old boss interfered. The guy said Brazier cleaned out the register the night he quit. He seemed eager to find him."

"What was his name?" Miller asks. "Brazier's old boss."

"Rene."

"Did you by any chance get a last name?"

"No."

Barton and Miller look at each other.

"What?" Remer says.

Barton nods and says to Miller, "Show him."

"Show me what?"

Miller removes something from the pocket of his field jacket and offers it to Remer.

A piece of paper, folded.

Taking it, Remer waits a moment, then unfolds it.

It is a photocopy of a marriage certificate from, according to the banner printed in bold at the top of the page, a Web site called government records.com.

The first line of the document lists the names of the bride and groom.

Mia Ferrara and Rene DeVere.

Below that are their birth dates, followed by the date of the marriage—October 15, 2008—and the town in which they were married, Bridgehampton.

Below all that is a residential address.

78 Magee Drive, Southampton.

"Jesus," Remer says. His voice is barely above a whisper.

"Spadaro found it first," Barton explains, "then tipped Tommy off."

Remer stares at Mia's name for a moment, then says, "I take it you've confirmed that Rene DeVere is Brazier's old boss."

"According to the owner of Pintauro's, yes."

"Spadaro talked to him?"

"Her, actually. Manfredi did, after he saw the tape of you and Mrs. Ferrara and realized that was where you started. According to the owner, her manager and one of her bartenders quit on Monday, the day after you were attacked."

"Rene and Casey."

"Yeah."

"The address DeVere gave her when he was hired was in Sag Harbor. That's the address Manfredi has."

Remer holds up the photocopy. "He doesn't know about this yet?"

Barton shakes her head. "No. It's Christmas Eve."

Again, Miller jumps in. "The whole thing kind of smacks of . . . overkill, don't you think? The bloody rug in the car, the directions to the murder scene right there on the front seat, you sitting outside, playing witness to the two of them going in together and then Brazier driving away. Add to all that the fact that the man who sent you there in the first place turns out to have recently married Mia in a civil ceremony, not to mention probably followed you when you chased after Brazier, and I think it's pretty obvious what you come up with."

It takes Remer a moment to process all that.

He understands everything being said, sees the pieces fitting neatly together, just isn't willing to draw the same conclusions.

At least, not yet.

"Maybe you should spell it out for me," he says finally.

"There are two ways to declare someone dead," Miller says. "The first is the easiest. Present the body of the deceased. But if for some reason there isn't a body, and let's say there was insurance money you wanted to collect and you didn't want to wait the seven years it takes for a missing person to be declared legally dead, you would need to go before a probate judge and prove what's called likelihood of death."

"Basically," Barton says, "you're asking the court to recognize that it is more likely than not that the reason a missing person is missing is because he or she is dead. An active murder investigation based on enough forensic evidence would help with that. As would a witness to actions that can only be explained as those of a murderer fleeing the scene of the crime."

Remer sees now exactly where this is going.

Seeing and *going*, though, are two different things.

"The Pine Barrens is a big place," he says.

"Manfredi had bloodhounds go through acres of it. Nothing."

"Brazier buried her body somewhere else."

"That's one explanation," Miller says. "Another is there is no body to bury."

Remer waits a moment, has to just get his head around this.

"You're saying Mia might not be dead."

"Think about it. Why would Brazier willingly make himself a suspect in Mia's murder? It could be that at this point in his criminal career, he doesn't care, he'd take any risk as long as the payout was big enough. If Mia, say, had a life insurance policy, and a big enough one, it's conceivable that Brazier's cut would be worth it."

"Insurance fraud?" Remer asks.

"We already know Mia doesn't have a problem stealing from someone she was supposedly in love with," Barton says. "Is it really that much of a stretch to imagine her being part of defrauding an insurance company?"

Miller steps in again. "In order for it to look like murder, there has to be a suspect. If Brazier were that suspect, and he and Mia had gotten married to make him beneficiary, he couldn't come forward to collect. He'd have to spend the rest of his life hiding. On the other hand, DeVere could play the role of bereaved husband, wait a few weeks or months, then petition a probate judge."

"Brazier was a scam artist, right?"

"Yeah."

"So maybe the marriage certificate was a fake. DeVere could have gone in with someone pretending to be Mia. That Casey woman, for example. Fake identification is easy enough to come by. And Mia and Casey are both Caucasian women with dark hair. They're around the same age."

By the way Miller and Barton glance at each other, Remer knows this is something they had yet to consider.

"That's not impossible," Miller concedes.

"Look, it's not that I want her to be dead," Remer says. "It's just that it seems to me just as possible that DeVere and Brazier worked together to actually kill Mia. Brazier is from Canada, and DeVere has a French accent. They could have known each other from before, picked Mia as a target, and planned this all from the start."

"I understand your wanting to believe that," Barton says. "If we're right, if Mia was in on this, then she had to know you were out there, watching. That would be a whole new level of cruelty, even for her. But we have to look at every possibility."

Remer remembers Mia crossing the lawn to stand toe-to-toe with Brazier.

The Mia he knew would never have done that.

The Mia he knew always ran from a confrontation—quick to start them, quick to leave them.

Could the drama outside the cottage on Magee have been for his benefit?

"Okay," Remer says, "but tell me this: How exactly did they fake it? I mean, all that blood—Mia's blood, for that matter."

Miller answers, "According to the crime scene report, between the bedroom and the rug there was less than two pints of Mia's blood spilled. That kind of blood loss isn't in itself fatal."

"The blow to the head could have instantly killed her. Once the heart stops pumping, bleeding slows, can even stop."

"Again, that isn't impossible. But you read Brazier's file. He worked as an orderly at a hospital, got fired for stealing. He could have learned how to draw and handle blood while he was there. They could have collected it over time and stored it in a refrigerator. People have done crazier things for money than draw their own blood and stash it away."

"But the reports concluded that the blood spatter on the wall was consistent with someone being struck in the head while on their hands and knees. How could Brazier and Mia have faked that?"

"They must have found a way."

"But how?"

Miller says nothing.

Barton quickly steps in. "Look, I understand this is upsetting. But I figured you deserved to know what we were thinking. I figured I owed you that much."

"But, Kay, insurance fraud? Really?"

"At least that would mean she's still alive." Barton pauses, then says, "The way I see it, that gives us a second chance to maybe help her."

"You still want to help her?"

"Maybe even more so now."

"Why more so?"

"You really think she came up with this idea on her own? I doubt they teach insurance fraud at Brown."

The only time Mia spent away from her parents, prior to her coming to Southampton and working for Remer at the age of thirty, was her four years in college.

On more than one occasion, particularly during the first months of Mia's employment, Barton had expressed surprise at just how little this Ivy League graduate knew.

Sheltered, naive, troubled, erratic—this was Mia. Barton had quickly taken the woman—at least a woman outwardly—under her wing.

How could Barton possibly abandon her now?

"If we can find her, maybe I can convince her to drop the whole thing before it's too late. I was aware of all her problems from the start. Like I said, Mia told me things she could never tell you. She was making real progress when she was with us, building confidence for the first time in her life. Then her father was killed, and boom, just like that she was back at square one. If I was able to help her once before, then I can help her again. And if Tommy and I are wrong and you're right, if she is dead, then I need to find the people who caved her head in with a baseball bat and buried her body somewhere. I need to do that because she was my friend and because it's my job."

Remer needs a moment before he can respond.

Then, finally, "So what exactly are you going to do?"

"It wasn't only DeVere's name that Manfredi got from the bar owner," Miller says. "The bartender—the one you think may have cracked your head with a blackjack—is named Casey Collins."

"How does that help us?"

"Spadaro searched the phone books for that name but came up with nothing. Then he looked through last year's books, and there it was, a Casey Collins listed at an address in Bridgehampton, 25 Main Street."

Remer looks at Barton. "What about Manfredi? I thought he had a strict rule against this kind of thing."

"Whatever we find we'll pass on to Spadaro, if possible," she says.

"And if it isn't possible? If we find something Spadaro couldn't have found on his own?"

Barton shrugs. "I guess we'll jump off that bridge when we come to it."

Remer looks at Miller again. "So you're just going to go out to 25 Main Street, Bridgehampton, and knock on the door? At midnight on Christmas Eve?"

"It's a place to start."

"The Casey Collins listed in the phone book might not even be the Casey Collins we're looking for. And if it is, the reason she's not in this year's phone book is probably because she moved."

"Or she could have just dropped her landline," Miller says. "A lot of people are doing that nowadays. If that is where she was living, though, and if she and DeVere skipped town on Monday, then it's a safe bet the place is still vacant. The earliest Manfredi will get out there is tomorrow afternoon. If we're lucky, maybe someone left something behind that will tell us where they went." Miller shrugs. "And if we're really lucky, we walk in on all four of them drinking eggnog."

Remer doesn't hesitate. "I'm going with you."

"I was hoping you'd want to," Barton says.

"We're going to have to take certain precautions," Miller points out.

Remer nods.

"And if the place is vacant and we do enter it, we'll be breaking the law."

"I don't care," Remer says.

Miller watches him a moment, then nods once and says, "Okay. So let's go."

15

In a black Jeep Grand Cherokee, Remer and Miller head east toward Bridgehampton.

The vehicle was parked in the lot behind Miller's building, next to Barton's unmarked sedan, when they arrived.

Ten years old, at least, and stripped of all its chrome trim.

When they turned into that back lot in Miller's pickup and Barton saw it there, she said, "He got that here fast."

So, not their vehicle.

Maybe it belonged to a friend, or maybe Miller—the son of a corrupt former chief of police, and a former private investigator—knew someone who could provide him with a "clean" vehicle on short notice.

The fact that Miller handed Remer gloves and told him to put them on before entering the truck was a good indication that this was a vehicle that could not be traced back to either of them, or maybe even anyone.

As they head east in silence, Remer looks at his watch, and he sees that it is past midnight.

Christmas, technically, though for Remer Christmas isn't really Christmas till morning.

Between now and first light, then, a kind of limbo—most everyone fast asleep, and all but a few businesses closed up.

Empty towns, empty streets.

No better time than this to roam into lawlessness.

On Remer's lap, a black canvas rucksack Miller grabbed from his pickup.

Inside it, a lock-picking kit, two pairs of rubber galoshes, and a digital camera in a rugged nylon case.

Everything they would need.

Nothing more, nothing less.

As a final precaution, both Miller and Remer power down their cell phones—Remer has his own as well as the prepaid one. If either were to get a call while in Bridgehampton, it could be used to pinpoint, should anyone care to in the future, their location by determining the cell tower nearest to them at the time of the call.

▪

It is twelve thirty when they reach the village.

Before they are even halfway through it, Miller announces, "There it is."

Remer quickly looks toward the driver's-side window and sees beyond it 25 Main.

It is a narrow building, two stories tall—the street level an upscale kitchenware store, the floor above almost certainly a residence.

The two upper windows overlooking Main Street are both dark.

"The front entrance isn't an option," Miller concludes.

He continues to the end of the long block, turns left onto the road to Sag Harbor, then pulls over to the shoulder.

After a quick scan, he makes an easy U-turn and, coming to a complete stop at the stop sign, turns right and backtracks through the village.

The building in question is on Remer's side now. He looks at it as they approach.

The two dark upper windows mean two things: Either no one is home, or someone is home and asleep.

Or, at least, in bed.

Miller passes the building yet again, makes the next right turn.

"Let's see if there's a back entrance," he says.

He makes another quick right, and then another, pulling into a narrow dirt driveway that leads to a small tree-lined lot.

Through the windshield Remer can see the rear of 25 Main. Attached to it is a set of plank stairs leading up to a small wooden porch and door.

"I think that's what we're looking for," Miller says.

He parks the Cherokee, turns off the lights and motor, but doesn't yet make a move to exit the vehicle.

Both he and Remer look around carefully. All Remer can see is the small lot in which they are parked, its entrance behind them, and the backs of three buildings ahead, all of which are dark. The building in the center is 25 Main.

There are no lights on back here, but some of the illumination given off by the streetlights on the other side of these buildings spills over their roofs.

"I don't think it's going to get any better than this," Remer says.

Miller asks for the canvas bag. Remer hands it to him. Opening it, Miller removes the galoshes, hands one pair to Remer, then bends around the steering wheel as well as his large frame will allow and reaches down to pull the other pair over his shoes.

Once they both have their galoshes on, Miller removes the lock picks and nylon camera case, putting the picks in one pocket of his overcoat and the camera in the other.

After pausing for one more quick listen and look around, the two exit the Cherokee, cross to the stairs, and make their way onto the small back porch.

Remer decides to survey the area from this elevated position. Standing with his back to the door, partly to block Miller's actions, he scans but sees, really, nothing he couldn't see from below.

Miller is looking through the window in the upper half of the apartment's back door.

"Well?" Remer says softly.

"It looks vacant to me."

Remer turns and joins Miller, looks through the glass for himself.

Immediately beyond is a bare kitchen, and beyond that, a brief hallway leading into a large room, also bare.

Based on the narrowness of the building, Remer believes this to be the entirety of the apartment. The light from Main Street coming through the two front windows at the far end is more than enough to see by.

Less than half a minute later, he and Miller are standing inside the kitchen. Miller quickly moves to the counter and begins opening drawers, looking for bills or pieces of mail, anything that might have been left behind.

The echo of each drawer, and the ease with which they slide along their rollers, tell Remer that they, like this place, are empty.

After that search Miller opens the upper cupboards two at a time. Again, nothing. Quickly searching the bottom cupboards, he gets the same results.

Miller then opens the refrigerator, activating the compressor. With nothing to absorb the steady hum of the motor, it, too, echoes.

"Guess I didn't need to bring the camera," Miller says.

Remer has left the kitchen and is standing in the brief hallway leading to the front room.

Miller enters the small bathroom off the kitchen. Joining Remer in the hallway just a few seconds later, he says to him, "Nothing there."

On one side of the narrow hallway is a closet door, and on the other side is the door that leads down to the Main Street entrance. While Miller checks the closet, Remer steps to the other door.

The chain lock is in place.

"Looks like the last person to leave went out the back door," he says. "Anything in the closet?"

"Just a water heater."

Together they move through the hallway to the front room. With the exception of a tangle of cable TV wires leading from a baseboard in the immediate left corner, this room, too, is utterly empty.

"If they were all staying here," Miller says, "I can see why Brazier and Mia might keep a mattress in that place in Southampton."

Remer says nothing to that; something else has caught his attention.

"Do you smell that?" he says.

Miller pauses. It takes him a moment. "It's bleach," he says. "They must have cleaned the place up good before they bugged out."

"Any idea how long the smell of bleach lasts?"

"No."

"It seems pretty fresh to me," Remer says.

Miller shrugs. "The windows are all closed. And maybe they had to use a lot for some reason."

There is another door on the far end of the front room, set in the wall perpendicular to the wall that faces Main Street. Miller crosses to it and pulls it open, but because of the way the door swings, it blocks the light coming in through the front windows, preventing it from reaching inside.

It is a closet, nothing inside but blackness.

A cord is hanging overhead. Miller reaches up, tugs it. A click, and then a bare bulb comes on, casting a sudden and harsh light.

"The electricity hasn't been shut off," Miller says.

Reaching for the cord again, he switches the light off.

Remer speaks quickly. "Wait a minute."

"What?"

"Turn that light back on."

Miller tugs the cord once again. "What's up?"

"Do you see that?"

"See what?

"There, on the wall."

Remer, standing in the middle of the room, is staring at a section of the left-hand wall.

"I don't see anything," Miller says.

"You're not at the right angle. Come toward me."

Miller steps away from the closet and follows Remer's line of vision. "I still don't see anything."

"Keep coming."

He takes a few more steps, then abruptly stops.

"What the hell?" he says.

There is a vague swirling pattern on the surface of the white plaster wall, visible in the glare caused by the closet light.

"This part of the wall has been scrubbed," Remer says. "That would explain the smell."

He quickly looks along the rest of the wall, adjusting his position to re-create the conditions necessary to detect the same pattern.

"And it's only this patch of wall right here. If you hadn't turned on that light, I wouldn't have seen it."

Miller crosses to the other side of the room. Standing at an angle to the opposite wall, he examines it.

"Nothing on this side," he says.

Remer traces an oval shape in the air with his right hand. "It's from about the height of my chin down to the floor. And maybe four feet wide."

He thinks for a moment, then looks at Miller.

"Am I crazy, or are those dimensions familiar?"

Miller nods. "It's the same coverage as the blood spatter in the cottage," he says. "Jesus." He removes the digital camera from his pocket. "Guess I needed this after all. I wonder if I can get a picture."

"Maybe if you turn off the flash."

Miller powers up the camera, switches off the flash, and aims at the wall. He takes a step to one side, then two more to the other, finds, finally, the proper angle and clicks the shutter.

He and Remer stand shoulder to shoulder and look at the photo on the camera's LCD display.

"You got it," Remer says.

Miller points at the small screen. "You can actually see the swirling," he says. "It looks to me like they used a rag or something like it, all wadded up. You can make out the lines left by the creases."

"The paint looks almost worn down in spots. They must have scrubbed pretty hard."

"So whatever this was, someone was eager to get rid of it."

Remer thinks for a moment, then looks at Miller. "Blood?" He can hear the doubt in his voice.

"Maybe. You don't happen to have a Luma-Lite on you, do you?"

"Left mine in my other coat," Remer jokes.

"Damn."

Returning to the wall, Remer stares at the markings for a few moments more, then leaves the front room to check the hallway wall.

Miller lingers behind, taking several more photographs from different angles, then joins Remer.

"Anything here?"

Remer shakes his head but says nothing.

"What are you thinking?" Miller asks.

"I don't know what to think. What about you?"

"At this point I'm trying to figure out a way to let Spadaro know about all this without setting ourselves up for a breaking and entering charge. Or without getting him in trouble."

"How would he have found this himself?"

"Exactly. If that is blood back there, and if this was Casey Collins's place, then this is a second crime scene connected to Brazier and De-Vere and Mia Ferrara. A second crime scene with an identical blood spatter. Despite all the cleaning that's been done here, I doubt they got every fingerprint. And if we can track down the landlord, we can find out who was living here and when exactly they left."

"Which brings us back to how to pass this on to Spadaro without screwing ourselves in the process."

"Right now I think we should go back and tell Kay about all this. I think we've pushed our luck enough for one night, don't you?"

Remer nods.

Outside, as they head back toward the Cherokee, Remer happens to glance back and spot a single garbage can under the porch steps.

He stops. Miller, too. Remer walks to the can and lifts its lid.

"Empty," he reports.

"Now, that's a surprise," Miller says.

Walking back toward Miller, Remer looks around the small lot and says, "If they were packing up to leave, wouldn't they have left garbage behind? Kitchen stuff, staples from the refrigerator, something?"

"Collins and DeVere quit their jobs on Monday. Assuming that's when they took off, there may have been a garbage pickup between then and now."

"That garbage can is store-bought, not the kind issued by a refuse company. I don't think they had pickup service."

"So they made a run to the dump on their way out of town."

Remer shrugs. "I suppose. If they had the time."

Miller continues toward the Cherokee. Remer follows. As they reach the vehicle, Miller instructs Remer to remove his galoshes. Doing so would ensure that no traces specific to that apartment that the soles of their galoshes might have picked up would be carried into the Cherokee.

Remer leans against the truck with one hand and reaches down for his boot with the other.

It is then that he sees what looks like a path running through the cluster of trees surrounding the small lot.

It isn't the path that catches his eye but rather what is beyond it: the rear lot of the building next door—and, just steps from it, an industrial-sized Dumpster.

Remer looks at it for a moment, says finally, "Hang on a minute, okay?" and walks to the path. Moving along it, he crosses this rear lot, larger than the one next to it. He reaches the Dumpster and hears Miller coming up behind him.

This building is home to a hardware store. Not far from the Dumpster is a stack of empty wooden pallets, some intact, others broken up.

Remer takes a quick look around, then lifts the metal lid.

Miller removes a Maglite penlight from the pocket of his field jacket and shines it into the Dumpster.

Inside are scraps of wood and several large dark garbage bags.

Beneath that pile of bags, though, is something white.

Climbing into the Dumpster, Remer moves the dark bags and finds below them two smaller white bags.

Household garbage bags.

He picks one up, hands it to Miller, then grabs the second one, opens it, and glances at its contents.

Condiments, in jars and bottles, some nearly empty, others close to full; an empty orange juice jug; a head of wilted iceberg lettuce; a bag of baby carrots; several to-go containers of rotting Chinese food.

Refrigerator contents.

He reaches and shifts through the items, spots below them what looks like a wadded-up rag.

He digs for it, grabs it, and pulls it free, holding it up.

Miller aims his light at it.

The rag is stained red and as stiff as cardboard. Even as Remer holds it by a corner, it remains a wad.

"It's not blood," Miller says immediately. "Blood would cake."

"So what the hell is it?"

Miller says nothing. Placing the penlight between his teeth, he begins searching through his bag, which, at first, seems to contain only strands and strands of shredded paper. Reaching past them to the bottom, though, he, too, finds something.

He removes it and holds it up, aiming the light at it.

It is a large sponge. Heavy-duty, porous, the kind used to wash a car.

One side of it is stained red and stiff.

"What the fuck?" Remer says.

Miller returns the sponge to its bag, takes the penlight from his mouth, and says, "I think we need to show all this to Kay."

Remer, as quickly and as quietly as he can, scrambles out of the Dumpster.

Back at the Cherokee, he and Miller remove their galoshes.

Pulling a large ziplock bag from the pocket of his field jacket, Miller stuffs his galoshes into it, then holds it open for Remer, who stuffs his pair in as well. As Miller pockets the ziplock, Remer tosses both garbage bags into the backseat of the Cherokee.

As they leave Bridgehampton, Remer notices Miller checking the rearview mirror.

Montauk Highway, though, in either direction, is as empty as it was when they headed into town just ten minutes ago.

The limbo that exists between midnight and Christmas morning.

▪

Just past the village of Water Mill, Miller steers the Jeep onto a back road.

Less than a minute later, when the vehicle has entered a dark and desolate stretch, he suddenly pulls over and shifts into PARK.

"What's up?" Remer asks.

Saying nothing, and removing the ziplock bag containing the galoshes from his pocket, Miller exits and hurries around the back of the Cherokee to the passenger side, then crouches down.

Remer watches as he shoves the bag through the opening of a storm drain.

Returning to the driver door, Miller takes a quick look around, paying close attention to the darkness behind them, then pulls himself in behind the wheel.

Continuing on that back road, taking the long way into Southampton, he removes his cell phone and powers it up.

It is a nondescript unit, identical to the prepaid phone in Remer's pocket.

Once it has detected a signal, Miller places a call to Barton, telling her they are on the way and explaining the thing she needs to do to get ready for them.

16

■

The kitchen table is covered with several layers of newspaper, and Barton is already wearing latex gloves.

Miller places his garbage bag on one end of the table and removes the stained sponge. Remer places his next to it and removes the wadded-up rag.

They lay the items side by side, and then Remer takes a step back.

"The apartment was cleared out," Miller tells Barton. "But we found these bags in the Dumpster behind the building next door."

Barton examines first the rag and then the sponge.

"Part of one of the walls in the living room had been scrubbed with bleach," Miller explains. "A lot of bleach. You could still smell it. The outline was pretty much identical to the shape of the spatter back in the cottage."

With her right hand, Barton carefully picks up the rag, holding it between her thumb and index finger. It continues to maintain its crumbled shape.

"This isn't blood, you know that, right?" she says.

Miller nods. "Yeah. But if it isn't blood, then what the hell is it?"

Placing the rag back onto the table, Barton rubs the tips of her index finger and thumb together, looks at them for a moment, then finally raises them to her nose and smells them.

She looks first at Miller beside her, then over her shoulder at Remer.

"Guys, this is corn syrup," she announces. "Corn syrup and food coloring."

"What the hell?" Miller says. "Why would someone spatter corn syrup all over their wall?"

Barton takes a step back. She needs a moment to think. Remer and Miller give it to her.

Then, finally, she says, "Jesus."

"What?" Remer asks.

"When corn syrup is wet it has the consistency of blood, even behaves like blood," Barton explains. "But it dries differently, especially on fabric. Blood cakes, eventually becoming flaky, almost powdery along the edges. Corn syrup, though, just turns into this hard, tacky film, almost like a shellac. It's the difference between paint and spray paint. But because it behaves like blood when it's wet, has more or less the exact same viscosity, corn syrup is used to re-create crime scenes, both in the classroom and in the lab. A lot can be determined by the way blood spatters—it can tell you whether a blow resulted from a stabbing or blunt trauma. It can tell you the force of a blow and often the weapon that was used. And it can tell you the position a victim was in when the blow was received."

"Shit," Miller says.

"If you have blood spatter at a crime scene," Barton continues, "and you want to reproduce it for the sake of a jury, prove beyond a shadow of a doubt what that pattern means, you'd re-create it in the lab using corn syrup. But it could also work in reverse. If you wanted to be certain what blood would do—if you needed to create a particular pattern so the police would conclude what you'd want them to conclude—you might first try it somewhere else with corn syrup."

Remer says, "How, though? How would you make it look like someone had been hit in the head while on his hands and knees?"

"Soak the sponge with the corn syrup, place it close to the wall, then hit it."

"It would have to be elevated, though, wouldn't it?" Miller says. "I mean, you couldn't just lay the sponge on the floor. The angle would be wrong, and if you hit it with force, there'd be a ding on the floor. That would pretty much give you away, wouldn't it?"

"Unless you laid something down," Barton says. "Or put the sponge on something—" Stopping short, she looks at Remer.

"Like a folding chair," he says.

She nods, then says to Miller, "I think we need to set up a little experiment."

Within a minute they have it ready to go: a sponge from the cupboard under the sink, similar to the stained sponge, soaked with water and placed on a chair from the kitchen table set a foot from a living room wall. Miller enters the bedroom, then returns seconds later with a baseball bat.

Standing beside the chair, he raises the bat over his head, then brings it down with force, smashing the sponge and cracking the wooden seat.

The scattering drops make a pattern on the wall that isn't an identical match to the blood spatter pattern back in the cottage, but it is close.

The three stare at it for a moment, silent.

"The viscosity of water is different," Barton says finally. "That's why it isn't a perfect match. And the chair might have been farther back." She shrugs, then looks at Remer and says, "At least we now know why Brazier took the chair with him."

Miller lowers his arm and touches the baseboard with the tip of the now-wet bat. It leaves a small watermark similar to the smudge of blood.

"Put a few strands of Mia's hair down there," he says, "and you're in business."

Remer looks at Barton. "So it was staged."

Barton nods. "They drew Mia's blood over a period of time, stored it, and brought it with them when they went to the cottage."

"But they went in empty-handed," Remer says.

"Two pints would easily fit in a couple of coat pockets. And they could have already stashed the sponge in a cupboard or something in-side. My guess is they used the kerosene heater to warm up the blood so it would behave exactly right. Temperature can affect the way blood behaves. Then they soaked the sponge with some of Mia's blood, enough to get the right amount of spray, and carefully spilled out the rest in the Persian rug and on the floor."

"But how would they know about any of this?" Remer says. "Blood spatter and using a chair to re-create an angle consistent with a rage killing. How would they know to do all that?"

"Lots of places," Miller says. "Books, the Internet. Or TV, from one of those true-life forensics shows. There are dozens of them on nowadays, and they're basically how-to shows for would-be criminals."

Remer recalls the cable wires coming out of the wall in that apart-ment's living room.

And he recalls again the argument between Mia and Brazier on the front lawn of the cottage.

There is no doubt now that the whole thing was for his benefit.

"You okay?" Barton asks.

Remer nods, but stiffly. "They must have been waiting for Mia's mother to send another team of investigators out looking for her. They ditched the last one in, what, October?"

"That's what Mrs. Ferrara said."

"So they had to have this plan ready for a while. They had to be all set to go at a moment's notice. Since Pintauro's was the place connected to Brazier, all they had to do was wait for someone to show up there, then send that person right where they needed him to be. Once that person was in place, all Brazier and Mia had to do was show up and put on their show."

"You know, it's possible Mia didn't know it was you out there," Barton says. "For all she knew it was just another one of the men her mother hired."

"DeVere had to contact Brazier and tell him I was at the cottage. He could have told Brazier, and Brazier could have told Mia."

"Did DeVere even know who you were?"

"Yeah, I told him."

After a pause, Barton says, "Okay, maybe she knew. Maybe at the last minute she was told. My point is, I don't think Mia planned for it to be you. And if Mrs. Ferrara had gone to someone other than Tommy, it wouldn't have been you."

"Why does it sound like you're defending her?"

"I'm not. I just don't want you to go into a tailspin because of this. Like you did the last time she mistreated you."

A *strange choice of word*, Remer thinks. *Mistreated*.

Still, it is better than the word Evelyn Ferrara used. "*That must have been . . . emasculating.*"

Neither says anything for a moment.

Finally, Miller breaks the silence.

"The question now is what do we do with this. How do we get this information to Manfredi without getting Kay or Spadaro in trouble?"

Remer doesn't hesitate. "We tell him I found it," he says. "I located the apartment and let myself in. I took the pictures of the wall, I found the evidence in the garbage, then came to Kay with it."

"But how did you find the apartment in the first place?" Miller asks. "Manfredi is going to want to know that."

"For all anyone knows, I caught Casey's full name the night I was at Pintauro's. When I started to suspect that Mia had faked her own death and set me up to witness it, I did what Spadaro did, looked up Casey's name in last year's phone book."

"You'd be admitting to breaking and entering," Barton says.

"I know," he says. "I want this to end, Kay. I want my life back." He pauses, then shrugs and says, "Her mother is right, Mia is dangerous. Maybe she does need to be locked away, before something really bad happens. Before this turns violent and someone actually gets killed."

Barton says nothing.

Miller returns to the kitchen and lays the bat on the newspaper-covered table beside the sponge and rag.

It is obvious to Remer that the guy is doing so to give Remer and Barton a degree of privacy.

"If Evelyn Ferrara wants me to testify that Mia stole from me," Remer says to Barton, "I will. But if she wants to find Mia, she's going to have to get someone else to do it. I'm done. I don't care about the money anymore."

"Was it ever about the money?" Barton asks.

Remer doesn't comment. "Call Manfredi tomorrow. Okay?"

"He'll want you to come in."

"I know."

"Maybe you'll get lucky and he'll agree to look the other way on the breaking and entering."

"I'll take whatever happens, Kay."

Remer removes from his pocket the prepaid cell phone and hands it to Barton.

"You'll want to get rid of this," he says.

Once that phone is disposed of there will be no record of their having talked since Remer's discharge from the hospital.

And Remer's visit earlier could be explained as him simply returning the clothes Barton had loaned him.

A cover-up, yes, but not the worst Remer has participated in, not by a long shot.

"You're sure you want to do this?" Barton asks. "There might be another way we haven't thought of yet."

Remer shakes his head. "This is the only way. Manfredi needs to know that he should be looking for a life insurance policy with Mia's name on it. And he needs to be ready in case DeVere comes forward and tries to collect. The sooner this is in Manfredi's hands and out of mine, the better."

"I'll call you after I talk to him."

"Okay."

"You'll be around?"

"Aren't I always?"

Remer extends his hand. Barton takes it.

"I'm grateful, Kay," he says. "For everything."

As he heads through the kitchen toward the door, Remer pauses to shake Miller's hand.

"It was good to finally meet you," he says.

Miller nods. "I'll walk you out, man."

"No, that's alright. I know the way."

Outside, Remer welcomes the cold air against his face.

Glancing toward the train station parking lot, he sees nothing but the same two vehicles that have been there all night.

Their owners, more than likely, took the train into the city for the holiday.

Good for them.

As he walks along Elm, Remer wonders if he is the only being out and about.

He wouldn't be surprised if his presence is the only one for miles and miles.

17

Home, exhausted but wide-awake.

His body dead, and his mind active—the exact opposite of the way he likes to spend his nights.

The way he needs to spend them.

He decides to take a dose of his blend, gets up to look for his vial but doesn't find it on the windowsill. He can't remember the last time he used it, but there is a lot since he came to in the hospital this morning that he can't remember. He steps into the bathroom to look for it there, but before he can begin his search, he catches his reflection in the mirror.

What he sees is the face of a man who is beyond tired—eyes red, black half circles beneath them. He sees, too, a cheek and chin in desperate need of a shave.

And above all that, just below his hairline, two flesh-colored Band-Aids barely covering a cut that has only just begun to heal.

The sight of all this helps him to realize that what he craves is something stronger than his blend.

There is a part of him that wishes he had taken the doctor who discharged him up on the offer of pain pills. But there is another part of him that knows he is better off without those.

He runs through the list of what he has at home—surprisingly little, for the owner of a liquor store—and comes to the conclusion quickly enough that just any old intoxicant won't cut it.

Let the tailspin begin.

▪

Parking his truck in the small rear lot, he enters his shop and deactivates the security system, then climbs the narrow back stairs to his office.

Turning on his desk lamp, he opens his safe.

Of the three bottles inside he chooses the oldest. Setting it on his desk, he closes the safe, spinning the tumbler.

On top of a nearby filing cabinet is a glass, a promotional tumbler given to Remer by one of his liquor distributors. Grabbing it, he places it next to the bottle, then sits at his desk, facing the window that overlooks his back lot.

He can see both his reflection and the dark lot beyond.

When he clicks off the light, his reflection disappears.

He fills the tumbler with a liquid the color of seawater. He has no sugar to cut the strong, almost bitter taste of licorice—the traditional method of consuming absinthe—but he doesn't care. One does not drink this for its taste.

The main ingredients of absinthe are anise, fennel, and wormwood. Nothing more, and nothing less. The anise and fennel give it the licorice taste and greenish color, and the wormwood, which contains the neurotoxin thujone, gives it the reported hallucinogenic property.

Remer, though, has never hallucinated from absinthe.

His reaction is, in fact, quite the opposite.

A *mind set adrift.*

This, combined with the high alcohol content, will get Remer to where he needs to be, and then some.

Leaning back in his chair, he takes a long sip and closes his eyes.

▪

He awakens on his small couch with no memory at all of having moved there.

But this doesn't concern him; what does is that it was a sound that stirred him from his drunken slumber.

He sits up and listens. The sound hadn't come from inside his building; he is sure of that much.

Rising from the couch, he quickly loses his balance and lumbers across the small room. It is as if his building were suddenly afloat on some rough sea. Grabbing the edges of his desk to brace himself, he looks out his office window.

To his surprise, he sees an East End snow squall—a white, almost blinding chaos. Despite the fury in the air caused by the falling flakes, each one melts as soon as it touches down. Grass holds them longest; pavement not at all.

This wild snow is all his aching eyes can make out.

He hears another sound, and there is no mistaking that this one came from outside.

It wasn't a distant sound, as far as he can tell, but one coming from somewhere within the municipal lot beyond the trees bordering his own lot.

He has to concentrate to pierce the snow with his eyes.

He sees, though, nothing.

And then, suddenly, something.

The fast sweeping of a car's headlights, the kind of sweep indicative of a vehicle making a wide turn quickly.

It is strange for someone to make use of that back lot at this time of night, not to mention on Christmas morning.

Nothing in town is open. Remer checks his watch; he sees that it is 5:00 A.M.

A delivery truck, maybe, dropping stuff off at one of the restaurants or delis.

But, again, not on Christmas morning.

Remer decides that whatever this is, it is none of his concern.

With that in mind, he grabs the bottle and is about to pour himself another glass to knock him out again when something catches his eye.

Through the snow, not motion now or even light, but a shape.

Something on the dark, glistening pavement that does not belong.

Remer hesitates, staring at it. The more he looks, the more the shape becomes something.

A heap, on the pavement near the small cluster of trees that separates his shop's back lot from the municipal lot.

It takes a moment, but finally Remer makes his way down the stairs, holding on to the rail with both hands as he goes. He doesn't reactivate the alarm, is just stepping out for a look at what is certainly nothing.

Moving through the door, leaving it open behind him, he crosses the back lot, can see the thing a little better but still can't tell what it is.

The fat, wet flakes he watched from the warmth of his office are falling into his eyes now, clinging to his lashes and all but blinding him.

Unable to blink the snow from his eyes, he holds up his right arm, as if against a strong overhead sun.

It is only then, with just a few yards left between him and the thing, that he sees what it is.

A body, sprawled out and facedown, motionless.

18

Remer's first instinct is to freeze and drop into a crouch.

Looking around, making a quick but thorough sweep of his surroundings—as thorough as the swirling snow and his drunken mind allow—he determines that he is alone.

Then and only then does he look at the body again.

By the clothes and the shape of it, it is obviously a man. Rising up from his crouch, bent at the waist as though under fire, Remer takes a few more steps toward it.

His wild hope is that this is merely some poor drunk—some holiday celebrant—who has lost his way and passed out.

For that matter, it could be a customer of Remer's, someone he knows and who wandered back to the source of his poison the way a true addict would.

Remer's mind, even as addled as it is, can't help but search for some explanation, something that would make this anything other than what his experience is telling him it is.

He has seen, after all, the body of a dead man before.

Seen it drop and land in a similar heap on the pavement.

The man's head is turned away from Remer. To see who this is will require Remer to move around to the other side, put himself between the man and the municipal lot.

He does so cautiously, then, taking another quick look around, drops again into a crouch.

There are enough lights on in the empty lot stretching out behind him for him to get a good look.

He recognizes the face immediately.

David Brazier.

Lids half open, his eyes staring but vacant.

Standing upright, Remer faces and scans the municipal lot.

Despite the snow, he can just make out the far edge a hundred yards away.

The vehicle whose lights he saw is nowhere to be seen.

Turning back to Brazier's body, he steps closer to it and begins to look for indications of the cause of death.

There are no wounds to the guy's face or head, nor any rips in what Remer can see of his clothing. More importantly, there is no blood.

Killed somewhere else.

Killed, then dumped here.

On the edge of the lot behind Remer's business.

There can be only one reason for that.

And the fact that this is the man Remer chased to the Pine Barrens— not to mention the man Mia left him for—only quickens Remer's understanding of what it is he has to do now.

It wouldn't take much for a cop—a smart cop—to look into Remer's past and put two and two together, see that Remer walked away from a lucrative career as a New York City private investigator on the same morning a Frenchman suspected of being an enforcer-for-hire was found shot dead in Brooklyn.

Considering what that Frenchman was known for, one glance at Remer's chest would be enough to undo him.

Explaining to Manfredi why he broke into the apartment in Bridge-hampton was one thing.

Explaining the presence of a dead body behind his business—this dead body in particular—would be something else entirely.

■

Hurrying to his pickup, he glances at his watch.

Two hours, at the most, till daylight.

No time to waste.

Opening the passenger door, he grabs a pair of cotton work gloves from his glove compartment, then removes a blanket he keeps for emergencies from behind the passenger seat.

At the rear of his truck he quietly lowers the back gate, then returns to Brazier's body. As he looks around once more, he opens the blanket and lays it out alongside Brazier. With his heart pounding against his sternum, adrenaline rushing through his veins, he rolls the body over and onto the blanket.

Faceup now, Brazier's unblinking eyelashes begin collecting the falling snow.

Remer sees nothing unusual about the front of Brazier's clothing—no tears or knife holes or bullet holes. And no blood, either.

But the cause of Brazier's death is the least of Remer's concerns suddenly. As he steps around to the other side of the blanket, about to fold it over to cover the body, something catches Remer's eye.

Something on the pavement.

As was the case when he initially saw the heap from his office window, Remer's first glance at this item puzzles him to the point of slowing his thoughts, then stopping them dead.

It is, as before, a glance at something that does not belong.

But the confusion and hesitation don't last for long.

On the pavement, where Brazier's body had been lying face-down, is a glass vial.

A blue glass vial.

His blue vial.

He whispers, "What the fuck?"

Then he just stands there, staring at it.

He thinks suddenly of the Chevy Avalanche that exited the train station shortly after he left Barton's place.

He thinks, too, of the hours he was away from his own apartment—at his office with Barton and Miller, then in Bridgehampton, and then in Barton and Miller's apartment.

Plenty of time for someone to let himself into my place and look for something that would no doubt hold my fingerprints.

Moving with even greater purpose now, he picks up and pockets the vial, then folds the blanket over the body like a shroud.

Crouching down again, he slides his arms beneath the corpse and lifts it. The thing is heavy, unwieldy, but he manages to stand straight and carry it to his truck. Easing it into the bed, he pushes it forward till it is all the way in, then closes the tailgate.

He has read enough coroner reports to know by the lack of stiffness in the limbs that Brazier hasn't been dead for long.

From his own Dumpster, Remer removes several broken-up and folded cardboard boxes, uses these flat pieces to cover the contents of his truck bed. He doesn't have to worry about the cardboard blowing off as he drives; he won't be going fast at all, not in this weather, and he won't be going very far.

He hurries to the back door of his shop, closes and locks it, then climbs into his pickup and starts the motor.

Just to be safe, he takes out his cell phone and powers it down, then removes the battery, placing both pieces in a cup holder in the center seat console.

At the end of the narrow driveway running between his shop and the clothing store next door, Remer turns right onto Job's Lane and heads for the streetlight fifty feet away. Reaching it, he waits for the light to turn green, carefully studying what can be seen of his immediate surroundings.

As before—or maybe even more so thanks to this snow—it is as if Remer is the only being at large.

▪

When the light changes, he turns left onto Pond Lane, follows that around Agawam Lake till it becomes Ox Pasture Road.

The last thing he needs, of course, is to lose sight of the road in this snow and crash into a tree, so he drives slowly.

He turns left onto First Neck Lane, and one block later—a long block lined with dark, hedged-in estates, more than a few of which have FOR SALE signs posted out front—he turns right onto Great Plains Road.

Finally, he makes one last left turn onto Cooper's Neck Lane.

Heading south now, with the ocean less than a half mile away.

Cooper's Neck ends at Meadow Lane, and Remer can see through his windshield the entrance of the parking lot at Cooper's Beach straight ahead.

The lot is empty—why would it be otherwise at this time of night and year?—but better than that, it is unlit and, unlike the lot back in town, the far edge of it isn't at all visible through the snow.

Remer enters the lot and steers toward the ocean side, which becomes visible only when he is twenty or so feet from it, and even then just partially.

A narrow roadway loops off the lot here, rising up and around a tall dune. It is long enough for four or five vehicles to park nose to tail and allow their occupants a view of the beach and ocean.

Pulling up onto to this narrow lookout, Remer parks his truck and hurries out.

The dune around which the road is built is high enough to block the view of any person who might enter the lot, or pass by on Meadow Lane. So even if this snow were to ease up suddenly or even stop, Remer will still be able to work unseen here.

Opening the tailgate, he lifts off the cardboard and pulls the body to the edge of the truck bed. Whoever placed the vial beneath Brazier might have taken something else from Remer's apartment and planted it somewhere on the body, so Remer quickly searches through his pockets. He finds, though, nothing.

Getting his arms beneath the body, he lifts it and crosses from the pavement onto the sand, where each step is a struggle to keep his footing.

The tide tonight is low, and the crashing of the waves, which Remer can only barely see in the darkness, sounds like the roars of angry giants.

As he reaches the shoreline, he can hear nothing else, not even his own labored breathing.

At the water's edge he crouches down and lays the shrouded body onto the damp sand. He doesn't expect it to be carried away by the incoming surf, but if it is, all the better.

What he really wants is for whatever trace evidence it might hold—incriminating fibers from his apartment, perhaps, that may have been planted on it—to be washed off by the force of pounding saltwater.

He rolls the body off the blanket. Brazier is once again facedown. After shaking the blanket out several times—it flutters in the steady winter wind like a loose sail—Remer carries it back to his pickup, quickly folds it up, and tosses it, and the cotton gloves, into the truck bed with the cardboard.

Steering down from the lookout, he catches himself holding his breath as the parking lot comes into sight.

To his relief, it is still empty.

■

On his way back to the village, following a different route from the one he took to get to Cooper's Neck, Remer pulls to the shoulder of a well-lit street and parks in the shadow of an old tree.

Opening the driver door, he removes his boots and claps their soles together till sand stops falling from them, then grabs a bottle of water from the seat console and pours half of it over the sole of one boot and the other half over the sole of the other.

He wants to be thorough, though, has to be, so he searches through the console for a foil-wrapped moist towelette he knows is in there somewhere. Finding it, he tears it open and wipes each boot down, then pockets the towelette and puts his boots back on.

Pulling the driver door closed, he continues on through the snow.

Back behind his shop, he returns the cardboard to the Dumpster, then heads inside and grabs a garbage bag from a utility closet just inside the door before climbing the steep back stairs to his office.

He opens his safe again. Despite the alcohol in his blood—not to mention the thujone playing havoc with his brain—he is thinking now with utmost clarity.

He puts the bottle of absinthe on its shelf inside the safe, then closes it and, sitting at his desk, fingers the touchpad of his notebook computer, awakening it from sleep mode.

The screen shows the four-way-split view from his four security cameras.

Activating the monitoring program, he pulls up the most recent activities and watches the digital recording that shows him entering just a moment ago.

A stamp at the bottom of the screen indicates the exact date and time, down to seconds.

He selects the erase option and, when prompted, confirms that he does indeed want to erase this recording permanently, then quickly moves to the previous activity captured by the camera inside his back door.

He sees himself exiting less than a half hour ago.

He erases that, then erases the footage of him entering two hours prior to that.

The next activities caught by the system are him leaving, then Barton and Miller leaving.

Then Barton and Miller entering, then him entering.

Remer erases those, too, till the most recent activity that remains is his employees closing up yesterday evening.

He then accesses his security system's logs and brings up all the enter and exit codes posted between yesterday evening and now, deleting them one by one.

He can't be seen leaving, nor does he want to leave an exit code, so he has no choice but to deactivate his four cameras, as well as the alarm system.

Of course, doing so will leave his shop vulnerable to a break-in and robbery, but this is the risk he has to take.

With the empty garbage bag in his hand, he moves down the steep stairs, exiting through the back door and locking it behind him.

A strange feeling, not activating the system, but he ignores it.

Just to be safe he uses the blanket to sweep the truck bed, damp now with melting snow, then stuffs it, along with the cotton gloves, into the garbage bag. Tossing the bag into the back of the truck, he pauses to take one last look around his rear lot.

Nothing, no one but him and the crazy snow.

▪

Just inside the entrance of his apartment building he removes his boots, tosses them into the bag, and climbs the stairs in his stocking feet.

In his apartment he empties his pockets—all he has is his wallet and the vial—then strips down, stuffing each article of clothing, including his North Face jacket, into the bag.

Carrying the vial into the bathroom, he flushes it down the toilet, waits till it disappears from his sight, then returns to his living room and grabs a change of clothes and a pair of sneakers from his closet.

Once dressed, he grabs his greatcoat and puts that on, stashing his cash and wallet in the deep inside pocket.

He thinks of packing a few things but doesn't bother; he isn't even sure where he is going, knows only that the safest thing for him to do is *be gone.*

Back in his truck he makes his way through the village to Sunrise Highway, the quickest route out of town, then heads west.

The snow requires that he keep his pickup to thirty miles per hour, though often he needs to go even slower than that. His headlights show nothing but white flakes blowing in one direction, then, suddenly, blowing in the complete opposite direction, changing like that countless times every minute. And every now and then, the snow seems to stall in midflight, creating a white wall that reflects his own headlights back into his tired eyes.

On the seat beside him is the garbage bag, and he wonders if his heart will stop pounding once he is rid of that. He remembers Miller stuffing the ziplock bag containing the galoshes down a storm drain. This bag is too big for that, however. There is only one place he can think of to dispose of it.

The Shinnecock Canal.

It seems to take forever to cross the few miles between the village and the canal. Remer is blind to almost all landmarks, blind even to the road itself, spends a good ten minutes thinking that the canal should be coming up any minute now. If it weren't for a sign made of reflective material that he manages to catch out of the corner of his eye, he might have driven across the bridge without even knowing it.

The instant he passes the sign he jumps out of his truck and hurls the open bag over the railing, doesn't even wait to hear its splash.

Getting back into the warmth of his vehicle, he brushes the fresh wet snow from his hair and grabs the wheel, continuing on at the same snail's pace.

He hasn't a clue where he is going. All he knows is that west is the way off Long Island. The quickest way, anyway.

His marine buddy, the man who had tracked down the French-man for him six years ago, lives in a small town in northern New Jersey. Remer wonders if that is where he is going.

He thinks of Angela, in her girlfriend's apartment in the West Village. How easy it would be to go to her: exit Sunrise Highway at Manorville, connect with the Long Island Expressway, follow it to the Queens Mid-town Tunnel, and once through that shoot down to Twenty-third Street, his old neighborhood, and from there crosstown to Seventh Avenue.

Just a handful of blocks south, and he would be entering the maze that is the West Village.

Once as familiar to him as the back of his hand. Every shop, every restaurant, every residence.

How much of it would even be recognizable to him now?

But he knows that, as much as he wishes to go there, he doesn't have what it takes to do that.

So northern Jersey, then.

He forces his mind to focus on the route there. The expressway to the Whitestone Bridge, then across the Bronx to the George Washington. A trip that would take less than two hours on a clear night.

God knows how long it will take tonight.

Remer settles in and runs through his mind everything he did be-hind his shop and at Cooper's Neck. He can think, though, of noth-ing that he missed or should have done differently.

As he leaves Hampton Bays and crosses into the Pine Barrens, he considers powering up his phone. Taking it and the battery from the cup holder, he is about to assemble them but pauses.

He knows not to call his friend now; such a call could be used to prove that he was on this road at this exact time. He'll make the call from a pay phone once he's over the George Washington Bridge.

And though there is no reason at all for him to expect an incoming call, he decides the best thing to do is keep the thing shut off for now.

It is as he is returning the phone and battery to the cup holder that he sees something in the rearview mirror.

Headlights.

Distorted and dim, little more than a yellow-white haze, but head-lights nonetheless.

The vehicle can't be more than a few yards behind Remer's. And the way it appeared suddenly tells Remer that it wasn't moving at a crawl, like his own midsized pickup, but at a much higher speed.

As soon as the vehicle appeared—as soon as its driver saw Remer's truck ahead—it slowed to match Remer's speed.

It remains behind Remer for a half minute, its lights filling the cab of his truck, then eventually begins finally to drift to the left.

Sunrise Highway is a four-lane road—two lanes westbound and two lanes eastbound, divided by fifty or so feet of scrub pine. The driver is obviously pulling into the passing lane to resume his previous pace and pass the slow-going truck in front of him.

Holding the steering wheel with two hands, Remer eases off the accelerator, slowing even more to allow the vehicle to pass without having to increase to an unsafe speed.

Watching the side mirror carefully as the vehicle pulls alongside, Remer sees it beginning to emerge from the chaotic snow.

A truck of some kind, but Remer knew that already by the height of the headlights.

Black, and big, the sound of its engine, as well as the sound of its tires on the wet pavement, quickly rising up and drowning out the sound of Remer's own vehicle.

It isn't till the truck is directly parallel to Remer that he sees a marking on the passenger door.

Bold silver letters spelling out the vehicle's model.

AVALANCHE.

Remer's instinct is to hit the brakes and let the truck continue past, but just as he does that and feels his own wheels locking up beneath him, the truck veers sharply and then turns so its large front bumper collides with Remer's driver door.

More than collide, though, it digs into Remer's door like a plow, all but folding the metal and driving Remer's smaller pickup instantly sideways.

There is nothing Remer can do but hang on to the steering wheel jolting beneath his hands and brace himself for the ride.

In a matter of a second, maybe two, his pickup is heading down a bank, the full force and weight of the giant Chevy Avalanche in control now.

Though his torso is buckled in, his arms are not, and once he loses hold of the wildly spinning steering wheel, they begin to flail about. Everything loose in the cab of the truck—including his cell phone and battery—is suddenly airborne, flying around him like shrapnel.

In all this Remer is somehow able to reason—if it is even reason— that the driver of the Avalanche is an amateur. A pro would have simply tapped the rear quarter of Remer's truck and sent it into a spin. Plowing full force, and turning the assaulting vehicle into an almost nose-first position against the target vehicle, is not something a trained person would do.

But there is something more pressing on Remer's racing mind.

The recognition that the driver of the Avalanche doesn't know what he is doing causes Remer to believe that the worst is yet to come.

To his own terror, he is quickly proven correct.

The Avalanche itself suddenly loses traction; Remer can hear the sound of its thick tires spinning wildly on the slick pavement, followed by the subsequent over-revving of its powerful engine. No longer the force driving Remer's pickup down the bank, the black Chevy is now following it, a ton-plus out-of-control hunk of steel racing toward the same inevitable abrupt stop.

Remer knows that in seconds his pickup will reach the bottom of the bank and put him directly between the still-moving Avalanche— mass plus speed equals force—and the winter ground at the bottom of a ditch.

His pickup will fold like an accordion.

A minimal amount of his vehicle's original forward motion has remained as it is being driven down the bank, but suddenly this energy dissipates and the Avalanche, locked with Remer's truck, begins to fishtail.

Remer can actually hear the Avalanche's bumper separate from his smashed-in door, a sound that gives rise to a wild hope that maybe the worst is not, in fact, inevitable.

At that instant Remer's pickup hits the bottom of the ditch, and he hears dirt falling around his vehicle like hard rain and feels the abrupt deceleration and the subsequent violent tug of the seat belt snatching at him and holding him in his seat.

He feels, too, the side of his head strike the driver door's window as he bounces in the recoil of the sudden stop.

A sickening thud fills his ears, followed by the sound of cracking glass.

Because it broke away as it fishtailed, the Avalanche does not crash into his truck, instead begins to spin out along the shoulder, ultimately turning around completely several times before finally sliding over the edge and into the ditch, shuddering to its own abrupt stop a good hundred feet ahead.

In its headlights swirls more soil than snow.

And for a long moment this chaotic mix of white and dark is for Remer the only motion left in the world.

19

Remer sees only blurs and shadows, hears for what feels like a long time only a dull but steady ringing in his ears.

The Avalanche has come to a stop perpendicular to the road, on the steep bank of the ditch, its tail at the bottom and nose at the top, its headlight pointing into the sky at an angle about halfway between forty-five and ninety degrees.

The engine of Remer's pickup has stalled. His headlights are still on, and the bits of churned-up earth lingering in them look less like dark snow now and more like drifting smoke.

He has no idea how long he has sat there, listening to ringing in his ears. The crash could have been seconds ago, and it could have been minutes. The Avalanche is just within the reach of Remer's headlights. He can see that its doors are still closed. Though it is hard for Remer to imagine that its driver is seriously injured—the truck is a large cage of steel—the multiple spins may have disoriented whoever is behind the wheel. That is the only thing Remer can think of to explain the stillness of the vehicle.

His own pickup has landed at an angle, its passenger side at the bottom of the ditch. Outside his driver door's window is nothing but dark winter sky. He scrambles for the door handle, finds it and pulls it, but the door won't budge, is too damaged to open. The only way out is through the window.

The glass is shattered but remains in place. Remer needs to break through it, looks around the cab for something he can use. As he does this he sees that his cell phone is in several pieces on the passenger door.

Shit.

Reaching down, he opens his center console and feels around inside till he finds the Gerber multitool he keeps there. Holding it like a an ice pick, he strikes at the glass till all the pieces rain down and the way out is clear.

He braces himself by wedging his feet under the dashboard, then releases his seat belt. As he reaches through the open window for something to hold on to he feels that his hands are slick. Looking at them he sees blood, but a quick search of his hands shows no indications that they have been cut.

It is then he realizes that the left side of his face is wet, too.

Snow, coming through the window?

He touches his head with his right hand, takes it away, and sees even more blood. He remembers striking the window with his head at the moment of impact.

Wiping his hands on his greatcoat, he reaches through the window again and places one hand on the roof of the truck and the other on the mangled door, then presses upward, pulling himself through the narrow space.

Finally out and sitting on the door, he rests for a moment to find the strength to continue.

Looking straight ahead, he sees the driver door of the Avalanche open and someone struggling to climb out—someone clearly in the same condition, give or take, as he.

Bloodied, disoriented, fumbling.

Despite having spoken to this man only briefly, in the dark parking lot behind Pintauro's, there is no doubt in Remer's mind of his identity.

Rene DeVere.

The passenger door of the Avalanche opens. Remer can't actually see that side of the vehicle, can only hear the door open.

This is his first indication that he is now hearing more than just the ringing in his ears.

It doesn't take long for this second person to make her way around the tail of the truck and enter Remer's line of sight.

Right there, just a hundred feet away, is Casey Collins.

She seems less troubled by the ride she and DeVere have just taken. *The boxer in her,* Remer thinks. She hurries to DeVere's side and stands close to him, bracing him.

The devotion of a lover, no mistaking that.

She checks his face, looking for the source of the blood streaming down it, but DeVere shakes off her concern and points a bit feebly—and a bit impatiently—at something beneath his seat.

Casey Collins immediately follows his instruction and reaches into that dark space and removes something.

There is, too, no mistaking what that something is.

A tire iron.

DeVere gestures in Remer's direction.

Remer hears a faint "Go. Go!"

Collins hesitates at first, doesn't want to leave her injured lover, but then does as she is told.

Tire iron in hand, she begins to make her way on steady legs along the bottom of the ditch.

Remer does the only thing he can think to do.

He scrambles the rest of the way out of his truck but then, lying flat on the door, reaches back inside the cab through the window.

Straining, he finds the steering column and feels along it for the long plastic rod. Once he finds that, he twists it forward.

His pickup's headlights, set on low beam for the sake of visibility in the snow, switch suddenly to high.

Casey Collins raises her hand, but it is too late; the bright light has already entered her eyes, and, instantly night-blind, she stops dead in her tracks.

▪

Remer has the advantage now, knows he will need to hurry if he is going to make good use of it.

He moves around to the back of his truck, stops there, and looks toward the Avalanche.

DeVere, too, is shielding his eyes against the high beams. Standing frozen, the man mutters, "Jesus."

Collins, with urgency in her hushed voice, whispers back to him, "I can't fucking see."

As a marine recruit in basic training, Remer was taught that looking into light at night can disrupt the rods and cones inside the human eye.

It is that very same training that tells him what to do next.

Scrambling to the top of the bank, where the surface is smooth—and where he will have control of the high ground—he quickly moves forward, closing the distance between himself and Casey Collins standing in the ditch below.

Then, from above, he rushes down on her.

By the sudden swinging of the tire iron in his general direction, he knows she heard him coming, but robbed of her sight she swings wildly and desperately, passing close enough to Remer's head that he can hear it cutting through the air.

Just as she did several nights before, Casey Collins once again means business.

Knowing she is a boxer, Remer has no intention of trading blows with her, so he immediately gets in close and goes for her throat, grabbing it with his right hand while hugging her right arm with his left. As he moves even closer to her, Remer traps her right arm between their torsos, rendering the tire iron, for the moment at least, useless.

He allows himself no hesitation, gives himself fully to violence of action by reminding himself of the damage that was done to his skull by this same person.

He senses all the muscles in her body tense—boxers are used to clinches being broken by the referee, but there is no ref here, and Remer has no intention of letting her go.

The hesitation the seizing of her muscles causes is exactly what he needs.

Holding her tightly, he drives her backward, causing her to run to keep from falling. He wants to close the distance between himself and DeVere in case DeVere is armed as well, and with something other than a blunt instrument.

Of course, DeVere, even if he weren't caught by the headlights and blinded, would at best see only silhouettes—or, more likely, a single confusing silhouette—rushing toward him.

Another advantage Remer must press.

Within seconds, he reaches DeVere and drives Collins into him, slamming them together. There is plenty of light for Remer to see what he is doing now, and he directs Collins so that the back of her head collides squarely with DeVere's face.

A sickening thud echoes, and both Collins and DeVere fall to the cold ground in a tangled heap.

Standing over them, Remer grabs the tire iron from Collins's hand, then drops to his knees and mounts DeVere like a schoolyard bully, raising the tire iron above his own head.

He is compelled by an overwhelming urge just to bring the thing down onto DeVere's skull, crushing it and killing the man, putting an end to this nonsense.

But despite every primal instinct telling him to let his hand fly, Remer resists giving in.

Semiconscious at the bottom of a ditch, DeVere is no immediate threat.

Remer's mind clears, and, as he did not an hour ago, in the lot behind his shop, he understands what needs to be done here.

While clubbing a semiconscious man's head is one thing, hobbling him so you can get away is another.

Adjusting his bully's mount, Remer takes a swing at DeVere's knee with just enough force to damage it without breaking it.

DeVere, brought into full consciousness by the pain, screams. Telling him to shut up, Remer flings the tire iron into the surrounding darkness and quickly begins searching DeVere's pockets, removing everything he finds and stuffing those items into the pockets of his own coat without even bothering to identify them first.

DeVere is simply too busy cradling his damaged knee to do anything to stop Remer.

Standing, Remer moves to Casey Collins and rifles her pockets as well.

She, unlike DeVere, is unconscious. At one point Remer notices that there is blood caking in her hair, probably where her skull collided with DeVere's face. It is, as best Remer can tell, a superficial cut, not at all life-threatening. Still, after he has claimed all of her belongings, he lifts her and carries her along the bottom of the ditch to his pickup.

Using the bank as a ramp, he is able to get her to the driver door's window and lower her inside the cab. Reaching inside, he kills the headlights, then searches for the ignition.

It is still in the ON position, so he has to turn it to OFF before he can switch it back to ON again. The motor catches almost immediately, and the heater, which was on full blast, resumes blowing a current of warmish air that will turn hot soon enough.

It isn't much, but it is the best he can do for her.

More, anyway, than she did for him the last time they met.

At least she is in no danger of freezing to death.

Remer makes his way along the bottom of the now pitch-dark ditch, heading back toward DeVere.

Standing over him, Remer wants to tell the man that this makes them even, but he doesn't bother. He thinks of the questions he should ask—*what the hell is going on? where is Mia? who killed Brazier and left him behind my shop?*—but he doesn't bother with that, either.

All he wants is to get out there, get somewhere safe—Jersey, if he can make it—so he leaves DeVere where he is and hurries to the only remaining means of escape.

Getting in behind the wheel of the Avalanche, he turns the ignition till the engine catches, then shifts into gear and eases down on the accelerator.

The Avalanche is an off-road vehicle equipped with a high suspension, four-wheel drive, and rugged tires. The steep bank, nearly frozen solid, poses no problem for it.

Remer is back on the level road in a matter of seconds.

Stopping at the shoulder with the vehicle facing west, Remer shifts into PARK and looks in the rearview mirror. He cannot see his pickup in the ditch—he can't, in fact, see anything at all to indicate there could be someone in need there.

He mutters, "Shit," and, turning his head, checks the backseat, sees something very familiar.

A large carrying case made of impact-resistant plastic.

Tools of the trade?

He spots beside this case what he is looking for. A blanket and a small emergency kit.

Opening the kit, he finds a battery-operated road flare. Grabbing it and the blanket, he exits the truck and makes his way back to the bank's edge.

He can barely see DeVere just feet below. When he switches the flare on, a blinking yellowish light illuminates the scene. Barely.

Tossing the blanket toward DeVere, Remer sees that it lands within the man's reach.

Close enough.

Releasing the flare's tripod, Remer sets it down on the edge of the pavement.

Back inside the truck, he finds a small pack of tissues inside the emergency kit. Tearing it open, he grabs nearly all the tissues it contains and presses them against the wound on his forehead.

The cold had slowed the bleeding, but now that he is inside the warmth of the truck cab, it is flowing again.

Examining himself in the rearview mirror, he sees that his stitches have all been torn, the gash that had only begun to heal ripped open again.

He holds the wad of tissues to his forehead with his left hand and shifts into DRIVE with his right.

Heading west, he once again moves at a crawl through the scattershot snow.

20

He doesn't make it very far.

A few miles, at the most; then he pulls over, has to because there is something wrong.

He knows by the handling of the vehicle that a tire has gone flat.

Removing the flashlight from the emergency kit, he climbs out to check.

The right front tire is almost completely deflated. A close look tells Remer that the tire stem has been damaged, most likely during the slide down the bank, creating a slow leak.

Standing there on the edge of that desolate road he realizes that he has no tire iron, so he couldn't swap this tire for the spare even if he wanted to, which he really doesn't; the ringing in his ears has returned, as has the pain deep behind his eyes.

And, deep within his gut, is a rising nausea.

Familiar symptoms, these.

Back inside the truck he grabs the emergency kit and the plastic carrying case. He doesn't want to wait for help to come along, wants only—still—to be somewhere no one can find him.

There is only one such place: Jersey.

But how to get there now?

Among the items he took from DeVere and Collins are two cell phones, but he doesn't dare use them. And anyway, who would he call?

In fact, the thought of the phones in his pockets compels him to remove them and power them down and detach their batteries.

Leaning into the Avalanche, he kills the motor and the lights. As his eyes adjust to the near-total darkness, he notices a faint smudge of hazy orange along the southern horizon.

Cutting through the falling snow, it looks almost like the glow of a distant fire. But Remer knows it can't be that.

So, what, then?

Lights. But it would have to be a lot of them.

The only thing this could be is the Suffolk County Airport.

Remer knows suddenly where exactly on Sunrise Highway he is. Not far ahead should be Old Riverhead Road. If he follows that south, it will take him to Montauk Highway, but before that it should cross the train tracks. Following those a few hundred yards to the west will bring him right to the Westhampton train station.

From there he could catch the early train into Penn Station. It would require a wait of an hour or so, but he could bear that. Once he reaches Penn Station he could make his way into New Jersey without even having to come up from underground.

And once in Jersey, all he needs is to find a pay phone and make a call.

Semper fi.

■

It takes less than a mile of walking for Remer to begin to doubt his plan.

The cold isn't the problem; in fact, it is the cold that keeps him alert and cools the heat he feels in his face and forehead.

It is the pain behind his eye and the ringing in his ears and the nausea and the dizziness and the growing weakness that stand together like very real obstacles before him.

A forced march while lugging heavy gear—this is something he has experience with. Or did twenty years ago—no, twenty-plus years ago.

But he was a kid back then, could take anything, *wanted* to take anything to prove himself.

He isn't a kid anymore.

His thoughts begin to wander, and he lets them—anything to distract his mind from his many agonies.

He remembers that kid he once was: no family to speak of, and no prospects other than a dead-end factory job in a dying paper mill town that itself smelled like death.

What other choice did he have but to sign up for military service? What other way of escape?

In four years the Corps took him all over the world. More than that, it gave him a few friends he could always count on no matter what.

It paid for his college and gave him the credentials necessary to pursue the career of his choice—private security at first, then several years as an in-house investigator for a law firm before starting his own business, a thriving business, one he could never imagine walking away from till that night in February . . .

Walking now—no, not walking, stumbling—his thoughts spinning out even further. Of all the people he could think of, he thinks suddenly of Evelyn Ferrara's bodyguard, sees in his mind's eye the man getting off the train at the Southampton station.

He remembers that fresh-out-of-the-military way in which her bodyguard carried himself, that dogface scowl Remer had seen on all the recruits around him—and on his own reflection as well.

A reminder of what Remer used to be.

Before the burn, and the six years of hiding and numbing himself.

For some reason this image forces Remer to push on. Competition with a younger version of himself? Perhaps. But whatever it takes. He believes there is less than a mile to go till he reaches the train tracks. He can do this—*one can always do another mile.*

Remer is able to see barely more than a few feet ahead, and he realizes that he has reached the tracks only when he finds them below his feet.

He walks a few hundred yards to the west on the hard ties and at last reaches the Westhampton train station. He doesn't see any hint of the structure as he approaches it, knows he is there only when the long platform is suddenly beside him.

It is, of course, empty. He can't even see the well-lit parking lot just beyond it. He knows now that he is shot, and though one is always supposed to be able to go another mile, a train ride into the city and then on from there to New Jersey is suddenly out of the question.

It isn't just his deteriorating condition that makes this journey impossible; in the shape he is in now, he will stand out, be too easy for a conductor or fellow passenger to remember, should it come to that, should someone somehow retrace the steps he has just now taken.

No, Jersey is out. There is no way around that. He needs a place to rest for a few hours.

Somewhere nearby, somewhere he can clean himself up and recover from the most recent blow to his head.

Not to mention the absinthe poisoning his brain.

Stepping onto the platform—the four steps may as well have been forty—he walks to the pay phone and, placing the carrying case at his feet, digs into the pocket of his jeans for change.

He can barely focus on the half-dozen coins in his palm. It takes, in fact, all he has just to determine that there are in that small pile at least three quarters.

Three quarters should do it.

He removes the receiver from the hook, puts it to his face. The hard plastic is cold, but his ear is burning, so it really doesn't feel all that bad.

To his surprise, he dials the number without even having to think about it.

Easy enough to remember, even in the worst states of mind.

Seven sevens.

A computer-generated voice tells him fifty cents is required to complete the call.

He drops two quarters down the slot with a left hand that is shaking.

■

The cab arrives fifteen minutes later, as the first hint of morning light begins casting pale shadows.

It isn't till Remer is in the backseat with the door closed that he recognizes the driver.

This time he doesn't need a quick glance at her hack license mounted on the seat to remember her name.

Brianna Ruocco.

That has to be a good sign, no? he thinks. *Remembering her name, considering everything—that has to be a good thing.*

He pulls his wallet from the inside pocket of his greatcoat, opens it, and removes a hundred-dollar bill. He hands it over the seat to her. His hand is still shaking.

He asks her to take him to the nearest motel.

Looking over her shoulder at him, Brianna nods and takes the money, placing it into the pocket of her fur-lined denim jacket.

Turning forward, she shifts into gear and pulls away from the train platform.

The snow has lessened and visibility is better, though only slightly. But Remer doesn't have to care about that now. He sits as still as he can in the backseat as the cab follows Montauk Highway toward Westhampton.

He is finally beginning to feel the warmth of the vehicle's interior as Brianna pulls into the lot of the first motel they come to.

It is a roadside joint—a long, single-story building, one end set very close to the edge of the highway, the other reaching into a dense woods of scraggly pine and scrub oak.

The office is located on the end nearest to the road. It is lit, and in its large window hangs a neon NO VACANCY sign. The VACANCY part is glowing, the NO preceding it dark.

Pulling another hundred from his wallet and offering it to Brianna, Remer asks her if she would mind checking in for him. By the way she glances at his head—bloodied, as is one side of his greatcoat—he knows that she understands what the problem is here.

People with fresh head wounds don't generally get welcomed with open arms at places like this.

Who wants to rent a room to someone who'll bleed all over the sheets and towels?

Or who has clearly just had a bit of trouble—trouble that might possibly be right behind him.

So, better the manager doesn't see Remer right now.

Again, Brianna nods and takes the money. "How many nights?"

Remer removes two more hundreds. "Better make it two."

An off-season Westhampton motel shouldn't be more than a hundred bucks a night. Just to be certain, he removes yet another hundred and hands it to her.

She looks at his shaking hand, then takes the money and exits.

Reaching the office, she enters; less than five minutes later, she is back behind the wheel with a room key in her hand.

Driving the cab to the end of the unit, she parks in front of the last room—the room farthest from the road—and looks at Remer in the rearview mirror.

"I figured you wanted the quietest room," she says.

Remer nods, even smiles slightly. "How much? For the ride, I mean."

He hears it, and so she must hear it, too: His words are beginning to slur.

"I think you've given me plenty already," she says. "You want me to help you get inside?"

He shakes his head, feels as he does a whole new wave of nausea overtake him.

More than that, he feels pressure against the inside of his skull, an expanding sensation that makes the roots of his teeth feel as though they are being pushed from their sockets.

He has to wait a moment before he can even consider making any kind of movement again.

Finally, Remer pulls himself together and opens the back door. Grabbing the handle of the carrying case, he pulls it across the seat as he gets out.

Once he is standing, though, the weight of the case catches him off guard and pulls at him like an anchor. But he manages to compensate for this and hold himself upright.

Brianna has gotten out, too, is standing face-to-face with him.

He sees that she is as tall as he is. A tomboy, maybe—now that he sees more than just what the rearview mirror can show, this is his impression of her. Athletic, certainly. *A boxer? Maybe? Jesus, I hope the fuck not.* She is dressed in green cargo pants and hiking boots, and under her fur-lined denim jacket is a gray sweater of densely woven wool.

She hands him the room key. The expression of deep concern on her face tells him that he, at best, looks the way he feels.

Taking the key, he tells her thanks and turns away.

He manages to take two steps in the direction of his room, has maybe five more to go till he is within reach of the door.

But it isn't long before he realizes that the two steps he has taken are simply two too many.

The will that has gotten him this far abandons him.

The case handle slips from his hand, and he is suddenly down on one knee.

The next thing he knows he is on his back on cold gravel, staring up at snow falling out of a graying sky.

Soon enough Brianna's face appears above him. He sees that her curly hair is beginning to fill with snow. She is saying something, but he can't hear what.

This goes on for a while—or what seems to Remer to be a while—and then Brianna grabs his right arm and wraps it around her neck.

Wedging herself against him, pressing her hips into his for leverage, she gets him to his feet and keeps him there, propping him up like a crutch.

He doesn't remember entering the motel room, but he realizes they must have done so because he is on his back again, only this time on a strange bed in a dark room, out of the cold and the snow and the rising morning light.

Above him once more is Brianna's face, looming like a shadowed moon.

The last thing he is aware of is the smell of her hair, wet now with melting snow.

21

Remer awakens to light.

A dim, somber light seeping around the edges of heavy curtains that are drawn shut, but light nonetheless.

Whether it is dawn or dusk he doesn't know, nor does he, at this point, particularly care.

He feels cool, clean sheets against his bare skin, and the comforting weight of several blankets weighing down upon him.

For now, what more than that does he need to know?

Eventually, though, he raises his hand to his forehead and finds there the crisp surface of a bandage held to his skin by adhesive tape. He smells something medicinal—antibiotic cream, he assumes—so he must be back in the hospital, no?

For a moment he wonders if it is possible that the events of the past few nights were nothing but a dream, and that his second ambush, as well as the events leading up to it, were nothing more than the ravings of a rattled, unconscious mind.

But soon enough he knows better. The hand touching his forehead—his left hand—is trembling.

From somewhere nearby a female voice says, "You're awake."

Remer lifts his head off the pillow, though by only an inch or so, and looks in the direction of the voice.

He sees not far from the foot of his bed a figure sitting in a chair, backlit by the weak light, her face invisible.

"Who's that?"

The woman rises from the chair and moves to the bed. Sitting on the edge of the mattress, she carefully places the back of her fingers on Remer's forehead.

As near as she is, he still cannot see her. For an instant—an irrational instant—he finds himself hoping that it is Mia.

A *foolish, self-destructive wish.*

"It's Gale," the woman says. "Do you remember me?"

Remer lays his head back on the pillow. "Yeah."

"Good. That's good."

Remer scans the room. What he can see of it doesn't look much like a hospital room.

"Where am I?"

"You tell me."

"What?"

"I want to know what the last thing you remember is."

It takes Remer a moment.

"Checking into a motel," he says.

"Where? Do you remember what town?"

"Westhampton."

"Good."

That's where I am, he thinks.

Gale switches on a bedside lamp. Remer winces against the brightness, expecting it to stab his eyes and cause an explosion of pain in his head.

But there is no such reaction. He feels, in fact, only the normal discomfort created when sudden light is cast immediately after waking.

He can view his surroundings in detail now. The room is large, and from what he can see, he and Nurse Gale are its only occupants.

"What's going on?" Remer asks.

Gale is dressed not in scrubs but in street clothes—faded jeans and a red T-shirt under a heavy wool button-up sweater as long as a dress. The room is cold—cheap motel heating. Instead of answering Remer, she removes a penlight from her sweater pocket and uses it to check his right eye, then his left.

"Your pupils look good."

"What's going on?" he asks again.

"You're okay, you're safe," she explains. "You reopened your stitches and aggravated your concussion. And, if you ask me, you were pretty much on the verge of alcohol poisoning." She pauses. "Holiday blues, maybe?"

"Something like that. How did you get here?"

"The cabdriver called your detective friend. Do you remember her? The girl who drove you here."

Remer nods.

"How about her name? Do you remember that?"

"Yeah."

"What is it?"

"Brianna."

"And your detective friend?"

"Kay."

Gale seems pleased. "Good. This is all good."

"Kay and Tommy called you?"

"No. The chief did."

"Manfredi?"

She nods. "There's a cop outside the door. Apparently, you're a very important person."

"What does that mean?"

"I was told to call Manfredi when you came around."

"What for?"

"I imagine he'd like to talk to you. He said it didn't matter what time of the day or night, I was to call him directly."

Remer remembers his activities prior to his attempt to leave town.

Brazier's body, the ride to Cooper's Neck, deleting video and log entries from his security system.

He remembers, too, the crash in the Pine Barrens and the long haul through the snow to the Westhampton train station.

Based on these few memories alone, there are a number of questions that Manfredi might want to ask.

A lot to keep straight.

Gale says, "Listen, if you want to rest some more, I don't have to make the call right away."

"How long have I been out?"

"Two days. But you've been in and out of consciousness a lot."

"I don't remember that."

"I'm not surprised."

"You've been here all this time?"

"Kay took a shift. Then her boyfriend did. Every time you came to when I was here, you said some crazy things."

"What kind of things?"

She shrugs, smiling assuredly. "It doesn't matter. You were delirious. We all agreed it wasn't anything any of us needed to pay attention to."

Remer thinks of all the things he could have said, the wild confessions he could have made.

He decides not to press the matter.

"What day is it?" he asks.

"Friday."

Remer wrinkles his brow. "Christmas?"

"No. Day after."

He glances toward the heavy curtains leaking pale light. "What time is it?"

"Almost four."

"Afternoon?"

"Yeah."

Remer nods but says nothing.

"You should probably rest up," Gale says. "A blow to the head is serious stuff, and you've had two in a matter of days."

"No, I might as well get this over with. Tell Manfredi I'm up and ready to talk."

"You sure?"

"I've slept enough."

Gale rises from the edge of his bed, walks past her chair to the desk by the door, and picks up her purse.

Looking at the door, Remer thinks of what's beyond it.

He wonders if the cop out there is to stop someone from coming in or him from leaving, is on the verge of asking Gale this but doesn't.

Holding a business card, she enters a number, saying as she does, "By the way, he took all your clothes again. Kay left you some things over there." She gestures toward the bureau.

On top of it is a pile of neatly folded clothes.

Yet more Tommy Miller hand-me-downs.

Remer remembers suddenly the carrying case he liberated from the Avalanche.

"I had a case," he says.

"Manfredi took that, too. In fact, he and Kay's boyfriend argued over it. The whole thing got pretty heated. They went toe-to-toe."

Sitting up, Remer begins to pull the sheet away only to realize he is naked. He stops himself and looks at her.

"Sorry," she says. She turns her back to Remer, giving him privacy, and holds the phone to her face.

Remer grabs the pile of clothes from the bureau top, notices right away that they are not hand-me-downs but rather brand-new, store tags still attached.

Black trousers made of thick cotton, a designer T-shirt, underwear, socks, and a dark wool turtleneck sweater.

On the floor by the bureau is a new pair of leather boots.

Well, at least I'll look good, Remer thinks.

Heading into the bathroom, he considers the two reasons why Manfredi would want his clothes.

To type the blood on them, and to pull fibers for comparison.

As much as this concerns Remer, what is foremost in his mind now is how many of those who took care of him over these past two days saw the scar on his chest.

More than all that, though, did Manfredi?

▪

His new clothes are a good fit, and he feels, naturally, less vulnerable after he is dressed.

With his hands in the pockets of his trousers, he waits by the only window, watching through curtains parted by just a few inches.

He can see the narrow parking lot stretching to Montauk Highway, and the patrol car parked a few doors down. That and the quickly approaching December night are pretty much the only things for his eyes to detect.

Turning away from the window after a few moments, Remer sees that Gale is writing in a small notebook. He asks her what she is writing, and she tells him that she is entering his current stats: the time he awoke, the response of his pupils, his ability to recall events, and so on.

As he watches her he can't help but think of Angela and her plan for a postdivorce life—her second life, *the thing she and Remer have in common.*

If it comes to fruition—if she completes her training and lands a job at Southampton Hospital—then she might work with this woman.

She and Gale might even go from co-workers to close friends, the way Mia and Kay had.

Would Angela and Remer socialize with Gale, the way he and Mia and Kay had?

Might Angela eventually live with him in his tiny place? Come to count on him for so many things the way Mia did?

Only to disappear on him one day.

Fleeting thoughts, and, ultimately, pointless ones, considering what should be on his mind now.

Looking out the window again, intending to distract himself from his concerns, he suddenly wonders where Angela is at this moment, and what she is doing.

Being Friday evening, she is likely beginning her shift at that restaurant on the Upper West Side. He can't remember the name of the place, knows only that it is one he never heard of and therefore must have opened in the years following his escape.

Tomorrow she'll catch the early train from Penn Station to Southampton, walk straight to Red Bar, and work her double shift. She puts herself through this so she can hang on to her affordable year-round apartment—not an easy thing to find. And out here, during the summer season, a good waitress can make a lot of money.

After her Saturday night shift, Angela will return to her room above his, change into her bathrobe and slip, then make her way down to his door and gently knock upon it.

This thought leads Remer to the inevitable question.

Will I be there to answer?

■

A few more minutes pass; then finally a car turns into the parking lot and heads toward the far end of the long unit.

The vehicle is an unmarked sedan, but its color, Remer can tell, even in the diminishing light, is a shade darker than Barton's.

It pulls in next to the patrol car and parks. A man emerges from behind the wheel. Medium height but broad, built like a tree stump. Midfifties, dressed in a department-issue parka and winter boots.

Chief Manfredi.

Remer watches as the man pauses to talk to the officer in the patrol car. Another vehicle pulls in, and Remer recognizes it immediately as Barton's.

As she gets out, Manfredi steps away from the patrol car. It backs out, and by the time Barton and Manfredi meet up, it has turned onto Montauk Highway and disappeared from sight.

Manfredi and Barton talk briefly—or rather, Manfredi talks and Barton listens, carefully. Every now and then she nods.

A dressing-down, maybe. Or maybe just instructions. Remer can't be sure.

As this goes on, another vehicle—a Jeep Wrangler—enters the motel's parking lot. It parks on the far side of Barton's sedan. A man emerges from behind the wheel.

Sergeant Spadaro, in street clothes.

Carrying a large manila envelope, he joins Manfredi and Barton. Manfredi points at the envelope and asks a question, which Spadaro answers. Hanging from his left shoulder is a nylon messenger bag, and by the weight of it, and the awkward way it bounced off Spadaro's hip as he walked, Remer's guess is that it contains a notebook computer.

Manfredi gives Barton and Spadaro one final set of instructions, then turns and leads them toward Remer's door.

22

∎

The three cops enter.

Manfredi removes an envelope from inside his parka and hands it to Gale.

She takes it, places it inside her purse, then grabs her coat. Putting it on, she looks at Remer, nods once, then leaves.

Remaining by the window, his hands deep in his trouser pockets, Remer feels a bit like a man suddenly face-to-face with a firing squad.

But he keeps his cool. It is the only hand he has to play.

Barton looks at Remer but says nothing. It is, no doubt, a significant silence, a form of communication in itself. But exactly what it means, Remer hasn't a clue.

What he is certain of is that this—whatever this is—is Manfredi's show.

The chief looks Remer up and down. Remer recalls seeing the man in the doorway of his hospital room, arguing with Barton.

The contrast between her being so vocal then and so silent now is notable.

"What's the date?" Manfredi says flatly.

"The day after Christmas."

"So that would be what date?"

"December twenty-sixth."

"Who's the president?"

"What?"

"What is the name of our president?"

"Bush is still in office. Obama is president-elect."

Manfredi nods. "So you obviously understand where and when you are. You're thinking clearly, everything's working the way it should?"

"Yeah."

"Good."

Manfredi asks Spadaro for the manila envelope. Opening it, Manfredi pulls out a stack of five-by-seven photographs and begins sorting through them.

Remer is silent at first, but he quickly grows tired of waiting and says, "What the hell is going on?"

"First we need to clear up what happened on Christmas morning," Manfredi says. "It's obvious that your pickup was rammed and run off Sunrise Highway by a Chevy Avalanche. What we don't know is who was driving the Avalanche."

"A man named Rene DeVere."

"Was he alone?"

"No. A woman named Casey Collins was with him."

"The same two people you believed assaulted you last Sunday night."

Remer glances at Barton, then back at Manfredi. "That's right."

"And in roughly the same area."

Remer pauses, then says, "More or less, yeah."

"But this time you actually saw them. Saw their faces."

"I did."

"They seem to have it in for you, don't they?"

Uncertain what to say—and what not to say—Remer shrugs and leaves it at that.

"Any idea what happened to them?" Manfredi says.

"What do you mean?"

"You obviously abandoned your vehicle and drove away in the Avalanche. Alone, I'm assuming. So how did you leave them?"

Remer's gut tightens. "Alive, if that's what you're asking."

Manfredi, still sorting through the photographs, nods, then says, "You abandoned the Avalanche after a few miles. Why?"

"It had a flat tire."

"And from there you walked to the Westhampton train station and called for a cab."

"That's right."

Manfredi nods thoughtfully, looks finally at Remer. "Would you mind telling me what exactly were you doing in the Pine Barrens at five in the morning?"

"I was on my way out of town."

"Heading where?"

"A friend's."

"Would this friend be able to confirm that you were coming for a visit?"

"No."

"Why not?"

"It was going to be a surprise. Listen, Chief, I might not be as on the ball as either of us first thought. You may have to dumb some things down a little for me here."

"Fair enough. I'll start with the basics. We know by the blood on the driver door of your pickup that you were driving it when it was rammed. And we know that the driver of that truck ran you off the road, then spun out and lost control. What we don't know is what exactly happened after that."

"We exchanged insurance information," Remer says. "What do you think happened?"

"So there was an altercation."

"Yeah."

"And things ended a bit differently this time around."

Remer says nothing.

"And you just left them there. The same way they left you."

"A little better than that, actually. I'm starting to think maybe I should have my attorney present."

"That's certainly your right. And, of course, you're not under arrest, so you're free to leave anytime you like. But you might want to stick around and hear what I have to say."

Remer glances at Barton. She nods once.

It takes a moment, but Remer looks back at Manfredi.

The chief selects a photo and pulls it from the stack, then holds it up for Remer to see.

"Do you recognize this item?"

Remer nods. "It looks like the carrying case I found inside the Avalanche."

"Do you know what it contained?"

"I didn't really have the chance to look inside."

"It was mostly equipment, none of it all that impressive. Night-vision binoculars, a lock-picking kit, a Maglite flashlight, black leather gloves, and a small digital video camera. If you ask me, the owner of this case was an amateur snoop; a pro's kit would have higher-grade equipment. The last item in the case, hidden under a panel beneath the black foam rubber padding, turned out to be more interesting."

Manfredi returns the first photo, then selects and holds up a second one.

It shows a small Hewlett-Packard Netbook computer, roughly the size of a thin hardcover book.

Remer doesn't immediately understand what is so interesting about this.

Manfredi returns that photo to the stack. "We dusted these items for fingerprints and found on every one of them just one set. Would you like to have a guess whose?"

"No, not really."

"Maybe this will help," Manfredi says. He pulls out and holds up a third photo.

This one shows a close-up of the face of a dead man.

Hair soaked and tangled, skin dotted with wet sand.

Vacant eyes staring, mouth agape.

David Brazier, just as Remer left him.

"Do you recognize him?" Manfredi asks.

Remer nods. "Yeah."

"His body was found Christmas morning. He was killed somewhere else, then dumped at Cooper's Neck beach. The coroner estimates his time of death to be around 4:00 A.M. Which, according to our timeline, is about an hour or so before your little incident on Sunrise Highway." Manfredi pauses, then says, "Anything you care to tell us about this?"

"No."

"What I'm asking right now, Mr. Remer, is if there's anything you can tell us about Brazier's murder. Anything at all."

"No," Remer says.

Manfredi doesn't hesitate, simply continues on.

"As I was saying, only one set of prints was found on the contents of the case. Brazier's. The outside of the case, however, had three sets. His, yours, and an as-of-yet unidentified partial print, which we are currently running through the national database. I'm sure you know, though, that can take days. I was hoping you might be able to save us some time and tell us who this third print belongs to."

Remer shrugs. "Sorry."

"So there was no third person in the Avalanche when it rammed you?"

"No."

"You're certain about that."

"Yeah." Remer thinks for a moment. "The third print could belong to Casey Collins. Or it could have been DeVere's."

"We were able to rule him out."

"How?"

"DeVere has a record up in Canada. That part was easy."

"And Casey Collins?"

"We found prints on a locker she kept at a boxing gym in River-head. We couldn't be one hundred percent sure they were hers, but just a little while ago we were able to compare them to prints found on a cable box that had recently been returned to the cable company. The store's surveillance cameras show Casey Collins returning that box on the day she quit her job and disappeared."

Remer glances at Barton. Again, she says nothing.

"My detective here filled me in on what you found at the apartment in Bridgehampton," Manfredi says. "She gave me the photos you took, and the items you claim to have found in the Dumpster behind a neigh-boring building. You should know that I don't much care for back-alley investigations."

"It was all me," Remer says. "Kay knew nothing about it."

"Is that so?"

"Yeah."

Manfredi nods, then says, "As it turns out, we got lucky. The cable box the Collins woman turned in was a DVR. Usually the cable company refurbishes each box by scrubbing the hard drive, then rents it out again. But because of the holiday their technician hadn't gotten to hers yet. We were able to recover a number of recordings, most of which were true-life crime shows from a channel called In-vestigation Discovery. One show in particular was about a murder-by-bludgeoning. It showed the forensic investigators re-creating the murder in the lab by laying a sponge soaked with corn syrup on a surface and placing it at the right height and distance from a wall, then striking the sponge with a baseball bat. Obviously, that's where they got the idea."

"So you agree. Mia faked her death."

"Yes. But, of course, now we have an actual murder on our hands, with an actual dead body in the morgue as proof. Someone killed David Brazier, brought his body to the beach, and dumped it there. The boyfriend of a woman who tried to fake her death turns up dead just hours after you break into an apartment that, until a few days ago, was the home of another woman you say cracked your head and left you on the side of the road." Manfredi shakes his head and laughs incredulously. "And what connects these two women is a man named Rene DeVere—one worked with him and disappeared the same day he did, and the other turned out to have secretly married him. And what connects all four of these lowlifes, Mr. Remer, is you. Do you see what I'm getting at?"

"Not really," Remer lies.

"Let me ask you again. You're certain there wasn't anyone else with DeVere and Collins?"

"Yeah. Why?"

"When the state police came up to the crash site, there was no one there. DeVere and Collins must have gotten away somehow."

"I doubt it was on foot," Remer says.

"Why's that?"

"I smacked DeVere's knee with the tire iron Casey Collins had when she came after me."

"No blackjack this time?"

"I would imagine she got rid of that after our first encounter."

"So you believe someone picked them up after you left."

"That has to have been what happened. We were miles from anywhere. And I took their cell phones, so they couldn't have called for help. Unless she tossed DeVere over her shoulder and carried him away, someone had to have come along." Remer pauses, then says, "You seem set on there having been a third person there, Chief. Why's that?"

"Four sets of footprints were found in and around the scene. The ground was frozen, but the snow softened up just enough of a surface layer for prints to be made. When the snow stopped, the surface layer refroze. Three of the four prints were definitely male sizes, and the fourth was likely female. They way I read it, that's you, DeVere, Collins, and an unknown male. Since DeVere left a print on the floor mat of the Avalanche, we were able to match that with one of the three male-sized prints. Your sneakers matched the second of those prints, and a pair of boxing shoes in Casey Collins's locker is a match, sizewise, for the female print. So that leaves a third male at the scene around the time of the accident—a male with a size thirteen foot, to be precise. If there wasn't a third person in that Avalanche when it rammed you, then that unknown male arrived after you left."

Remer needs a moment to take all this in. Then, "I take it the size thirteen print was side by side with DeVere's print at some point."

"As if helping him out of the ditch to a vehicle?" Manfredi nods. "Yeah. As for the phones you took, both were prepaid and had their calling histories cleared out—that is, with the exception of the one with Collins's fingerprints. It had a single call in its history."

"What was the number?"

"Untraceable. Most likely from another prepaid phone."

"Incoming or outgoing?"

"Incoming. Time-stamped at little before 4:00 A.M. Around the time the coroner estimates Brazier was murdered."

Remer says nothing to that, then asks, "How was he killed, by the way?"

"His neck was broken."

"It takes a certain kind of person to be able to do that," Remer says. "Not to mention a certain degree of strength."

"The kind of strength one would expect from a man with a size thirteen shoe."

Remer nods. "Would you mind if I ask a few questions?"

"Go ahead."

"Was the Avalanche stolen?"

"Yeah. Just like the Scirocco."

"Any fingerprints in it?"

"No. Wiped clean."

"How about the apartment in Bridgehampton?"

"Same thing. According to her landlord, the Collins woman lived there for two years." Manfredi returns the stack of photos to the manila envelope. "Listen, it is obvious that DeVere and his girlfriend were intent on keeping you from leaving town. Which means they had to have been watching you. Any idea why they would be doing that?"

Remer shrugs. "If they were watching me, they probably knew I was onto them. And I don't think they were trying to stop me from leaving town. I think they were trying to kill me."

"David Brazier at 4:00 A.M., and then you at five. Lucky for them you didn't decide to visit your out-of-town friend an hour earlier."

"I'm starting to get tired, Chief. Are we almost done here?"

"There are two more things I'm curious about. Maybe you can clear them up for me."

"What?"

"Apparently Mia Ferrara stole a large sum of money from your safe on the night she first disappeared. Eighty grand, I believe. Yet you didn't report it. Why not?"

"It was a private matter."

Manfredi nods as if to convey that he'll accept that explanation. "That's a rather large sum to just keep around, though, don't you think? I mean, I like to keep some cash handy, too. You never know, right? But eighty grand? Don't you trust banks?"

"You're welcome to have a look at my tax returns anytime. Every penny I take in gets reported."

"I'm sure it does. You live in a cheap apartment, walk to work every day, own a pickup that's close to ten years old. And you own the one business that seems to be recession-proof. Perfectly reasonable for you to have saved that much over six years."

Manfredi pauses, then continues. "The other thing I'm curious about is that when you came out here six years ago, it seems you left behind a fairly lucrative career as a private investigator. In fact, the manner in which you walked away from everything you had was rather . . . well, abrupt. I can't help but wonder what would make a man do that. What made you leave the city, come out here, and buy, of all things, a liquor store?"

"It was time for a change."

"So, boom, just like that?" Manfredi says.

"Yeah. Just like that."

"If one needed, for some reason, to get out of town quickly, eighty grand would not only let one do so in style but leave plenty left over to start a new life somewhere else. Another new life."

"If you have something to say to me, Chief, just come out and say it."

Handing the envelope to Spadaro, Manfredi says, "Six years ago you ran from one life and started another. And not just a new life but a completely different life. You went from someone who invades the privacy of others to a man who, by all accounts, guards his own at any cost. Maybe, like you said, it was just time for a change. Or maybe it was something else. And maybe the money Mia Ferrara took from your safe was your life savings. Or maybe it was your get-out-of-Dodge money, just in case you needed to run again, which, the way it looks to me, you did two nights ago. You tell me it was to surprise a friend on Christmas morning, so okay, that's what it was. But I still can't help asking myself, what would make a man run? A man like you? You're a private man, though, and I respect privacy. It's a fundamental right, if you ask me. But the next time you take matters into your own hands, the next time you pull a stunt like you did in Bridgehampton, I won't be so inclined to look the other way. In fact, I'll have no choice but to start digging, and as deep as I have to. Do we understand each other?"

Remer understands, though only partially.

As always, he is left to wonder how much is and isn't known.

Still, he nods and says, "Yeah, I think so."

Manfredi turns to Barton, in a way that indicates he is handing things over to her.

As the chief looks back at Remer, Spadaro slides the messenger bag from his shoulder and places it on a nearby desk.

"Kay's going to show you what we found on Brazier's computer," Manfredi says. "It should bring you up to speed."

Spadaro opens the bag and removes a large Sony notebook computer. Finding the outlet behind the desk, he plugs in the cord, then powers up the computer.

"Considering your experience," Manfredi says, "and the fact that you were once intimate with the Ferrara girl, I'd be a fool not to ask for your input on this matter. If any of what Kay shows you strikes you as significant in any way, I would appreciate you sharing it with her. Even the smallest thing could help us out."

Remer nods.

Gesturing toward the computer, Manfredi says to Barton, "Bring that back when you're done."

"Of course."

He takes one last look at Remer, his eye briefly shifting to the bandage on his forehead, then says, "I'll see you around town, Mr. Remer."

He and Spadaro head toward the door.

The chief steps through it, followed by the sergeant, who pulls it closed behind himself.

In the brief silence left behind, the computer completes its start-up.

23

■

"This might be difficult for you," Barton says.

More difficult, Remer thinks, *than what just occurred?*

Whatever, exactly, that was.

He says, though, only, "Why?"

"Just know that before you start, okay? When I watched it I couldn't help but feel a little bit like a . . . voyeur."

She sits on the edge of the bed not far from the desk and places her right hand on the top of her round stomach.

Remer pulls out the desk chair and sits.

Looking at the computer, he sees several icons on its desktop.

"There should be an AVI file with Brazier's name under it," Barton says.

Remer spots it.

"A number of videos were found on Brazier's computer," she

explains. "Our tech guy strung copies of them together so they'd play as one clip."

"What kind of videos are we talking about, Kay?"

"You'll see."

Remer hesitates, then proceeds to select the AVI file.

Windows Media Player opens instantly. The player's screen remains dark for a moment, and then, suddenly, it is filled by a video image.

Remer is looking at a kitchen. Bright, nicely furnished. Stainless-steel appliances, brass pots hanging from hooks above a center island with a butcher-block top.

An upscale place, no doubt.

The view is from some kind of surveillance camera. The image, however, is color, not black-and-white, as Remer's cameras are. And there is background noise, indicating that the camera is capturing audio as well.

So, not surveillance gear but a video camera. Digital, by the quality of the image. And by the angle, hidden on a shelf or on the top of some tall piece of furniture or appliance.

Within seconds of the video starting, a man appears in the frame, walking from one end of it to the other. He has obviously just hidden the camera and is testing its range.

The man is David Brazier.

He then steps out of frame, and a second later the camera is jostled a bit, indicating he is shutting it off. There is brief gap of blackness as the first clip ends, and then the second clip begins.

Entering the frame, Brazier quickly sits down on a stool at the butcher-block island. His movements give Remer the impression that the activation of the hidden camera was not only done in secret but in a hurry as well.

Soon enough Remer understands why.

A second person enters the room. Remer at first hears only the sound of footsteps on the tile floor.

Then, finally, the person to whom those footsteps belong enters the frame.

But he already knows who that person is—knew it by the sound of her steps and the length of her stride.

Mia, with that cowgirl's walk of hers—as though she were strutting down some narrow line.

That walk, and those leather harness boots.

This must be the kitchen of the apartment she and Brazier shared.

He can't help but wonder if his eighty grand helped pay for it.

Pushing these thoughts from his mind, Remer focuses on what is before him. He quickly finds himself looking for clues to the location of the apartment, as well as indications of when this recording was made.

He can see no window, only the brightness spilling in from somewhere beyond the frame.

Mia is dressed in black jeans and a black sweater. So, a colder month, then. But her skin is nowhere near as pale as it got in the dead of winter. There is, in fact, still a hint of color in her exquisite face.

So maybe a chilly night in late summer. Or early autumn.

Leaning forward in his chair, Remer carefully watches as the video plays.

▪

"So you really want to do this?" Brazier says.

Remer gets the impression that Brazier and Mia began this conversation in the other room, and that it was moved by Brazier into the kitchen, where he restarted it.

A conversation, then, that Brazier obviously wanted a record of.

"I can't live like this," Mia says. "I'll keep waiting for her to find me again."

She is standing on the other side of the butcher block. Seeing her now is for Remer as strange as it was to see her outside the cottage on Magee.

No, he thinks, *this is even stranger.*

This is Mia and the man—the kid—she left him for in a private moment in their home.

I couldn't help but feel like a voyeur, Barton said.

"What could she do, though?" Brazier asks. "I mean, you're a grown woman."

"You don't know her," Mia says. "You don't know what it's like to be hated by your own mother. With my father gone, there's nothing to stop her."

"What we're talking about is high-risk, though."

It is clear to Remer that Brazier is trying to guide the conversation.

"You're the one who suggested it."

"I know. If it was just us, I wouldn't be worried about it. But we'll need help. One more person, at least."

"Who could we get?"

Brazier shrugs. "Rene."

"You trust him?"

"Yeah. And actually, it was kind of his idea."

"What do you mean?"

"He and I were talking one night at work, and he brought up this plan he'd been working on for years, how to fake someone's death and collect on life insurance. We talked about it for a few nights—you know, just the general theory of his plan, what problems it would pose and how to solve them. Eventually I realized I was hearing the solution to all of our problems."

Mia thinks about that, then says, "When can we talk to him?"

"I'll have him come over."

"I don't want him to know where we live."

"I really think we should do it here. I know him, he'll feel more relaxed in our home."

"No, let's do it somewhere else. You know the rules. At least till I know I can trust him."

Mia is silent for a long time. Even with the camera positioned where it is, Remer can see her face clearly.

A trace amount of adrenaline hits his blood.

"We don't have to decide right now, do we?" Mia says.

"It'll take a while to get everything arranged. I'll have to lay low while we do, so I won't be able to get another job. Do you have enough money to last us for a few months?"

"Can't you get a job off the books?"

"I could try to find one, but it's not the time of year to look for work out here. And there's the risk that the men your mother hired might find me again. There aren't that many restaurants and bars out here, so all they'd have to do is check out each one, then follow me home one night, and we'd be right back at square one."

Mia is silent again.

During this pause, Remer wonders if the money Brazier is asking about is the money Mia took from him.

Finally, Mia says, "I should have enough to last us three or four months. After that, we'll be completely broke."

"So we'll talk to Rene and see what he has to say. The sooner, the better, I think."

Mia nods.

There is another gap of blackness that is followed immediately by the start of another scene.

Remer quickly uses the touchpad to move the cursor to the pause button, then left-clicks.

The playback freezes.

"We should have seen him get up and switch off the camera just then," he says. "Did your guy edit this?"

"No. I noticed that, too. Brazier must have trimmed these after he uploaded them to his computer."

"So you've seen all the videos? In their entirety?"

"Yeah." Barton nods toward the computer. "What do you think?"

"It was made after Mia disappeared on her mother in October."

"That's what I think, too."

"She obviously doesn't know the camera is there."

"Anything else?"

"It wasn't Mia's idea. It wasn't even Brazier's, apparently, either. This evidence alone is enough to shoot down their whole plan."

Barton nods but says nothing.

Facing the computer screen again, Remer left-clicks and the playback resumes.

There is no shot of Brazier activating the camera, just a cut to him and Mia gathered at the center island. The camera is in the same hiding place as before.

By the lack of brightness coming from out of frame, and the fact that the overhead track lighting is lit, it is clearly nighttime.

And by the nearly empty bottle of red wine on the butcher block, and the two glasses at various stages of emptiness between them, it is obvious that Mia and Brazier have been talking for a while.

Another edit by Brazier.

But for what reason?

To prevent self-incrimination? Manipulate the facts? Or perhaps for the sake of the limited storage space on the mini computer?

Again, Remer watches.

■

"What place can we use?" Mia says.

"There's a house I know of, over by the college. The guy who owns it is about to walk away from the mortgage. The way things are now, it'll probably take a while for the bank to even get around to foreclosing on it. So it'll just be sitting there, empty."

"How do you know this?"

"The guy who owns it used to come into Pintauro's a lot. A regular, one of those losers who sits at the bar and tells you his fucking life story night after night. The house is an investment property—he doesn't live in it, just rents it out for big bucks in the summertime, and then to kids from the college during the off-season. But no one rented it for this winter, and that, combined with the money he lost when the stock market tanked, leaves him with no option but to walk away. Just like that, overnight, this guy everyone thought was richer than God is suddenly flat broke. Rene's going to change my contact info and records at work, make that address my address. He's even going to make it look like that was the address I gave him back when he hired me."

"Why do that?"

"In case the cops come around afterward. After Rene has left. He says it'll give them nowhere to go. A big fat dead end."

Mia thinks for a moment, then asks, "How much longer will all this take?"

"I don't know. There's a lot we still need to figure out and plan for. Why?"

"It's just my mother's life was a house of cards before the market crashed. She has got to be getting desperate. I know my father had stock in a lot of the lenders that have gone bust. Unless she sold them . . ." Mia doesn't finish her thought.

Watching her, Remer gets the sense that she is hesitating at saying what is now on her mind.

It seems to him as though for her to speak this thought would somehow cause her pain.

Finally, though, she says, "It bothers me that you're not working. I understand why you can't, but it still bothers me. I feel like you're taking advantage of me."

"I'm not, Mia. I would never do that. You know that."

She shrugs. "I can't help it. We need to do this soon, okay? Because I'm starting to . . . resent you."

Saying nothing more, Mia sips from her glass of wine. It looks as though Brazier is about to speak, but the video cuts again.

Remer pauses the playback, sits there for a moment. Finally, he looks over his shoulder at Barton.

"I never told you the last thing Mia said to me the night she left. I figured it was just so bizarre, you know, came right out of nowhere, that it didn't really have anything to do with anything. Now, though, I'm not so sure."

"What did she say?"

"That she believed her mother was going to have her killed. Did she ever say anything like that to you?"

Barton shakes her head. "No, never. I knew she thought her mother hated her. And I knew she had memories of her mother doing terrible things to her. But she never said anything like that."

"What memories?" Remer says.

"If Mia misbehaved in any way, her mother would lock her out of the house. I'm talking about a four-year-old who didn't mind her manners at the dinner table being pushed out the back door by her mother, who then locked it and wouldn't open it for an hour, sometimes longer. There's this little kid sitting outside in the dark, shut out by her own mother."

"Do you really believe she could remember something that happened when she was four?"

"If it was traumatizing enough," Barton says. "I knew it wasn't bullshit because whenever she talked about it, she'd get upset. I mean, as upset as if it had just happened an hour ago. I know enough about traumatic stress to know that's one of the symptoms."

"What do you mean?"

"If an event was truly traumatizing, then talking about it often causes the victim to relive it. Even if it took place twenty-five years ago, the victim can feel the fear all over again. It can be paralyzing. Mia would actually tremble when she talked about the shit her mother did to her, and you could hear the anguish in her voice. Her fear was palpable. I mean, there were nights that I had to give her some leftover Valium I had."

Remer recalls the only time he came close to confessing to a lover the true origin of his scar.

To Patti, the wannabe healer who introduced him to what is now *his* blend.

Back during those weeks when she helped to wean him off the pain pills he was hooked on.

Even thinking about speaking the truth to her all but put him back in the Brooklyn warehouse where he screamed in agony while six letters were burned into his skin.

Now, remembering coming close to uttering those words to another causes his heart to race just a little.

He pushes those thoughts away and focuses his mind.

"Where was her father during all this?" he says.

"From what Mia told me, it only happened when he was away on business, which I guess he was a lot. Whenever he was around, her mother was perfectly loving and civil."

"Mia freaked out after he died."

Barton nods. "Exactly. It wasn't just getting locked outside, there were other things. Years and years of all kinds of crap. All of it done in the name of discipline, of course, but all of it bordering on cruel at best."

Remer shrugs. "I didn't know about any of this."

"Mia didn't want you to. She wanted her new life to have nothing to do with the life she was trying to leave behind." Barton pauses, then says, "I spent a year hanging out with her. Almost every night after work, we'd go out or she'd come over. I told you, she was like a sister to me. We talked about everything. She told me stuff she never told anyone, not even her doctors, and made me promise to never tell a soul, which is why I haven't said anything to you till now. It was her secret, and even if the truth might have helped you out after she left, it wasn't my place to give it away." Barton nods toward the computer. "Things, of course, are different now."

"If you knew her mother was so terrible, why did you want to help her find Mia?"

"Like I said, I wanted to help Mia. And if you found her, as opposed to some private investigator hired by her mother, there was a chance I could get to her first."

"You could have told me that at the time."

"Not without breaking my promise. This was all very private stuff to Mia. You of all people should be able to appreciate that."

Remer says nothing.

Barton gives him a moment, then says, "Mrs. Ferrara was right, boss, Mia was a narcissist. She showed all the characteristics, every one. But what Mrs. Ferrara failed to mention is that narcissistic personality disorder is generally believed to be caused by—okay, let me get this right—the systematic deprivation of affection from infanthood up through adolescence. Basically, narcissism is extreme overcompensation—if no one loves me, the child thinks, then I'll just have to love myself. The problem with that logic is that it is based on the assumption that one is unlovable to begin with. Every act of overcompensation reinforces that premise. Eventually, the narcissist breaks with reality, has to just to survive. They tell lies that they themselves believe; they use people while at the same time they fear being used. They become distrusting, and from there it's just a short trip to out-and-out paranoia. I mean, we just saw it on the tape. Mia, who took advantage of you by stealing your money, was afraid that Brazier was taking advantage of her by living off the money she stole from you. Though she knows intellectually he wasn't, she couldn't help but feel that way, and when push comes to shove, narcissists trust their feelings, no matter how irrational. It's that separation from reality swinging into action. 'Things are what I say they are. And everyone who doesn't agree with me is wrong. Or worse, they are in some way out to get me or take advantage of me. After all, I'm unlovable, so why else would they be with me in the first place?'"

Remer needs another moment, then says, "Yeah, okay, I get all that. I really do. But she went to a tremendous amount of trouble to hide from her mother. I think it's pretty obvious that's why she wanted to fake her own death—so her mother would stop looking for her. She must have believed she was in danger."

"I'm sure she believed it," Barton says. "I'm sure she was convinced of it. You were just her boss for that first year, so you didn't see the level of paranoia she was capable of. By the time you two got together, she had chilled out a lot. In the last weeks of your relationship, after her father died, that's when you started to see the old Mia returning. Narcissists are very suspicious of anyone who wants to love and help them. They can't help it. After she got the news about her father and snapped, didn't she start to turn on you? The more you tried to help her, the more she pulled away."

"But from what I can tell she ran from me and straight to Brazier. Why?"

Barton shrugs. "I can only guess that she thought he could do something you couldn't. He could help her hide." A pause, then she says, "She could use him."

Remer looks at the computer screen. "How many more clips are there?"

"A few."

"Do I need to see them?"

"I think you might," Barton says.

"Why?"

"You'll see."

Remer reaches out for the touchpad and restarts the playback once more.

The new clip shows the same angle. It is nighttime again, but instead of wineglasses, Mia and Brazier are seated in front of plates of Chinese food and to-go containers.

On the edge of the butcher block is a cluster of gourds and minia-ture pumpkins, one of which, carved into a jack-o'-lantern, has already begun to rot.

■

"Rene is right," Brazier says, "your blood alone won't be enough. There needs to be a witness."

"But you'll be making yourself a suspect."

"We'll make enough to disappear on. I mean, really disappear, leave-the-country disappear. And anyway, you won't actually be dead, so there isn't really that much of a risk in me looking like the bad guy here."

"But can you trust Rene with all that money?"

"If he collects and doesn't pay, he knows I'll find him. Remember, I tracked him all the way to Bridgehampton. Besides, if he screws us, he'll have the FBI *and* your insurance company on his ass."

"And you really think it shouldn't take longer than a few months?"

"I've looked into it, and yeah, insurance companies have to pay out once a judge declares a person dead. One woman's husband got drunk, went for a late-night walk on their honeymoon cruise, and never came back. Even though his body was never found, she collected on his life insurance three months later. Rene's story is a real tearjerker—his brand-new wife was murdered by her obsessed ex-boyfriend, me. It'll be that much easier for his lawyer to sell the story if the police believed you were murdered, too."

Mia thinks about that, then says, "I'm not sure we can last three months on what I have left."

"Rene said he'd stake us with ten grand while we waited, take it out of our share when he collects. *That's* how sure he is this is going to work. We'll have to live close to the bone for a while, that's all. And the friend who's going to help us across the border says he can give us a place to stay if we need it. That'll help. Plus, things are a lot cheaper up there."

Another moment, then, "How soon can you get the ten grand?"

"He said he'll have it December first."

"That's almost three weeks away."

"I warned you this would take time, Mia. Everything has to be set up just right. And a lot depends on what your mother does. If she still has men looking for you, and if they know what they're doing, they'll run a standard document search and find the marriage certificate, see it as proof that you might still be around. DeVere and his girlfriend will stay at Pintauro's until someone shows up there looking for me. It'll work, Mia. We just have to be patient."

Mia takes a sip from her glass of water.

Another cut, and then the next scene begins.

The kitchen again, daytime, Mia seated on one of the stools, Brazier standing in front of her.

She is wearing black jeans and a black bra, no top.

Brazier is drawing her blood. On the butcher block beside Mia lies a clear plastic plasma pouch. It is connected to her forearm by plastic tubing.

"You okay?" he asks.

She nods. "Yeah."

Yet another cut, and yet another scene.

Brazier is talking on a cell phone. Mia's boots can be heard somewhere off camera, and then she enters the frame.

She and Brazier look at each other as Brazier listens intently. Several times he says, "Okay," and then, once, "You're kidding me."

Mia whispers, "What?" Brazier holds up his index finger and continues to listen.

Finally, he closes the phone and says to her, "It's time."

"Someone came to Pintauro's."

Brazier nods. "Rene sent him to the house."

"Who is it?" Mia asks quickly.

Brazier hesitates, but only briefly. "Just some guy your mother sent," he says.

There is a moment between them. Remer reads it as silent awe. *Here we are, finally.* Brazier steps close to Mia, grabbing her hips with both hands and pulling her closer still.

She smiles, seems to Remer genuinely happy.

"We need to get ready," she says.

"We have time," Brazier replies.

They kiss, and Brazier begins unbuttoning her shirt.

Remer reaches out for the touchpad, but instead of pausing the playback, he quickly moves the cursor to the red X in the upper right corner and closes the program.

Neither he nor Barton speaks for a bit.

Finally, Barton says, "Our tech guy edited out what happened next. Not sure why Brazier didn't do that himself. Obviously, he made these recordings for his own protection, in case this went bad. Apparently he felt compelled to include a sex tape."

Remer closes his eyes, takes a breath, then opens them again. "Is there more after that?"

"Yeah."

He turns to her. "I think I've seen enough, Kay. Maybe you can just tell me the rest."

She nods. "Yeah, sure. There's just one more recording anyway. It was made right after they faked Mia's death. Everyone is all worked up and shouting at once. Mia is upset that the guy they left on the side of the road turned out to be you, accuses Brazier of knowing it was you and not telling her. Brazier doesn't understand how you followed them to the Pine Barrens, which apparently wasn't part of the plan, so he and DeVere go at it about that. It almost comes to blows at one point. It turns ugly when Mia loses it and starts accusing DeVere of being in cahoots with her mother. You can just see her . . . snap, you know? You can see the paranoia just take over."

"How does it end?"

"Mia says she wants to call the whole thing off, and Brazier tries to talk her out of it. He finally gives in and tells DeVere they want out. DeVere says if they're calling it off, he wants his ten grand back. He gives them to the end of the week to pay him."

"And that's it?"

"More or less. You can see it all start to fall apart. Conspirator turning on conspirator. No one trusting anyone. I'll tell you one thing, Mia wasn't happy about them leaving you out in the middle of nowhere. She wanted someone to make an anonymous call to the police and tip them off. And all the while, DeVere is trying to convince them it might be a good thing that it was you, that the cops might think it was you who killed Mia and not Brazier. He really tries pushing that, even gets Brazier thinking about it. But Mia doesn't want to hear it. And Casey Collins just wants Mia to shut up." Barton pauses, then says, "Like I said, you can see it all starting to fall apart."

It takes Remer a moment to process all this. "DeVere could have killed Brazier over the ten grand."

Barton nods. "That's what Manfredi is thinking."

"Any sign of Mia?" Remer knows that if there were, someone would have said something by now. Still, he has to ask.

"None. And no sign of DeVere and Collins, either."

"DeVere could have had a friend helping him out," Remer says. "Someone big, to intimidate Brazier into paying up. That might explain the size thirteen boot prints."

"But you said it was only DeVere and Collins in the Avalanche. And you took their cell phones. So this friend just happened to come along after you took off?"

"Maybe he was supposed to meet them after they ran me off the road but got delayed because of the snow. They probably would have known they weren't going to drive out of there in the Avalanche, that they'd need someone to pick them up. Just like Brazier needed DeVere and Collins to pick him up when he abandoned the Scirocco."

"So they kill Brazier around four, dump his body on Cooper's Neck, then, what, wait for you at your place? That's a pretty tight time frame. And it would mean they got to your place just as you were driving off. That is pretty damn lucky for them, don't you think?"

Remer says, "Isn't everything just luck, Kay?"

"Maybe." A pause, then she says, "Is there anything you want to tell me, boss?" There is concern in her voice.

Remer shakes his head. "No."

"Because in all the time I've known you, I don't really recall you ever leaving town. I don't even think you've ever taken a vacation."

"Just because you don't know about it doesn't mean it didn't happen."

"I'm just trying to be your friend here. If there's anything you want to tell me, now would be the time. Do you understand?"

"There's nothing else to tell you, Kay. I had a little too much to drink and decided to visit a friend. That's all."

Barton nods, watches Remer for a moment. "Are you going to be okay?" she says. "It must not have been easy for you to watch that."

"Yeah, I'll be fine. What day is it again?"

"Friday."

Tomorrow is Saturday, Remer thinks.

In a little over twenty-four hours, Angela, dressed in her bathrobe and white slip, will be knocking on his door.

He suddenly craves her smell.

"I seem to keep finding myself having to thank you for things lately," Remer says. "You and Tommy, that is."

"Don't worry about it."

"Where is he, by the way?"

"Home. Or at least he'd better be."

Remer smiles at that, takes a breath, then lets it out. "Home sounds pretty good to me right now."

"You feel up to the drive?"

"Yeah."

"So let's get you out of here."

■

In the warmth of Barton's sedan, Remer tries to relax.

The ride from Westhampton to Southampton shouldn't take longer than a half hour.

Not a long journey home, but in his condition, one that has become all too familiar, it is long enough.

24

Alone in his apartment.

He makes toast with butter and eats the pieces standing by his window, can think of no other entryway back into his life.

His cell phone was smashed in the wreck two days ago, and the loss of it presents a few problems: It contained all his numbers, but it was also his most direct connection to his employees and security system. Should the thing he fear most actually occur—someone gets injured, or worse, during a robbery—he would not be informed, at least not instantly.

So, nothing to do right now, as closing time once again nears, but to listen for the sound of sirens.

There is another problem that he needs to face. His pickup having been, no doubt, totaled, he is currently without a vehicle. Even if it hasn't been totaled, then it is in need of serious repairs, the kind that can take a while.

He tells himself that he needs to make calls in the morning, find out where his vehicle is, and its condition, then contact his insurance company so an adjuster can be sent out. Depending on what the adjuster determines, he'll either need to arrange for a rental car or walk to one of the three dealerships in town and purchase a new vehicle.

He has plenty of money for that—all of it, with the exception of the few grand he always keeps in his wallet, kept in a bank these days—so he won't have to wait for the check from his insurance company for the blue book value of a nearly ten-year-old pickup.

Once all that is sorted in his mind, Remer starts to think about Mia.

Would she come forward, or simply disappear again?

And if she was going to come forward, wouldn't she have done so by now?

Believed dead, then proven to be alive. Now, status unknown.

If she is alive, would she know who broke into Remer's apartment and took his vial?

Had whoever done that spotted the vial and decided to take it, or had she told that someone to look for it?

Another concern suddenly enters Remer's racing mind.

Might Mia know the truth about Brazier? That his body, with evidence implicating Remer, was left behind Remer's shop?

Might she tell Manfredi that?

Remer eventually begins to consider that another attempt at leaving town might not be a bad thing.

Checking his clock, he sees that he has missed the last train out of town. He considers calling a cab and offering the driver two hundred dollars over the fare to take him to the city, but with his luck Brianna would be the one to answer that call, and it is clear where her loyalties lie.

And even if it was someone other than her, cabbies keep records.

No way to run for now. No choice, then, but to stand here and wait.

A few minutes after this, Remer sees a pair of headlights make the

turn into his driveway, sweeping fast, like searchlights, across his courtyard.

He half expects it to be Manfredi, or one of his men. Or several.
The vehicle, though, isn't a sedan or a patrol car but a pickup.

Miller's pickup.

The vehicle pulls into Remer's empty spot, and Miller exits, crossing the courtyard and heading toward the door below.

His movements, to Remer's eye, are those of a man with a purpose.

■

They stand face-to-face, Remer in the open doorway, Miller in the
dimly lit hallway.

"Kay sent me," Miller says.

Though Remer wouldn't have thought it possible, this serious-
looking guy looks even more serious.

"C'mon in," Remer says.

Miller enters, taking a quick look around as he steps toward the
center of the room.

Remer closes the door, Miller turns, and they are facing each other
again.

"What's going on, Tommy?"

"Kay wanted to come herself, but she had to stay with Manfredi."

"What happened?"

Miller hesitates.

"Tommy, what's going on?"

A long pause, then he says, "They found her. They found Mia." He
hesitates once more. "I'm sorry to be the one to tell you this, I really
am. But she's dead."

It takes Remer a moment to ask the inevitable question.

"How?"

"She was bludgeoned."

"Jesus. Where did they find her?"

"In a house out on Millstone Brook Road."

Remer knows the neighborhood. A winding back road behind the Shinnecock Hills Golf Club in Southampton. Several miles long, lined with upper-middle-class homes, many of them Mock Tudors set on multiple acres. Landscaped, bordered with trees.

"How did they find it?"

"Spadaro tracked the serial numbers on the night-vision binoculars in Brazier's case to a mail-order company in California. He got the address the binoculars were shipped to and went to check it out. When no one answered the door, he went around to check out the back and saw her through the kitchen door. She was on the floor."

Having seen that kitchen in Brazier's hidden-camera videos, Remer can't help but see the scene in his mind. Vividly.

Mia, dead, blood all around her.

He needs a moment. Miller seems ready to give him all the time he needs.

Finally, Remer asks, "What does Manfredi think happened?"

"Kay only had time to tell me so much. She didn't want Manfredi to know she was calling me. What I do know is there are three sets of footprints outside the house. DeVere's, one that matches the female print from the site of your crash, and that size thirteen male print. DeVere's, and the print that matches Collins's, enter the house but only go as far as the mud porch. The size thirteen prints, on the other hand, are all over the place."

"So our mystery man killed Mia."

"Yeah."

"Were there signs of a struggle?"

"Not in the kitchen, no. It looks like he got in undetected and sneaked up on her."

"But elsewhere?"

"Some of the furniture in the living room was overturned."

"So you're thinking Brazier was killed there, too."

"Yeah."

"What else?"

"That phone you took from Collins had one call in its call history. An incoming call from another prepaid phone, around the time Brazier was believed to have been killed. What if that call was the killer telling DeVere and Collins that he needed their help moving Brazier's body?"

"It could be. Or it could be a call telling them he found Brazier's carrying case."

"With the incriminating videos inside."

"Exactly."

"How would they know about that, though?"

Remer shrugs.

It is a moment before Miller speaks. "What I don't understand is why dump Brazier's body at Cooper's Neck but leave Mia's behind. The only thing I can think of to explain that is the fact that Mia's body was bloodied while Brazier's wasn't. His neck was broken, and there were no marks on his face or anything, which means his killer knew what he was doing, got him in a choke hold fast and, boom, snapped his neck. But, again, why go to the bother of dumping Brazier's body at all? Why not just leave it there?"

Remer says nothing at first, then, "Unless Brazier wasn't killed there. He could have been choked unconscious and taken out of the house. His killer might have wanted something from him, or wanted to get information from him before killing him."

"Yeah, that could be."

"I'm curious, what kind of boot print was it?"

"Again, that's the thing. It's just an outline, not an actual print, no tread marks at all."

"So our man was wearing something over his boots."

Miller nods. "Yeah."

"Manfredi said there were three different fingerprints on the carrying case. Brazier's, mine, and an unknown partial. It's doubtful that unknown print would be his. I mean, if he knows to wear something over his boots, then he obviously would know to wear gloves."

"Unless he removed them at some point. They might have been bloody, or he could have panicked and screwed up. I don't care who you are, after you kill someone, your heart has to be pounding. You could easily miss something. But, yeah, I doubt the print is his."

"So he sneaks in and kills Mia, wrestles with Brazier in the living room, then calls DeVere and Collins, who show up and take Brazier, either dead or alive, along with Brazier's case. An hour later, Brazier's body is dumped, and DeVere and Collins end up with the case in the Avalanche. They had to have known what was in it, then, don't you think?"

"If those recordings were Brazier's insurance against all this landing on his head, I doubt he'd go and tell the people who could leave him holding the bag all about them."

"Unless he was cashing in on his insurance. He could have told DeVere about the recordings and what they show."

"Why?"

Remer shrugs. "A way, maybe, of getting DeVere to forget about the ten grand. By killing Brazier and Mia, and getting his hands on the case, DeVere eliminates everyone and everything connecting him to the whole mess."

"Why stick around, then?" Miller says. "Why not just take off? For that matter, why follow you and run you off the road?"

More than that, Remer thinks. *Why leave Brazier's body—and an item linking Remer to it—behind Remer's store?*

To pin Brazier's murder on him, obviously, or at least make him a suspect, if only briefly.

But what could DeVere possibly gain from that?

"You alright?" Miller says.

"Yeah. Just thinking. I wonder if our friend with the size thirteen boot is a buddy of DeVere's or someone DeVere hired."

"What do you mean? Like some kind of professional fixer?"

Remer shrugs. "Something like that, yeah."

"Where would he find one?"

"He was a career criminal, right? He would know all kinds of low-lifes."

"Can you really trust a stranger, no matter how much you pay him?" Miller pauses, then says, "I think it would have to be someone he knew already and trusted. Someone he could count on to keep his secret. Either that, or someone with a vested interest in all this. Someone who had something to gain by helping him and keeping his secret."

Remer looks at Miller but says nothing. He is suddenly frozen.

"What?" Miller asks.

"Who put this in motion?"

"What do you mean?"

"The night I went to the cottage, who sent me there?"

"DeVere."

"Have you seen the recordings Brazier made?"

"No."

"In one of them he says they were just waiting for Mia's mother to send another wave of investigators looking for her."

"Okay."

"The plan was to send whoever showed up at Pintauro's to the cottage, and then Mia and Brazier would arrive and do their little show. They didn't know it would be me. Brazier found out right before they went there, and Mia didn't know till after it was over."

"So?"

"This wasn't Mia's idea. And it wasn't Brazier's. It was DeVere's. On one of the tapes Brazier tells Mia that DeVere brought it up one night at work. It was a slow night; he and DeVere were just two scam artists talking. DeVere said something about this scheme he had for insurance fraud, and the more Brazier thought about it, the more it sounded like the answer to his and Mia's problems."

"Hang on. Are you saying DeVere set them up?"

"He's Mia's husband, as far as the insurance company is concerned. With Mia and Brazier dead—actually dead—he wouldn't have to split the money with them. And he wouldn't have to worry about Brazier ever coming forward and implicating him. If you watch the tapes, you can see that DeVere basically called all the shots. He'd tell Brazier what needed to be done, and Brazier would tell Mia."

"Yeah, but what does this have to do with the man with the size thirteen shoe having a vested interest?"

"Mia disappeared on her mother in October. When Mrs. Ferrara hired me, she said the firm who found Mia in Bridgehampton prior to that went bankrupt. That's why she was looking for someone new. But that was two months *after* Mia disappeared. Her mother could have gotten someone at any time, but she waited over two months, and those two months gave Brazier and Mia and DeVere just enough time to get everything ready."

"Wait. You think she was in on it? You think Mrs. Ferrara helped Mia?"

"Not Mia."

It takes Miller a moment. "DeVere?"

Remer nods. "You gave Manfredi the videotape you guys made of my meeting with Mrs. Ferrara, right?"

"Yeah."

"I know I would have made a copy first. Just in case. Please tell me you did."

Miller nods.

"Do you mind if we go to your place and take a look?"

"What are we looking for, exactly?"

"The man who got off the train," Remer says. "Mrs. Ferrara's bodyguard. He was a big guy. And I would imagine he has the feet to match."

25

In Miller's apartment by the train station, Remer stands at one window, Miller in another, both watching as Barton walks Manfredi back to his unmarked sedan.

She and the chief talk the entire way to the vehicle, pause beside it to talk for a few moments more. They continue to talk even after Manfredi has opened the driver door.

Unlike the last time Remer saw them together, outside his motel room, Barton is the one doing most of the talking.

Finally, Manfredi nods and gets in behind the wheel. Barton is already across the street by the time the chief pulls away from the curb and drives off.

Back inside, Barton says, "He's going to make the necessary arrangements."

"Mrs. Ferrara hasn't been informed about Mia yet?" Remer asks.

"That she's dead again? No."

"So I'll call her first thing in the morning and try to get her to meet me."

"Tommy and I are going with you."

"Does Manfredi know that?"

"Yeah," Barton says. "Call us after you talk to her. We'll be ready to go."

She pauses, then hands Remer a slip of paper with Evelyn Ferrara's numbers on it.

"She might not answer or even return your call."

Remer looks at the paper. The numbers are marked *landline* and *cell*. The landline has a 212 area code.

New York City.

Remer folds and pockets the paper, says, "I'll just keep calling till she does answer. Anyway, if we're right, I'd imagine she's waiting for someone to inform her that Mia's body has been found, ready to put on a show of her own."

"Try to get some sleep, boss," Barton says. "You look like you need it."

"Thanks, Kay."

"Hey, what are friends for, right?"

■

Outside Remer checks the train station parking lot out of habit, making note of the vehicles parked there.

As he heads down Elm Street he listens for the sound of a car engine starting, hears only his lone footsteps echoing on the pavement.

Back in his apartment, as spent as he is, he cannot sleep. Sitting on the edge of his bed, he thinks of making up a new batch of his blend.

The half-dozen tinctures containing the various ingredients are all in the cupboard above his sink. The process would occupy and distract him, for a few moments at least.

But he decides that he doesn't want it. No distractions tonight.

As he waits for morning, he moves about his room—from his bed to his window, from his window to his desk, back again to the edge of his bed. He sees the blackness of 4:00 A.M., the first hint of morning light, the literal crack of dawn—a line of silver as fine as a knife's edge—along the low East End horizon.

Waiting till nine o'clock to make the call would be the proper and professional thing to do, but by seven thirty Remer knows he can wait no longer.

Taking the paper from his pocket, he unfolds it and dials the first of the two numbers, the one marked *landline*.

Four rings, and then voice mail picks up. In his ear is Evelyn Ferrara's voice, just as he remembers it. Soft, deliberate, deep—not unlike Mia's. Remer identifies himself, says only that he needs to talk to her as soon as possible, then leaves his number and hangs up.

He dials the second number, but before it can begin to ring, his call waiting beeps.

He clicks over. "Hello."

"This is Evelyn Ferrara."

"Sorry to call so early, but I was hoping you and I could get together to talk sometime today."

"What about?"

"I have some information I need to share with you. About your daughter. Just the two of us, and I think it would be better if we didn't discuss it over the phone."

"My weekend is pretty crowded."

"I'm coming into town this afternoon and could meet you anywhere you want. It won't take too long, fifteen minutes, tops."

A silence, then she says, "Do you have my cell phone number?"

"I do."

"It's possible I could meet with you around four. Why don't you give me a call at three and we'll see how I'm doing. Maybe we can set something up then."

"I appreciate it."

"We'll talk again at three."

The line goes dead.

It takes Remer a while to remember to return the receiver to the cradle.

26

■

A two-hour ride west, Barton behind the wheel, Miller in the passenger seat, and Remer behind him.

They make it through the Pine Barrens—past the site where Remer was left for dead and then the site where he had been forced off the road—then connect with the Long Island Expressway at Manorville.

From there, it is a straight run, more or less, to the Midtown Tunnel.

Each mile they cross brings Remer closer to the place he once knew well but has not seen in almost six years.

As she drives, Barton informs Remer that Brazier's hair, along with fibers from his clothing, was found in the back of the Avalanche, indicating that it was DeVere and Collins who deposited Brazier's body on the beach.

Remer barely listens. And, of course, he does not correct the flaw in their thinking. He never will.

It seems now that the only people who can contradict his account of Christmas morning are two people who have not been seen by anyone since leaving Pintauro's on Sunday night.

And whose last activity—*assumed* activity, but it is a safe assumption—was over forty-eight hours ago.

Remer knows that a lot can happen in forty-eight hours.

The rest of the ride is made in silence, everyone lost in thought.

Remer tries to imagine all the ways the city could have changed. He tries, too, to imagine how it will feel to be there again.

It isn't till he sees the entrance to the Queens Midtown Tunnel ahead that he gets his answer.

A twinge of fear hits him like a fist to the gut.

Passing through the tunnel, isolated suddenly from all signs of the world, his thoughts drowned out by the noise, Remer closes his eyes and takes a breath, keeps it for a moment, and then lets it out.

Opening his eyes again, he sees that Barton is watching him in the rearview mirror.

■

A suite in the Grand Hyatt Hotel has been made available for them.

The location is perfectly chosen, Remer notes as they enter the lobby, since below the Hyatt is Grand Central Terminal, and even though it is Saturday, there are enough people coming and going for the three of them to blend into.

It is 2:00 P.M. when they enter the suite, which is on an upper floor. The window faces east, offering a view of the river and, beyond it, Brooklyn.

Remer doesn't go near the window, however, choosing instead to sit in a chair in an out-of-the-way corner and wait for three o'clock.

As he does, a number of people come and go. He observes the commotion.

First to arrive are two New York City detectives, a male in his forties and a female in her thirties. They go straight for Barton, aren't even introduced to Remer, and talk with her in the corner farthest from

Remer—cop stuff, last-minute logistics, their voices hushed. Occasion-ally, though, the female detective glances at Remer.

Miller is in the bedroom, on his cell phone, has been since the moment they arrived. Remer can hear him clearly, but Miller doesn't say much, is busy listening carefully and transcribing into a Mole-skine notebook what he is being told by whoever it is he's talking to.

At two thirty Manfredi enters, bringing another detective with him, a male in his fifties. By the reaction of the other two cops, it is obvious to Remer that this man is their superior.

Manfredi spots Remer sitting in his corner across the room and gestures toward him. The senior detective looks at Remer for a mo-ment, then joins Barton and his subordinates.

Manfredi and Remer stare at each other for a while longer. Finally, Manfredi nods once, then joins the cops in conference.

Shortly after this, Miller ends his call and comes out of the bed-room. Pulling a chair into Remer's corner, he sits facing him. He leans close, indicating that this is to be a private conversation. Remer leans forward to meet him.

"That was Spadaro," Miller whispers. "Man, when this is over, I think you just might get handed the keys to the city."

"What do you mean?"

"The man Evelyn Ferrara introduced to you as Smith is really An-drew Hill. He's a private security consultant, a freelancer, though it seems for the past three years he has worked exclusively for you-know-who. Actually, he was hired by Mr. Ferrara when a former business partner made some serious threats. It appears, however, that Hill and Mrs. Ferrara have more than a professional relationship."

Remer remembers the gesture he witnessed as the man he was in-troduced to as Smith guided Evelyn Ferrara to her waiting Mercedes-Benz.

So, an intimate gesture, after all.

"That's got to suck," Miller says. "You hire someone to protect you, and he and your wife end up killing you."

"Is there proof they killed Mia's father?"

"No, but these cops here were pretty certain that Mrs. Ferrara and Hill had something to do with it. They spent six months trying to build a case, but the evidence just wasn't there."

"He was killed in a car crash, right?"

Miller nods. "For some reason, while driving back from a business trip in Boston, he decided to mix sedatives with booze."

"You're fucking kidding me."

"According to the coroner, he would have been incapable of turning the ignition, let alone driving. But Mrs. Ferrara and Smith had rock-solid alibis for that night, so . . ."

"Of course they did."

Miller nods toward the gathering of cops. "Anyway, what makes you their hero today is Manfredi ran the unknown print from Brazier's case—the case you grabbed from the Avalanche—against Hill's concealed weapon permit. It was a match."

"Jesus," Remer says. "How could he make a mistake like that?"

"Most of the criminals in prison right now wouldn't be there if they hadn't made at least one stupid mistake. Anyway, like I said, you kill someone in cold blood, it has to fuck with your thought process."

Remer says nothing.

"This print finally gives these cops what they need to apply real pressure on Hill," Miller says.

"Offer him a deal if he testifies against Evelyn Ferrara."

"Exactly. The question is, will he crack? He certainly looks tough, and he's got himself an impressive résumé. He was a marine, like you, then spent several years as a mercenary. Hard to imagine a guy like that caving. But if he was panicked enough to leave a print on Brazier's case when he handed it to DeVere, then maybe he isn't as tough as he seems." Miller shrugs, then says, "And there's always the chance Mrs. Ferrara is using him. Manipulating him with sex. For all we know, the guy could be feeling in over his head."

Or, Remer thinks, *he could be loving it.*

He knew the type when he was in the Corps: young men—boys, really—who dreamed of killing bad guys, or, for that matter, anyone, simply for the thrill.

Their approach to women was just as childish and violent.

Those who weren't tempered by their training and years of service generally pursued—or at least talked of pursuing—work as mercenaries.

So which kind of marine was Hill?

"Does he have his own place?" Remer asks. "The print should be enough for the cops to get a warrant and search it."

"No. The address on his most recent permit renewal is Evelyn Ferrara's residence on the Upper East Side. It seems those two are pretty much inseparable, which means you're dead-on with this plan of yours."

"If it works. She hasn't agreed to meet me yet."

"Considering everything she's done, she has to be wondering what it is you've come to town to tell her."

Remer nods, then says, "Anything else?"

"While she was out there last week, Evelyn Ferrara and Hill stayed at a hotel. Two rooms were taken, but according to the housekeeper, one of them hadn't been used at all."

"Why didn't she stay at the house in Southampton?"

"She hasn't made a mortgage payment in five months."

Remer thinks of what Mia said to Brazier about her mother's life being a house of cards.

He thinks, too, again, of the last thing Mia ever said to him.

The poor girl had it right all along.

She was, in fact, the only one who did.

When she ran from me, Remer thinks, *she was really running for her life.*

An act he understands well.

"Apparently Mrs. Ferrara had a good chunk of her money with that investor who got busted a couple of weeks ago," Miller says.

"Madoff?"

"Yeah. She was already in deep financial trouble last summer, before the market crashed. Now she's got to be in real bad shape."

"Then this has to be over something more than the payout from a life insurance policy."

Miller nods. "It is. A long time ago Mr. Ferrara set up a pension fund for his daughter. I guess he was worried that she wouldn't be able to provide for herself in her old age. The only person who could have touched it was Mia, but not till she turned fifty-eight. With her dead, control of the fund goes to her mother."

"Did Manfredi find this?"

"Yeah."

"How much is it worth?"

"Almost four million dollars. There was more before the crash, of course."

"So there it is," Remer says.

"What I don't get is why Mrs. Ferrara didn't just take the money and run. Wouldn't Mia thought to be dead and Mia actually dead provide her with the same access to the trust fund?"

"If she's in that much trouble, maybe she couldn't wait the months it would take for DeVere to get a probate judge to rule Mia legally dead. Having her killed by Hill, and leaving her body to be found, would get her that money much more quickly."

"And since the first rule of any conspiracy is to kill the conspirators, Hill breaks Brazier's neck and for some reason has DeVere and Collins dump his body at the beach."

Remer nods.

Miller thinks for a moment, then says, "But DeVere could have had a claim on Mia's trust fund, couldn't he? He was her husband, legally."

"Which is why I wouldn't be surprised to find out that DeVere and Collins are dead and buried somewhere," Remer says. "Hill probably picked them up after they tried to kill me. He could have murdered them after that. Maybe their bodies are hidden, or maybe they just haven't been found yet."

"And Mrs. Ferrara gets control of Mia's trust *and* the payout from Mia's life insurance."

"Exactly," Remer says. "And in the process she gets to inflict the ultimate punishment on the daughter she hated."

"And to everyone it looks like Mia simply got mixed up with the wrong sort and paid the price." Miller shakes his head. "Jesus."

"There's just one thing I don't understand," Remer says.

"What?"

"Who approached whom? If Mrs. Ferrara and DeVere were working together on this, they had to have met or at least communicated at some point. Our whole theory depends on that. Did he approach her? Did he plant the seed in Brazier's head, get things rolling, then seek her out and offer her a deal? With Mia and Brazier dead, there's no one he has to split the life insurance with. And she gets full control of Mia's fund. Or did she approach him? Was she the reason DeVere baited Brazier into doing this in the first place?"

Miller shrugs, and before Remer can say anything more, Manfredi announces, "It's time to make the call."

Remer walks to the center of the room, where he is met by a half circle of cops. Miller stands but stays back in Remer's corner.

Manfredi makes the introductions. The senior detective is Watts, the other male detective Hutton, and the female detective is Hernandez. Since she isn't Hispanic and is wearing a wedding band, Remer assumes it must be her married name.

As they all watch, Remer removes the paper from his pocket and sits at the desk by the east-facing window.

The hotel phone is rigged with a speaker so everyone can hear and a mini digital recorder so the call can be recorded.

Hernandez activates the recorder as Remer dials Evelyn Ferrara's cell phone number.

It isn't till halfway through the fourth ring that Evelyn Ferrara finally answers.

Their conversation is brief—Remer, in fact, says barely more than a few words. Evelyn Ferrara asks him where he is, he answers, and she tells him that a car will pick him up in fifteen minutes at the corner of Forty-second Street and Third Avenue and take him to meet her.

After Remer hangs up, Watts says, "You didn't say anything about meeting her alone."

"She knows that. I told her this morning. Saying it again would have only made her more suspicious than she already is."

"We need them separated," Hutton says.

"I know that. I'll do what I can."

Hutton hands Remer a cell phone. "We'll be able to track you with this. And the mike remains hot even when the phone is shut off. The range is limited, though, so make sure you aren't too far away from her. We need her on tape. Do you understand?"

Taking the cell phone and looking at it, Remer ignores the question; he suddenly has something more important on his mind.

"I should have a second phone," he says.

"Why?" Watts asks.

"Because Hill is going to ask me to surrender my phone."

The cops look at each other.

"So give it to him," Watts says. "We'll still be able to track and hear."

"Not if he removes the battery, which, if he's smart, he'll do. I'll need a decoy, a second phone to hand over."

Miller steps forward, holding out his phone. "Take mine."

Remer does, and thanks him.

"Keep her talking as long as you can," Watts says.

Pocketing the two cell phones, Remer says nothing.

He is beginning to feel crowded and makes no attempt to hide his annoyance.

"I think the guy knows what he's doing," Manfredi says.

Remer moves toward the door.

Looking at Barton, he says, "See you on the other side, Kay."

She wishes him good luck as he leaves.

▪

At the corner of Forty-second and Third Remer looks south.

Twenty blocks down is Gramercy, the neighborhood he once called home. But there is no time to remember anything about that life because within a half minute of Remer reaching that corner, the same Mercedes Mrs. Ferrara drove to the Southampton train station appears.

Pulling to the curb, it stops in front of Remer.

In the backseat, Remer looks at Hill via the rearview mirror. Though he can really see only the man's eyes, Remer can tell that he has the same hard sharpness that Remer observed when they were introduced six days ago.

"I'm going to need your cell phone," Hill says.

Remer nods and removes Miller's phone from his pocket, handing it forward. He watches as Hill detaches the battery, then lays the now-dead device on the seat beside him.

They head north on Third for several blocks, then turn west. Being Saturday, there isn't much traffic.

And being a cold winter day, the sidewalks are nowhere near congested.

As they cross town, Remer removes the other cell phone from his pocket and, never taking his eyes off the eyes in the narrow mirror ahead, begins discreetly keying in a number he has memorized.

The only number that was found in the phone Remer had taken from Casey Collins.

The number of the incoming call received by Casey Collins at the time Mia and Brazier were killed.

Once the number is entered, he presses TALK and waits.

A few seconds pass, and Remer is about to end the call when a buzzing is finally heard coming from inside Hill's overcoat.

A phone set on vibrate, in the inner breast pocket, Remer guesses.

Hill reacts to the buzzing by absently bringing his hand up and reaching into his coat. It is automatic, almost a reflex. But then he quickly stops himself and lowers his hand.

Their eyes still locked, Remer presses END and, as discreetly as he removed it, returns the cell phone to his pocket.

Just feet from him now sits the man who killed Mia.

Got you, Remer thinks.

Then, suddenly, that isn't enough. He feels an overwhelming desire to lean forward and reach across the seat—moving swiftly, with deadly intent—then wrap his arm around the man's neck and choke the life out of him.

Crush his windpipe, interrupt the flow of his carotid artery and starve his brain of oxygen, twist his neck till it snaps—whatever it takes to kill him.

He was, after all, as dangerous as the Frenchman.

Or maybe more so; as far as Remer knew, the Frenchman never cracked the skull of a defenseless woman.

A *woman running for her life.*

But Remer remains still, keeping from his face any hint of emotion.

One secret—one mistake born of rage—is enough.

Turning left onto Seventh, the Mercedes heads south. Remer sees Hill checking the sideview mirrors every now and then, looking to see if they are being followed.

"It's just me," Remer tells him.

Hill ignores that.

They pass Forty-second Street and continue south. Remer looks away from the mirror and watches as the streets pass.

Thirty-ninth, Thirty-eighth, Thirty-seventh.

Soon enough he is counting his way down from Twenty-ninth. He wonders if they are bound for the meatpacking district. Or maybe the West Village, where Angela lives, though she isn't there, should be in Southampton right now, working her double shift at Red Bar.

For an instant he forgets all about his imminent destination, and what needs still to be done, wonders instead if he will be home in time tonight to greet Angela when she knocks on his door.

Hill makes a right on Twenty-third Street, and they are once again heading west.

So, Chelsea, then, Remer thinks.

The Mercedes slows just before Twenty-third ends at the West Side Highway. Parking on the north side of the street, Hill nods toward the building directly across from them on the south side.

Ten stories high, all the floors, save for the ground floor, a series of tall, arching windows.

"Go to the tenth floor," Hill says.

Remer studies the building, has no idea from looking at its outside what its inside contains.

He looks back at the reflection. "Aren't you going to check me for weapons? What the hell kind of bodyguard are you?"

"No need for that," Hill says. "I'll take you back to your hotel when you're done."

Confused, Remer opens the door. There is a part of him that doesn't want to let Hill out of his sight, now that he knows what he knows. He will never have this chance again.

But they need Hill—need him here, waiting, and alive—if there is to be any justice for Mia.

Remer gets out, takes one last look at Hill, then crosses Twenty-third and enters the building.

▪

Exiting the elevator into the tenth-floor hallway, there is only one place to go.

A heavy steel door to the left on which is printed CHELSEA MINERAL BATHS AND SPA.

A young woman, dressed in white slacks and a white T-shirt, is standing behind a counter in the reception area. Her hair is short, and she is rail thin. She smiles brightly at Remer as he enters. He tells her who he is here to meet, and she calls through an open doorway behind the reception area.

A man, similarly dressed, emerges from the back room. The young woman hands him a prestacked pile consisting of two folded towels and a folded white robe.

The man escorts Remer to the men's locker room.

"We have a no-technology policy," he explains. His accent is Eastern European, dense. He is as large as Remer but has the thick forearms and large hands of a masseuse. "So all cell phones and pagers and handheld gadgets are to be left with your clothing."

The man leads Remer to a row of lockers, all of which are empty, then points to a door at the other end of the changing room.

The top half of this door is a window, opaque with what Remer assumes is condensation.

By this, and by the pile the man hands him, it is obvious to Remer what is beyond that door.

"She is through there," the man says.

He turns and starts to leave.

Remer inspects the two towels, then the robe, thinking maybe one of them contains some form of bathing suit. None of them does.

"I didn't bring any trunks," he says to the man.

Without turning back, the man replies, "It is not a swimming pool."

Saying nothing more, he exits the locker room.

Remer looks again at the items in his hands.

Well, she and Hill know what they are doing, that much is certain.

Removing the cell phone from his pocket, Remer places it on a shelf inside the locker, then begins to undress.

A minute or so later, with nothing on but the robe, and nothing in his hand but one of the folded towels, he heads toward the door with the opaque window.

It reminds him suddenly of the windows back in that Brooklyn warehouse.

Pausing a moment, he finally pushes open the door and moves through.

27

■

A floor of small black and white tiles. A hundred years old, at least, they create an intricate Mediterranean-style mosaic.

But there is so much steam in the air that Remer can't even begin to see the entire picture laid out beneath his bare feet.

Still, he knows what this place is: an old Turkish bath redone into an upscale day spa.

The room, roughly the size of his entire apartment, has a high ceiling. A small pool set in the center, the steam, and the immense, hollow echo of a cave are, as far as he can tell, its only contents.

From the other side of the room he hears a door open and close, followed by the sound of bare feet on the hard tile. The softness with which these feet pad tell him that it is a woman.

The footsteps stop, and Remer can see that a figure is standing at the opposite end of the pool.

He approaches his end and, as he reaches it, finally sees the figure clearly.

Evelyn Ferrara, in a white robe, her dark hair pinned up.

The pool between them is about as long as a king-sized bed and twice as wide. The water it contains is clear, its surface, from which the steam rises steadily, as flat as a mirror.

"I appreciate you meeting me here," she says. Her deep voice echoes sharply. "I didn't want to have to give up my appointment."

"It's no problem."

"They bring this water in from a spring upstate. It's supposed to have tremendous healing properties. I figured you might enjoy that, after what you've been through this week. I know I will."

Remer glances at the water. It shows a near-perfect, though upside-down, reflection of her.

"Thanks," he says.

She smiles a warm, welcoming smile, seems to Remer confident and at ease.

The good manners of the wealthy, he thinks.

Or a woman skilled at deceit.

"I only have the room for a half hour," she says, "so I hope you don't mind if I soak while we talk."

She unties the sash and opens the robe, sliding it from her shoulders. It falls into a half-circle pile around her feet.

Naked, save for a long, knotted string of pearls around her neck, she stands there for a moment, boldly facing him.

Letting him get a good look.

The pride of a woman who has clearly worked to keep herself attractive.

He does not need to move his eyes to see her from head to toe. Yet he detects something on her lower abdomen and can't help but look directly at it.

A long, thin line running between her sharp pelvic bones.

A cesarean scar.

Mia's mark on her.

Stepping carefully into the water, Evelyn Ferrara moves down a set of wide stairs till she is immersed to her waist. Then, sitting on the steps, she is up to her chin.

She looks up at Remer.

"Please," she says. "Join me. You look to me like you need this."

It takes a moment, but finally Remer drops the folded towel, unties and removes his robe, then starts down the steps into the water.

It is almost too warm to bear.

As he lowers himself in, Evelyn Ferrara's eyes first scan the length of his body, then quickly come to rest, as his eyes did on hers, on his scar.

The way she stares at it is all too familiar to him.

A little stunned, she clearly wants to say something but does not dare.

Soon enough he is seated and up to his neck as well. The water is strangely silky. Small bubbles collect in the hairs on his arms. He feels a buoyancy he has never known before.

"You'll be a new man after this," she says.

There is a sparkle in her eyes, but that could just be, Remer thinks, a trick of the water and steam and late afternoon light coming through the high windows.

Or it could be sheer delight.

Without the cell phone Hutton gave Remer, there is no way the cops can hear or record what is said between him and Evelyn Ferrara.

Still, Remer is supposed to keep her talking for as long as possible.

And anyway, he wants to hear it for himself, and from her, inadmissible in court or not.

"Chief Manfredi informed me the other day that my daughter faked her own death," she says. "He said you found proof of that. I'm assuming you want to keep looking for her under our previous agreement."

"That's not why I'm here," Remer says.

"So why are you?"

"You and your boyfriend made a mess of things, you know that, right?"

Her polite smile doesn't fade, and she almost laughs. "I'm not really sure I know what you mean by any of that."

"You do," he assures her. "You got desperate, I understand that. But you got careless, too."

"You've obviously come here to tell me something. Please, why don't you just say it."

"I know what you're up to, Evelyn. You and your bodyguard. I know that he killed Mia and David Brazier in their home on Christmas morning. And I'd bet everything I have that DeVere and his girlfriend are lying dead somewhere. I also know that the cops are standing around and scratching their heads, trying to figure all this out. I could help them, I could tell them everything I know, but what good would that do me? You know what your daughter did to me, so you know I don't care what happened to her. All I care about is what happens to me. That's a concern I'm sure you can understand."

Evelyn Ferrara glances at the bandage on Remer's forehead. "I think you may need an X-ray," she says.

"The one thing I can't figure out," he says, "is how exactly you and DeVere got together. At first I thought you probably approached him and set this whole thing in motion, had him plant the whole idea in Brazier's head. But now I realize that's giving you too much credit. Someone who could see a picture that big wouldn't screw up like you did. I think now that it was DeVere who approached you. He knew all about your relationship with Mia, heard all about it from Brazier, and figured, hey, why fake her death for a share when he could actually kill her and keep the whole thing. So he contacted you, and you two made a deal. What he didn't know was that it was a deal with the devil." Remer pauses, then says, "You planned all along to betray him and keep the insurance *and* Mia's trust fund for yourself, didn't you?"

"I sensed you were an intelligent man, Mr. Remer. I had no idea you had such a vivid imagination as well."

"Let's cut the shit, okay? You know what I want. The eighty grand your daughter took from me. The eighty grand you promised to pay me if I found her. Out of several million, eighty grand is nothing, a drop in the bucket. Pay me that and you'll never hear from me again."

Evelyn Ferrara's smile has faded, but only slightly. "The problem with paying blackmail," she says, "is there's no guarantee your black-mailer won't keep coming back for more. And, please, don't tell me I'll have your word you wouldn't do that. I mean, if, as you say, we're cutting the shit."

"If I wanted more, trust me, I'd ask for it right now. And for that matter, where's my guarantee that I won't come home one night and find your attack dog waiting for me inside my place? Or I won't sud-denly see another set of headlights in my rearview mirror?"

"I know a bluff when I hear one, Mr. Remer. And I know a lie, too."

"What lie?"

"That you don't care about what happened to Mia. I saw it in your face at the train station. And you wouldn't have gone tearing after Brazier the way you did when you thought he had killed her if you didn't care about her."

"So you were a part of this," Remer says. "How else could you know that I went 'tearing after Brazier'? Since you weren't there, someone had to tell you that. DeVere, maybe? Or maybe your bodyguard was watching me watch them."

Evelyn Ferrara says nothing.

"I have the carrying case," Remer says flatly.

"I don't know what you're talking about."

"The case your bodyguard killed Brazier for. That case. The one with your bodyguard's fingerprint on it. The one he handed to DeVere an hour before DeVere ran me off the road. Is that worth eighty grand to you?"

"I think I need to ask you to leave right now, Mr. Remer. I would prefer not to have to call the attendant and make a scene."

"Your bodyguard's name isn't Smith, it's Hill," Remer says. "After leaving the Marine Corps, he worked as a mercenary, then entered the private sector. He was hired by your husband for protection, but that didn't really work out the way it was supposed to, did it? And since your husband's tragic death, Hill has been living with you in your apartment here. There's one document so far to prove that. I'm sure if I look a little deeper I'll find more. And if I can't, I can always ask the police for help."

"I feared for my life. I told you that. I suspected that my daughter was up to something, and I wanted twenty-four-hour protection."

"You could have at least made it look like Hill slept in his own bed."

Her brow suddenly furrows. It is an unmistakable mix of anger and concern. "I'm sorry," she says, her tone indignant.

"You rented two hotel rooms when you came out last Sunday night. According to housekeeping, one of the rooms hadn't been used."

Evelyn Ferrara says nothing.

Remer lets that sink in, then says, "And I know about the house in Southampton. That wasn't difficult to figure out. If you had a home out here, why did you need hotel rooms? I know it's about to be foreclosed upon. I know you're almost broke." He pauses. "And I know you hated your daughter, and always have."

There is a shift in her attitude, one that tells Remer that he has broken through her pretense of civility.

The real Evelyn Ferrara—perhaps even the Evelyn Ferrara Mia knew—is about to show.

Remer wants very much to see it, experience it face-to-face.

She watches him, her eyes, which a moment ago sparkled with delight, now wild with rage.

Still, she does her best to contain it.

"The best I can do is offer you a job," she says. "Andrew is planning on starting his own business. Private security. I'm certain he could use a man like you."

"I already have a job, thanks."

Another moment of Mrs. Ferrara struggling to contain her anger—*narcissistic rage?* Remer wonders—then she says, "Is the case in town with you?"

"Yes."

"In a safe place, I hope."

"Very."

"And its contents?"

"You mean the recordings of your daughter and Brazier."

She nods. "Yes."

"They're all there."

"No copies? For future reference, perhaps."

"None."

"I'm supposed to just take your word on that."

She makes no attempt to conceal her contempt for him.

Her hatred is palpable.

"Like I said before, if I wanted more, I'd ask for it now," Remer says. "All I want is what you promised me when you sent me looking for Mia."

"I don't have that kind of cash available right now. But apparently you know this already."

"It doesn't have to be your money. Hill must have savings. He must have made some decent cash when he worked as a mercenary. And he hasn't had to pay rent for a while now."

"Shaking me down is one thing, Mr. Remer. You might want to think twice about shaking him down."

"I'll take my chances."

She thinks about that for a long time, seems to be sizing Remer up.

A second look at a man she underestimated.

Then, finally, "I'd say the three of us have something to discuss. Meet me downstairs. We'll take you back to your hotel, discuss this on the way."

"Sounds good to me."

Evelyn Ferrara stands and turns, water rushing down her smooth, tanned skin.

Climbing the stairs, she pauses on the rim of the pool. Crouched down to pick up her robe, she looks over her shoulder at Remer, then stands and walks naked, the robe over one arm, into the churning steam.

Gone from his sight.

The door to the women's locker room opens and closes, and then Remer rises from the water. He hears only the many echoes created by the drops falling from his body and onto the tile floor.

▪

Barton and Hernandez are standing just inside the entrance to the main lobby.

They look expectantly at Remer as he steps off the elevator.

He sees through the glass doors behind them the first hint of winter twilight, and below it a street filled with a mix of patrol cars and unmarked sedans.

As Remer heads toward the door, his friend and her colleague take several eager steps to meet him.

"They weren't able to hear any of it," Barton says.

"I know," Remer says. He hands Hernandez the cell phone. "Still, it felt good to hear her say it."

"So she went for it?"

"Yeah."

"That doesn't do us much good," Hernandez says. "It's just your word against hers."

Remer looks through the windows, sees the Mercedes pinned in by two patrol cars. After a quick scan he spots Hill in the backseat of one of the unmarked sedans.

He isn't alone, though; Watts and Hutton are with him, Hutton beside him, Watts up front and looking over the seat.

By the way Hill is seated—leaning forward, his head bowed slightly—Remer knows that his hands are cuffed behind his back.

"You've got him," Remer says. "If he's smart, he'll take the deal."

"He's already talking." Barton holds up a handheld radio, indicating she has been listening to what has been said inside the sedan. "The first thing he offered to tell us is where DeVere and Collins are buried."

Remer now knows exactly which kind of marine this Hill was.

More importantly, he knows that his latest secret—that DeVere and Collins dumped Brazier's body behind Remer's shop and that Remer moved it to Cooper's Neck—is safe.

He feels a sense of relief move through him like a wave.

"Is Mrs. Ferrara on her way down?" Hernandez asks.

"Yeah."

"It would probably be better if you stepped outside."

Remer nods. "Okay."

"Tommy's down the block," Barton offers. "You can wait with him."

Remer faces her and pauses. Before he can say anything, she smiles and touches his arm.

"What are friends for?" she says.

Stepping outside into the cold, Remer looks at Hill in the backseat of the sedan, sees the man talking, and fast.

Like a man who has let fear in.

Turning first to his left, and then to his right, Remer finally spots Miller standing alone halfway down the block, beyond the perimeter set up by a third patrol car, this one parked in the middle of the street.

Beyond that, at the far end of the block, is another patrol car parked in the same manner.

Remer reaches Miller.

"You alright?" Miller asks.

Remer nods. "Listen, Tommy, I'm going to head out."

"Where to?"

"Home."

"Wait around and drive back with us later."

"No, that's okay. I'll make my own way."

"They're going to want you to give a statement."

"I've got nothing they can use. And there's someplace I need to be in a little while. Someone I want to meet. Anyway, it can wait till Monday."

"Don't you at least want to stick around and see her brought out in handcuffs?"

Not really, Remer thinks.

I've seen enough.

He offers his hand, and Miller takes it.

They shake.

"I'll see you around, Tommy."

"Yeah. Hey, as Kay would say, 'Don't be such a stranger.'"

Walking away, Remer checks his watch, sees that it is just past four.

Eight hours till midnight.

Plenty of time.

▪

After a few blocks, twilight crossing quickly into full night, Remer, just as he did six years before, flags down a cab.

He offers the driver two hundred dollars above the fare to take him to Southampton.

But the driver tells Remer he can't, a drive like that would break him, so Remer doubles his offer, showing the bills to the man, who nods grudgingly and says, "Lucky for you I just started my shift. Get in."

On the way to the tunnel Remer looks out his window and sees all that has changed about the city, and those few things that haven't, that maybe never will.

A business here, a landmark building there.

To his surprise, though, he has very little interest in that. All he wants is to be home, waiting in his chair, when Angela comes through his door.

He wonders what she will say, the questions she will ask, when she sees the wound on his forehead, so fresh it has yet to scar.

He wonders, too, what he will tell her about it.

What will he say about the things he has seen since he was last with her, and the things he has done?

What can and can't be said?

As with New York, there are things about Remer that will change, and some that won't.

That can't.

He decides, though, that he doesn't need to think about what he will tell her right now. He doesn't need to think about anything. Not Evelyn Ferrara or Hill, not DeVere or Brazier or Casey Collins, not even Mia.

He'd like to feel free of all that, at least for the two-hour ride home.

Still, the thought of the woman he is heading to meet—a woman determined to make a second life for herself, a better life built upon the ruins of her previous one—doesn't seem to want to leave his mind.

And why should it have to?

The cab makes several turns, then enters the Midtown Tunnel. Remer is surrounded suddenly by a rush of overhead lights and a clamorous, echoing noise.

It isn't long before the cab clears the tunnel and all that chaos ends and Remer can see again the vast, clear night sky stretching out above.

Sitting still in the wide backseat, he settles in for this journey eastward.

A journey that is both familiar to him and, thankfully, not.